LOSS OF
SEPARATION

Also Conrad Williams
Decay Inevitable
One
The Unblemished
London Revenant
The Scalding Rooms
Rain
Head Injuries
Nearly People
Game
Use Once Then Destroy

LOSS OF
SEPARATION

CONRAD WILLIAMS

SOLARIS

First published 2010 by Solaris
an imprint of Rebellion Publishing Ltd,
Riverside House, Osney Mead,
Oxford, OX1 0ES, UK

www.solarisbooks.com

ISBN: 978 1 906735 56 2

10 9 8 7 6 5 4 3 2 1

A CIP catalogue record for this book is available from the
British Library.

Designed & typeset by Rebellion Publishing

Printed in the US

For Rhonda. I burn for you.

Acknowledgements

Thanks to Laurence Davy for opening doors in the plot; Tessa Kum for telling me straight, and wearing my book for a hat; Adam Nevill for support and helpful comments even as the nappies mounted up; Shaun Hamilton for pain management information; Tracy Savin for insights into a nurse's routine; Corrie Colbert for sending me air disaster links; and Peter Skinner, my old mate, who somehow manages to avoid flying passenger jets into mountains for a living.

Thanks also to Nicholas Royle, Graham Joyce, Jonathan Oliver, Darren Turpin, Sarah Pinborough, Susan Tolman, Carol Cummings, Rhonda, Ethan, Ripley and Zac.

Loss of separation between aircraft occurs whenever specified separation minima are breached. Loss of separation may ultimately result in a mid air collision.

Source: www.skybrary.aero

PART ONE
CHEYNE STOKING

Flight Z

DEPARTURE

THE DEAD CAPTAIN peers through cockpit windows flecked with blood and the fear-spittle of screams. Vomit, like panic paint. The wipers work at this grue, smearing, turning the control tower into a Grimm's windmill with ghost sails. This monster should not be able to fly.

– Roan ground from Flight Z on stand Lima Three-Zero requesting start-up clearance.
– Flight Z is cleared to Tamara Airport. Your initial routeing is Dunwich One-Niner. Cleared to line-up and hold on runway One-Niner Left.
– *What are you doing? We can't just leave him like this. We have to…*

Engulfed by black carbon, two giant passenger jets have become fused together in an unimaginably violent collision. The shark's head of a Jumbo jet seems to erupt from the mangled wreckage of a Boeing 777, like something struggling for air. One massive wing hangs from this convolvulus of aluminium, dragging and sparking on the apron as the molten shreds of the landing gear carry the jets along the taxiway. Its blistered engines – nacelles flayed open to reveal the weird anatomy of these powerhouses – stutter with flame, drizzling aviation fuel across the tarmac. Humours haze the black hulk, rendering its shape uncertain. Fractures in the fuselages are bonded shut by human glue.

The aircraft is the pilot; the pilot is the aircraft. The captain feels the jet a part of himself, as all pilots do. Must. He might look down and see his body blend sinuously with the seat, a molecular marriage of biology and mechanics. The blasted airstrip: pockmarked and strewn with skulls and naked, wrenched corpses bearing astonished expressions. He aligns the jet with the runway, and the engines clear their throats. He plays the throttles against the brakes and feels the tonnage pulling against them. The aircraft wants to be back up there, screaming in the night.

– Flight Z, this is Roan ground, you are cleared for take-off. Wind two five zero at fifteen.

Setting power. Brakes off.
We have to what?
We have to finish him off.

Gathering pace, Flight Z grinds over the runway. Skulls and ribcages pulverise beneath the massive wheels; clouds of bone dust rise in their wake.

Eighty knots... one hundred fifty one knots...
Vee-One...
... one hundred fifty eight knots
... Rotate...
He's dead. Look at him. He's dying. Leave him.

Engines screaming, the nose lifts and Flight Z arches into the night, wings flung out like something in the act of capitulation.

... Vee-Two... Positive rate of climb...
... Gear up...
We can't leave him. What if someone comes? What if he wakes up?

The bay doors wail open, fighting against the buckle of that previous impact. The howl of wind as drag is increased. Body parts fall away like titbits picked from a tooth. The bogies retract. At 300 feet the crosswind slams into the fuselage and the aircraft turns into it, crabbing against the airstream, inviting turbulence.

I can't do this. I can't do this. I won't do this.

The 777 hangs from the body of the Jumbo like a forgotten stillbirth. This abomination shrinks into the violet night, guided by a heartbeat beacon, otherwise flying blind. No porthole lights. No pre-flight safety announcement. No in-flight entertainment. A troubled, monotonous banshee call rises into the troposphere. And then, after a short while, even that is gone.

Chapter One
THE DEAD BABY

WHILE I WAS in a coma, surgeons operated on my spine. Cancellous bone chips were harvested from my iliac crest (they told me later) and placed carefully between the damaged dorsal vertebrae. Wires and glue held these plugs in place. They stabilised the spine with a metal brace to assist the fusing of the damaged spinal column. I was an Airfix kit for four months. At least I didn't know anything about it. The hit-and-run left me with so many broken ribs. It left me with a punctured lung; I almost drowned in my own fluids. Both femurs fractured in three places; the bones of my lower leg had impacted up through the patella in my left knee. I came off the bonnet and my face was the first thing to hit the ground. There are fourteen bones in the face, not counting the teeth, the *ossicula auditus* and Wormian bones. The orbit of my right eye turned into so much calcium dust. When I revived, six months of my life had been pissed through a catheter and my muscles were porridge. They took the bandages off and I found myself wishing that they would just keep unravelling, to a point where I would no longer fill the shape they had suggested. I didn't look at myself; I still haven't, three weeks later. I was no longer capable of crying.

'Where's my girlfriend?' I asked – or tried to ask – the surgeon, while he was prodding my back with a pencil, telling me how extremely lucky I was. My mouth felt alien, as if it had been grafted on to me, courtesy of a donor. Perhaps it had. I felt as if my skin had been removed and then stretched back over me the wrong way around. Nothing fit; nothing felt comfortable. Everything hurt, even the space that I occupied.

I had no idea what an iliac crest was.

THERE WAS A gull lying on the beach, trying to move its broken wings, making a pathetic sound among the pebbles. I wondered if it had been attacked by a seal. Surf frothed beneath the bird's throat, turning pink. I might have gone to help, If there was anything I could have done, but I was just as ruined. Out of hospital three weeks and I was determined to celebrate. *Here's to pain*; I raised the miniature bottle of rum and swigged it down. All along the beach, fishermen were switching off the ochre lamps in their tents, thoughts turning to breakfast. Rods were dismantled and stowed in tackle bags, old bait heaved into the sea. Beyond them, the land took over, flat and unyielding, save for the jutting thumb of an abandoned mill stuck on its own in a fallow field.

The idea of nightfishing had horrified me as a child, before I realised what it really was. I used to imagine hooks spiralling into the sky, cast by madmen. Barbs snagging on the velvet, tearing it open, tearing it down. It bothered me that anyone would want to do that, let alone try. Precious little bothered me now. A dying bird on the beach. A metal rod in my spine. Nearly three hundred people on a flight out of Heathrow airport missing death by seventy feet. You begin to learn how to keep a lid on it.

After the fishermen had gone I noticed there was another figure, much further along where the sand gives way to greater fans of shingle, and the dunes with their punk tussock hairstyles rear up between the beach and the caravan park. It was hooded, staring out to sea, stock still. Some time later it moved off in the direction of the harbour and something in the way it moved called to me. It was as if the figure was aping my shuffling gait; but then, it could just have been the unstable shoreline, dotted as it was at this hour with the detritus the surf coughed up.

I returned my attention to the job at hand. I shifted in the shingle and stared at the box for a long time. It was an Umbro shoe box, a new one. Someone with size 9s had bought something coloured LIGHT SILVER/VAPOUR/BLACK GOLD. I patted my jacket pocket for matches.

BURN THIS FOR ME.

I don't spend too much time on the contents. It's too much like prying. But sometimes you can't avoid the objects that tumble out; they contain their own force, a fearful potential. A map of Alaska slashed with black biro. Aeronautical charts (which gave me pause) with their dense codes, vectors and warnings to pilots. *CAUTION: Severe turbulence may occur over rugged terrain. CAUTION: Numerous windmills. CAUTION: Intensive aerobatic practice area.* A letter so old the page is as fragile as an insect's wing. A cat's collar. A photograph of a man in khaki shorts whose ice cream has fallen from its cone. Something grey, excised, rattling in a clear plastic tub. A promise, or a threat, of fidelity.

It takes to the flame every time, first match in. It goes up as if it were created for this moment. I get a few looks from the fishermen as they trudge up the beach to their kippers and their coffee, but some of them keep their eyes averted and in this way I know that I have burned secrets for them.

PLEASE GET RID OF THIS FOR ME, PLEASE?

A while yet before the sun comes up. Its colour surprises here, where the skies are so big you could be forgiven for seeing a curve to the horizon. The flames change. They bend and arch and quiver. The things they eat into produce unnatural colours; belches of black, chemical smoke. It all ends up as ash. When it's spent, I toe it into the sand. I go out in the dark only. I haven't yet the guts to show my face in daylight.

It takes me an hour to get back, whatever that means. On the way I find an infant's blue romper suit, washed up by the tide.

Dist.

Black cellulose. Purple sky. Silver rain. Grey skin.

Distance. I was always good at judging how far off a car was at night, in the wet. Coming on. Speeding. I could tell. Look both ways. Look both ways again. Swell of headlights. The growl of the engine.

I was fascinated, when I was a kid, by this thing called the dichotomy paradox. It was a daft thing, really, easily disproved by mathematics, but theoretically difficult to argue against. It was all about how getting from A to B was actually impossible. All motion is an illusion. The car can never get to where it needs to be because, to paraphrase Archimedes, it must first make it half way before it reaches its destination. But before you can get halfway there, you must get a quarter of the way there. Before that, you must travel one-eighth; before that, a sixteenth; and so on, ad infinitum. But you can't tell a ton of metal this. You can't reason with it.

Black cellulose. Grey skin. Red bone. White light. White pain.

Dist. Distance Is Speed times Time. Forty miles an hour. Fifty. Sixty. Ear to the ground. Nose to the grindstone. Back to front. Hell to pay. How far from me was it when I realised what was going to happen? Six months. Where did all the distance go? Inside me. That's where. I paid it out jealously. It filled me up so completely there was hardly any space left for life.

Deceleration. Stall warning. Brace for impact. Controlled landing into terrain.

The road. The car. The rain. The shine. The engine. The chest. The collapse. The pain. The blood. The hiss. The engine. The drowning. The glass. The eyes. The kiss. The blanket. The love. The engine. The dark. The engine. The heartbeats. The cry.

Acceleration. Diminishment. Flatline.

I'M PAUL ROAN. I *am* Paul Roan. I used to be First Officer Paul Roan. Now I'm plain Paul Roan, but that's good, I suppose. By rights I should be Paul Roan RIP. I clocked nearly 4000 flying hours with

Lufthansa, the German airline. I was in command of a Boeing 777 when it was involved in what we call an airprox incident. There was what we call a loss of separation caused by what we call a level bust that resulted from poor communication and a lack of coordination on the flight deck. Density of traffic. Simultaneous transmissions. Lack of hearback. Bottom line: I was tired and not paying as much attention as I should. There was what we call a fuck-up. We nearly hit a 747 en route to New York out of Madrid. Nearly never counts. But it does in this industry. There was an enquiry and I was suspended from my job. I was encouraged to appeal, but I lost my nerve. I couldn't stop thinking about what might have happened had I pulled back a little more on the control column. There were 412 passengers and crew on the 777; 289 on ours. That amounts to nearly 800 gallons of blood redecorating the cabins on impact.

I walked.

After that, whenever I was close enough to an airport to see a jet taking off I'd feel a cold choker fasten around my throat, even as I was running through my mind the procedure the pilots were likely to be following at that moment as they climbed steep and fast, adjusting trim, thanking air traffic control before being passed on to their next point of contact.

I had to move away from London. I became convinced that a jet would come out of the sky, plough into homes, through my living room, dragging an orange forest of flaming aviation fuel with it. Tamara, my girlfriend, was happy to move. She had not settled, despite having arrived from

Ukraine four years previously. She found it difficult to make new friends; she found the women in the city too inattentive.

'Like butterflies,' she described them. Her friends from home were loyal, stuck fast. She couldn't understand meeting someone just for coffee; she expected to spend the day with them, sometimes longer, shopping, cooking meals together. 'Everyone's in such a rush to get on. To get to next thing. Nobody ever looks at you.'

So we sold our two-bedroom flat in Camden and decided to use the profit to buy something modest on the coast. A B&B that needed a bit of work. A new life. Away from the flight paths.

I'M ON THE beach every day, but not always to burn secrets. Part of my physiotherapy involves walking. I was told by the doctors at the hospital that walking in sand was much better than on any other surface. I put in the hours. I walk until my back is on fire and the shape of my legs has been forgotten. I know I'm gritting my teeth because a thin layer of sand builds up on them. Every so often I'll jar my foot on a concealed rock and swear I can feel the brace in my spine grate against the vertebrae. An illusion – the steel is fused with the bone – but I can't shake it.

I'm a badly constructed Jenga tower. I've lost weight. I've lost height. My legs are so scarred they resemble snakes winding around thin boughs. My face feels punched in and carved out. A bruise in the shape of a 7 sits low on my torso; it hasn't faded in almost seven months. I'm convinced there's a dusting of rust compacted into the flesh. My left eye is permanently bloodshot. Even if I wanted to go back to flying, I'd never be allowed near a cockpit. I'm in persistent pain. I take strong opioid drugs. I take so many, I have a special plastic drugs case to remind me what to take and when. Some tablets I take every four to six hours. I take Solpadol to combat pain. I'm addicted. Addiction is the alternative to killing myself. I sit and watch far too much TV and take none of it in. I drift, only coming to when I drool on my bare knees, or when Ruth comes in to rouse me with a fruit smoothie, or a cool hand on mine.

There's a story, though, in the news, that finds its way through. Possibly because the footage spoken over by the reporter (favouring emphasis on consonants rather than vowels) is of Southwick beach, and the pier. In some footage I can clearly see the black, ashen pits of my own bonfires. A child was killed here, recently. I was still in hospital at the time. Kieran Love, his name is. Was. I watch a Detective Inspector wearing a hat, like some Chandler reject, reciting policespeak to the cameras: appeals for witnesses. *If anybody saw anything... it's imperative that we catch this man... I'd ask that he think hard about what he's done and give himself up... We fear he may strike again.*

THE LAST TIME I remember being with my girlfriend. We'd spent a few hours apart. She wanted to buy me something from the junk shop. *Go mad*, I said to her as she leaned in, giggling, and kissed the tip of my nose.

While she was gone, I wandered through the village, nodding at people, trying on the size of the place, wondering how long it would take for me to feel comfortable calling it home. I picked through trinkets in an antique shop. I bought a postcard and drank tea in the Rose café, where a woman in a black pinafore brought me a paper napkin and a bone china cup and saucer.

I bought a newspaper at the corner shop and turned left, up towards the junk shop. I peered in through the window and saw Tamara chatting with the proprietor, who sat in a deep, tatty armchair behind the counter. She was holding a brown paper bag. I went in and moved towards their murmurs, picking things up, putting them down. There were layers of junk. Some of them were so deep behind shelves and furniture that it was impossible to reach them, or make out what they were. I wondered how long they had been there.

Tamara saw me and waved me over. She introduced me to Ray, who told me he had owned the junk shop for twenty years. I wanted to ask him about the stuff that was buried, but Tamara was already saying goodbye, shooing me out of the shop. We went to the pub where she bought me... and then she gave me the bag... and I put my... or did I kiss her first? And then I opened the bag... and she said... or did I say?...

I can't do this.

The first time I saw my girlfriend.

She emerged from the first class lounge at Heathrow holding a Selfridge's bag between her teeth. She was so beautiful that I laughed out loud.

Chapter Two
BIGHTS, ENDS AND FALLS

THE BOOKSHOP IS on a road running parallel to the beach. It is hardly ever open. The only clue, when it is, is not in any door sign but in the presence of a chocolate-point Siamese cat lying on a blanket in the window. Go through the door and there's a long corridor of books, too narrow for more than one person at a time. An old school desk with a cash register, a plastic molded chair and a hand-sewn cushion. A notebook, a volume of non-fiction, a mug of something that will cool to tepid before being drunk.

The shop is empty. I don't know where Ruth is. I've asked her why she doesn't lock the shop when she nips out to buy a snack from the delicatessen, or fruit from the greengrocer's in the square. But she just gives me this pitying look and pats my hand. It's the look people who have never lived in London give to Londoners. It's a look that says: yes, there really are places left on Earth where you can go out and leave the door unlocked. There's an honesty box on the windowsill, next to the slumbering Vulcan, but it's always empty.

'Because people are stealing your stock,' I tell her.

'Because it's winter. There are no visitors,' she counters.

She opens the shop because she likes to sit there at her desk and read with the portable heater and a short-wave radio tuned to something far away, exotic, faded, unintelligible. She comes here too, to look after me, to keep me company.

'You're very kind to me,' I say, again.

'Shush.'

At the end of the corridor is a room where Ruth keeps the children's books, the science fiction and fantasy novels. There is a door that says STAFF ONLY. Behind it is a staircase up to Ruth's living quarters. There is another door next to a small bookcase with a cardboard bat glued to it and a legend: MASTERS OF MMMWAHAHAHAHAHAAA!!! The bookcase is crammed with paperbacks by Stephen King, Ramsey Campbell, Clive Barker, Peter Straub. There are warped and foxed copies of The Pan Book of Horror in a cardboard box. Fifty pence each. Five for two pounds. Skulls and candles and snakes and rats. I slide a key into the lock and turn the handle. I go inside. The horror room. The room where I exist.

There is a CircOlectrio orthopaedic bed, a chair and a small table. An en-suite bathroom contains a sit-in-bath, a toilet with a raised seat, a red emergency cord and a saucer of pot pourri. This extension to the bookshop had been added to house Ruth's mother, who died a few days after moving in, having funded its construction. I've been here for the best part of three weeks. I've seen Ruth's certificates. She wanted to look after me. She felt as if she had been chosen for the task because she had saved my life after the hit-and-run.

'I found you on that B road, just on the edge of Bailey's Hollow,' she told me. 'It was a miracle I was out at all that night. I shouldn't have been. My God, neither should you. Terrible storm. Winds gusting hard, fast. Trees down all over the county. A Range Rover, or something similar I think it must have been. One of those big 4x4s anyway, going too fast, drifting out over the middle of the road. It clipped you. You flew through the air. It was hard to believe you broke so many bones when you looked as if you didn't have any.'

I'd asked her where my girlfriend was, apparently, before the pain grew so big I could no longer hold it inside me. I couldn't remember where I'd left her or where she'd gone. I asked her again when I came out of the coma, half a year later. It might have been seconds. Ruth's hair was long. Her belly was big.

She took me home, even though I'd told her I would be all right. I said I was going to live at the B&B – Tam's Place, we were going to call it – but she insisted. She brought me back here and read to me. My life was measured out in chapters. I'd dread the moment the bookmark was slid into place and the book closed. I was worried I might die before we reached the end of the stories she was reading me. But it hasn't happened yet.

Tamara was gone. I should be dead, but I survived. I was alone. How could she leave someone, her man, her love, so wrecked? Did she leave me when she saw how destroyed I appeared? Perhaps she thought I would be a vegetable for the rest of my life and could not live with the responsibility of that. Did she stay for long? Was there any kind of vigil? Did she light a candle? Did she cry? Did she kiss my cheek? Winners and losers. Heroes and villains. Who was wearing which mask? I couldn't even begin to take a guess.

I drew a bath; it didn't take long. It was the only bath that would fit this space, Ruth told me, and anyway, her mother would never have been able to use a conventional tub.

After Ruth was raped, she used this bath all the time. It made it easier to hide the bruises. This style is popular with the Japanese, apparently. It looks like a ceramic well. There are steps up the side.

I poured in some bath foam. I don't like it; it irritates my skin, but, like Ruth, I don't want to see anything of me beneath the waterline. Somehow, I managed to undress. My clothes smelled of smoke. I couldn't bend down to clear them from the floor. Somehow, I got in. There are occasional, panicky moments when I feel I've not healed, that there are cracks and splits in me that will leak into the bathwater, turning it red. I feel like a thin bag filled with knuckles of bone. I feel like something continually on the brink of failure.

In coma, in that place, inhabiting that blind country, I suffered four heart attacks. As with the nightfishing, when I was young I saw this differently: I imagined the heart being set upon by marauders, gremlins sent by death through the veins and arteries to wage war. When you died from a heart attack, they opened you up and found the heart slashed and stabbed and burning. I can imagine it in my chest, scarred and exhausted, reduced. I wonder how many beats it has left now.

There's a window next to my head. It's frosted, low: the building sits next to a rising road. When I bathe I have it open – just a crack – and can see the occasional pair of legs, the swing of an arm, as people walk by. No matter how much cold I pour in, the bath is always too hot. Either that or my skin is still too tender to deal with any temperature above lukewarm.

I closed my eyes and waited. Presently, I heard movement from within the shop. The door opened and I heard her sigh. I heard the click of her knees as she bent to recover my clothes. A change in air pressure, a deepening of the shadow behind my eyelids. I thought of Tamara as the sponge glided over my shoulders and back. I thought about how long we'd been apart. Six months since the crash; three weeks since I emerged from coma. Before she went missing, we had spent every night together. We had been talking about who would make the breakfasts and who would change the bedding. We had been talking about chocolates on the pillow, or not? What to put in a full English. Herbal teas, or was that just too London?

She saw me, dried blood on the linen, intubated, catheterised, and thought, *what future is in this shell?* I can't spend my days sponging him clean while everything draws inward, his hands, his feet, his life. I won't watch him waste away.

Was that how it was?

'What was that?'

'Nothing,' I said. 'Daydreaming.'

She helped me from the bath, endlessly patient. She dried me with a towel, wrapped me in a bathrobe. Now I could open my eyes.

Ruth is the kind of woman who appears different every time you see her. Her hair is dense, Japanese black; she wears it always in a slightly new style, or her makeup is brighter, or darker. One day her freckles are prominent, another her skin seems unblemished. She doesn't have a general way of dressing. You wouldn't call her a jumper-and-jeans kind of girl, although she will wear them. She'll wear a dress with a pair of jeans underneath, if the mood takes her. I know she likes wearing expensive underwear and wooden jewellery.

Now she had her hair up, big plastic crocodile clips keeping it off her face. She was wearing Agnès B glasses with black oblong frames. A sleeveless, caramel-coloured summer dress. Her swollen belly was as tight as a drum. I could see the shape of her navel, proud against the fabric. The ebony bangles on her wrist clacked together as she dried her hands on the towel.

'How do you feel?' we both asked each other at the same time.

I wonder about the pain. I wonder if I'll ever recover enough to be able to not feel it any more. And will my body look like it used to? How could it? How could it remember the way it was? It's hard for me to remember. Did my chest always feel so lumpy? Or is it the scar tissue wound around my fingers suggesting the illusion? I say I'm fine. She's says she's fine. We both know that we're not.

The car punched me into the air. I put out a hand and it was buried in glass up to the elbow. My skin came off like the unravelling of a silk glove. I lost two pints of blood before the ambulance arrived. Ruth had been out walking in the storm, wondering whether to keep the baby. When she found me, the decision was made for her.

'How many more chances might I have?' she asked me, one night shortly after my revival. 'I'm forty-two. I'd need to meet the right man in the next few years. It might not happen. I might have an accident, like you. The odds are stacked.'

Seeing me lying, dying, had banished any relevance the rape might have had, she said. But I have my doubts. Her chameleon looks mask a lack of any bloom. Her skin is grey and tired, beneath that make-up. It is as if the pregnancy was separate, something that is going on apart from her. As much as she is trying to convince herself that she is doing the right thing, she has the look of someone who has made a mistake, with no time left in which to make amends.

She has large, very watery blue eyes. She seems for ever on the verge of crying, or in the grip of a cold. Her beauty is something scared, scary. Sometimes I think that if I were to touch her face, it would fall apart like something a child had made from sand on the beach.

I felt better after the bath. Restored. We ate breakfast together and I pushed away from the table, thoughtful, decided.

She saw some of this in me. 'What?' she asked. Her left hand stroked the bump of her belly. I thought I saw movement. Maybe a kick.

'You know,' I said. 'I think I'm going to go out for another walk.'

Humour and concern in her face. Before she could try to warn me off, I rose. Slowly. 'You don't have to mother me, you know,' I told her. 'You don't have to feel responsible for me.'

'If I'd been a bit quicker,' she said, 'I might have been there before it happened. It might not have happened at all. The driver might have seen me and slowed down.'

'Or hit you instead,' I said. 'Anyway, what does it matter? I might as well be dead. If I was dead, I'd probably be in a better state.

'Don't talk like that,' she said, jabbing a finger into the bridge of her spectacles, something I noticed she did a lot when she was agitated. I was struck by how strong her feelings for me were. I had to keep reminding myself that she had known me far longer than I had known her. She had saved my life. I was still getting used to the village, the people, my unreal role. Hot emotions were something I was unused to. Everything in my life was slow since I came out of the coma. My recovery, my new timetable. Even the shock of Tamara's abandonment nibbled agonisingly into me like the tide at the uppermost reaches of the shoreline.

I spread my hands; I had nothing to say.

I opened the door and the seagull with the broken back was before me, pinned cruciform to the lilac sky, blood fizzing from its opened beak and cloaca, trying to flap its wings and succeeding only in jerking its wrenched body from side to side. I blinked it into mist and moved up the lane to The Fluke. My mind was throwing up all kinds of visual treats since the hit-and-run – memories, nightmares, fantasies all spliced together and given the full widescreen, 3D treatment – but that didn't mean it was getting any easier to deal with.

Movement behind the frosted glass. Cleaners getting the pub ready for opening time.

I reached into my pocket and pulled out a length of yellow string. My fingers were gnarly and stiff. The doctors had suggested I do finger exercises; and try to use my hands as much as possible. Make bread, they suggested. Take up pottery. But Charlie had put me on to knots. The intricacy of it, as opposed to the vagueness of dough or clay, was difficult to overcome and my fingers grew tired very quickly, but I felt the benefit in them. They were always painful, but slowly I was reclaiming the dexterity I'd lost. Thankfully, the right hand, which had plunged through the windscreen, had suffered very little in terms of nerve loss. The lacerations, and how they'd healed into thick worming scars, were the problem. It felt, all the time, as if I was trying to thread a needle while wearing a thick mitten.

Charlie had given me the string, and a photocopied leaflet containing five basic knots to learn. 'Get thems mastered and you'll make fishman yet,' he told me, fins of silver hair flapping around his head like something he'd caught and ditched in a bucket. 'I'll have y'out on morning tide pullin' in y'dinner with us afore y'knows it.'

I hobbled on to the sand. I knew the reef knot from school, but I worked it now, liking its simplicity, the symmetry in the construction of it, the finished appearance. Left over right, then under. Right over left, then under.

The figure of eight. A stopper knot. Sometimes doubled to add weight to an end for throwing. I tied that one a little harder than I meant to and struggled for five minutes trying to get it loose. The tips of my fingers were already beating. They no longer seemed like my fingers. One of the nails had a warp in it that would not correct itself. Trapped blood formed black half moons under others. It bothered me that the nurses had not thought to extract it, as if they predicted I would not be concerned with looking my best again once I was up and about. How much time could a shattered man have for vanity?

I sat down in the sand and with the yellow string tied a sheet bend into my shoelace. A stiff wind swept the surface of the beach into skirls and skrims. Moments of foam out to sea. Gulls hovered or stood on the exposed groynes, staring west. Their beaks were open, black spike tongues. It was as if they were tasting the weather. I glanced west too. Invariably I walked up the beach; it was easier with the prevailing wind at my back.

Now I decided it was time to walk down it, against the weather. It would be harder, but that was good, necessary. There was a pub at the end of this stretch, and it would be open by the time I reached it.

One more knot first. I found a piece of driftwood and secured the string against it with a clove hitch. These five basic knots I felt I knew now. I could do them without thinking, the bowline without its mantra: the rabbit comes out of the hole...

I put the string in my pocket and struck along the beach, eyes beaded against the stinging hiss. The wind blew the creases out of my clothes. I felt the urge to lean into it, like the gulls, and allow myself to be propped up by its muscle. I wasn't feeling it quite so much; moving against the wind was distracting me from the basic pain that lifting and planting my legs produced. It felt good, even though I knew my bones would be aching by the end of the day. I could bathe again. And I could finally take up Ruth on one of the massages she kept offering me.

Shadows had shortened by the time I reached the harbour wall and I was feeling hungry. I decided to walk up to the abandoned mill and take a rest before trundling to the pub for lunch. I had reached the end of the harbour track, bypassing the gift shop and the boat repair centre, the land falling away to scrubby paths, razor wire and open fields, when I heard a call behind me. Charlie stepped out from one of the shacks and waved.

'How's thems knots coming along then, kidder?' he asked, when he had caught up.

I smiled at him. I liked Charlie. He had done as much for me, in his way, as Ruth had done with her intensive care.

'Not too shabby,' I said. I tied him a bowline with my eyes shut. 'What's next?'

'We'll get y'on to some decorative knots, maybe. Tricky stuff. Keep y'fingers busy. Tire 'em out. Where're y'off to?'

'Just walking.'

'Pushing too hard, chief,' he said. His sunblasted face was a fascinating map of seams and slots and wrinkles. 'Y'going to end up going backwards. Int there something about rest in this programme the doctors got y'on?'

'I rest enough,' I said. 'I was on my back for six months.'

He nodded, looked as though he might add something, and then hooked his thumb back in the direction of the harbour. 'I'm taking her out later,' he said. His boat, the *Gratitude*, was a stubby, bobbing mass of dull colour and portholes in the water. 'Goin fer sea bass. Come with? Get y'sea legs sorted.'

I shook my head. It would be good to get out on the ocean, pull some of that air into my lungs, but I wasn't ready. I felt as though my life was being measured in terms of a bed, a bath and a fire under the pier. My roads didn't stretch beyond these things. Not yet.

'I will, soon, thanks,' I said. 'But I don't know how much help I'll be.'

He shook his head. His soft hair echoed the movement. 'Don't worry bout it. I've been doing this alone so long I forgot what the help is sposed to do anyway. Need some hooks baiting, though, if y'up to it.'

We walked back towards Charlie's shack.

'You saved me from getting muddy, at least,' I said, taking a last look back over my shoulder at the dun fields and the crippled mill. Charlie nodded and laughed and walked at my pace. He told me about sea bass. And he told me about Gordon, his son.

RUTH MADE DINNER. I sat at her kitchen table, sipping a Bloody Mary with way too much Worcestershire sauce and Tabasco, just the way I liked it. I smacked my lips and blew my cheeks out. Ruth made good Bloody Marys. She used celery salt and dry sherry and grated horseradish. It didn't matter how crummy the vodka was after that.

I watched her waddle around the kitchen. She had jointed a chicken and was browning it off in a big pan of smoking oil. A heap of chopped vegetables sat on a board, waiting to be added to the cooking pot. I was hungry. For half a year of my life I had been nourished by injected fluids. I had vowed never to leave anything on my plate again. I nibbled on breadsticks and listened to the noises my body made.

'Don't you miss London?' Ruth asked. I hadn't realised how long we had gone without saying anything. I was happy with the silence. It felt comfortable. Perhaps not for her.

'I don't know,' I said. 'I don't feel as though I've had enough time away to come to any kind of decision. I'm just coming out of a sequence of giant wrenches to what seemed to be a straight, uncomplicated life. I don't have much time, or much stomach, to think about what went before.'

She nodded her head. She clacked at the thighs with her tongs. They sizzled and spat in the pan.

'You overdid it a bit today.'

'I'll be the judge of that.' I didn't mean to sound so short, but some sentences, no matter how you butter them up, still come out sharp and nasty.

'Well, actually,' she said, her tongs in the air, her back still to me, 'your physiotherapist will be the judge of that. And when you turn up with a prolapsed disc he'll be really impressed that you tried to go cross-country running three weeks after waking up.'

I snorted. 'It wasn't exactly a cross-country run.'

'No, but it wasn't exactly a stroll in the sand either. Charlie said if he hadn't pulled on your reins you'd have ended up in the middle of Cold Acre Marsh with a long walk back whichever direction you looked at it.'

'I wouldn't do it if I felt I couldn't manage it.'

Now she turned around. I could see she was upset, but there was also some matronly steel in her. She didn't like being argued with. It was funny seeing that in a young woman. An attractive woman. Maybe that was what turned you mean, after a passage of years.

'Paul, the weather's unpredictable. You only need to find yourself a couple of miles from home, a storm, or the cold coming in, and you're in trouble. The weather here, it changes fast. It gets ugly quick.'

'Point taken,' I said, irked, and unsure whether my dented features were able to hide it from her. She didn't seem to mind that; she must have come up against surlier tossers than me in her line of work.

She transferred the chicken to the pot and added the vegetables and stock. The slam of the oven door was some kind of end to things. When she turned to me again, she was smiling.

'I might be pregnant, but nursey reckons one glass of wine won't stunt growth.' She uncorked a bottle of Cabernet Sauvignon and poured a hefty glug.

'Has Charlie ever talked to you about Gordon?'

'Of course he has. He's not one to hide his grief, Charlie. He's seen plenty in his time, quite a bit of it unpleasant. He knows how to deal with tragedy.'

'It helped. He talked to me about it today. About the car crash. It helped me.'

'It was before seatbelts, of course. Everyone did the same. Everybody had a child who bopped about on the back seat, or leaned forward to chat in between Mum and Dad. When you think of the appalling injuries, windscreens and the like, well, it's beyond me how the law didn't change years before it did.'

Charlie and his then wife, who had left him after the accident, had been driving home to Peterhead, where Charlie was first mate on a prawn trawler. Their six-year-old son Gordon was in the back. Charlie was a good driver. He never drank. He always observed the speed limit. But the tread on their tyres was worn and the road was wet. The brake discs had not been checked for a while – they had skipped the last service because they couldn't afford it. It was a newish car; they weren't too worried about doing it just that once.

Music in the car. One of Carol's old tapes. The Ink Spots. They had all sung along to *If I Didn't Care* and *Do I Worry?* Later, Charlie would sit with the album sleeve alone at home, staring at the track listing, the last three songs of which were *Life is Just a Gamble*, *Forever Now* and *You Always Hurt the One You Love*. It might have been funny, beyond belief, if it hadn't happened to him. Charlie had noticed the spongey brakes a moment before they failed completely. Their car, an Austin Princess, slid through a T-junction and into the side of an articulated lorry, he and Carol had suffered whiplash injuries, and Carol had sustained a broken leg when the dashboard collapsed into her thighs.

Gordon had been catapulted past them. Charlie heard a popping sound, two in quick succession, even as the wreckage of the car drew in around him. He saw his son impact against the windscreen, his face spread into it, moments before it shattered outward. He realised that the popping sound must have been something in Gordon's legs giving way – his knees or his pelvis – to allow them to fly free of the footwell in the back. The popping noise disturbed him more than anything else; more than the visit to the morgue to identify the body. Carol turned to dust inside. She stopped speaking. She withdrew so far that she seemed for ever on the verge of turning around.

We both drank our wine a little too quickly, talking about this awful accident. I motioned to Ruth's glass, and though she looked reluctant, she nodded her head.

I reached for the bottle of wine and felt my spine crack. Grey mist drizzled across my vision. The bolus of mashed breadsticks in my mouth caked the back of my throat; I couldn't swallow it. Through the grain I saw the beak of the broken gull, bloodied and shuddering. I heard bubbles of air being sucked through wounds. The gull bent the spar of its wings and lifted from the sand; black, blood-wet clumps hung or fell from the chicane of its body.

And then Ruth was doing something to my back and the pressure relented and I was able to swallow and colour came back to my world.

'It's all right,' she said. 'It's okay. Just a spasm. A muscle spasm.'

'Christ,' I said.

'Not that I'm going to say "told you so", or anything like that.'

I shook my head. 'That was more painful than being hit by the car.'

'Just take it easy. There's plenty of time for you to up the ante. There's no rush.'

She reached across me for her glass. Her face

glided past my own, inches away. I smelled her, fresh and good and pregnant, and wondered where Tamara was, what she was doing. Was she thinking of me? Was she dissolving in her own acid guilt? I wondered if she would recognise me, should she turn up, racked with remorse. I couldn't bear to be rejected twice. It was better that she was lost to me.

I went out again after dinner. I felt full and, somehow, braced against further injury, as if the swell of food in my belly was acting as a buffer against my spine. Ruth had gone to bed with a cup of raspberry leaf tea and one of her non-fiction books about the indomitable human spirit of survival. She was obsessed by the human capacity to endure. If we were reading together in the same room, she'd break into my concentration with some excerpt about life in extremis: seriously injured mountaineers who crawl thousands of feet to safety; the story of the Japanese man lost on a winter hill who broke his pelvis and went into hibernation.

I made sure I shut the door quietly, not wanting another lecture on the fragility of my body and mind. I was coming back, I was healing, but so much of that was only going to happen if I regained control of myself. I felt, sometimes, like some piece of meat being tossed about by Ruth's tongs.

The air was splinter cold. I thought I could smell woodsmoke on it, but I was always smelling smoke these days. I couldn't tell if it was real or some olfactory breakdown courtesy of the accident. I stood and looked at the cleaned-out sky, massive above the village. Stars everywhere. The longer you stared, the more made themselves known. They were there on cloud-packed days of storm. They were there when you fell in love with a woman you no longer knew. They were there for her now, wherever she was.

I had never walked the beach at dead of night. It would be fun to do so, to see the colour and glow in those fishermen's tents, watch the loose particles on the surface snake across the packed sand like spindrift. But I was dog-tired. My back was seizing up; my legs felt as though they'd been dipped in quick-drying concrete. I thought of the beach further south, how it was collapsing into the sea, as it had done since the continents were formed. No amount of bulldozers and boulders were going to stop it. This entire bulge of East Anglia was sinking. In ten thousand years or so, the map of the UK would look as though a shark had bitten off its backside.

Ruth in bed, warm with her books and her tea. She was my riprap. She was my water barrier. I wondered what was stalling the tide for her. Not me. I was too weak. But I might, in time. I wanted to. But I needed to find out what had happened to Tamara, first. I needed to hear her version of events. I felt itchy, cuckolded, left out of some crucial loop. I felt like what I was: someone who had lost six months of his life.

Far off, above the lights of the oil tankers fastened to the horizon, the glitter and flash of aviation lights: a jet at cruising altitude chalking the night. If I stopped breathing, I could just hear its call.

I went back inside, fast as I could. It was if the heat from the engines, no matter how many miles away, and counting, had scoured out the back of my throat. My bowels were suddenly loose as soup.

Tragedy accreted. Layers of it pressing down, a geology of misery. If I'd thought the near miss would be subsumed by the hit-and-run, I was wrong. They held hands together and laughed; siblings reunited after too long apart.

I had gripped the control stick so tightly, I left fingermarks in it.

Chapter Three

THE PAIN NURSE

RUTH WAS DRESSED for work by the time I had struggled out of my bed. With her nurse's uniform on, she seemed fussier, more driven. She bustled about the living room, collecting things for her bag. I sat in the stiff, upright armchair that nobody else used and sipped tea, watching her, getting tired out by her industry. She was ordering me in that mock serious way of hers to relax today. I was not, repeat not, allowed to walk on the beach. The most effort I was expected to expend was in raising my arm to pour medicine, or fix myself lunch, by which time she would be back to check on me.

I gazed at her face and tried, again, to come to terms with what was happening here. Everything was new to me; it was not to her. She was clued up. I had been assimilated into her routine and was a part of her life now. I was three weeks into the biggest shock I'd ever experienced. Her face was at once the most familiar and the most foreign to me. I needed her, but I didn't know how much. At that obvious level, the nurse tending the healing, but I was beginning to feel something deeper, something uncoiling in me as it had when I first met Tamara. I was at a loss. I knew this sort of thing happened. Wounded soldiers were always falling in love with the angels who patted cold compresses against their fevered brows.

I sat there sipping tepid Typhoo, huddled in my musty old bathrobe, feeling cheap and nasty and unfaithful.

Ruth kissed my cheek, snatched up her keys and opened the door. A hesitation, a slight stiffening, then she was gone. I waited a minute or two, until I heard the struggling engine of her old Ford recede down Surt Road, and then hobbled to the door, thinking that even if I wanted to go to the beach I couldn't physically hack it.

On the doorstep was another shoebox. Blue. This had held a children's pair of all-terrain boots. The words Snow Field were written on the top of it. Whoever owned these shoes had bought them in France, where their foot size was 26. *1er Prix,* the box boasted: *12,90€.* I picked it up and brought it inside, smelling it first to check there was nothing on the turn. I had once been left a polythene bag of what looked like regurgitated chicken livers. A woman brought me ten garden refuse sacks filled with the soiled nappies of her six-week-old daughter. She had wanted to save everything, but it had overtaken her life, her home. People left me uneaten dinners congealing on paper plates. They left me dead pets.

Today there was nothing like that. A bunch of letters, some formal-looking documents, unmarked CDs in booklet-free jewel cases, a birthday card, a toy elephant, a toy car.

I felt a shiver as I thought of the person driving the car that had hit me. I wondered if he or she were local, whether they were aware of who I was, whether I had burned something of theirs. Maybe I had burned evidence that would have inculpated them. It wasn't worth thinking about; it would tear me up. But I decided to start paying more attention to the objects laid at my door, and to who was collecting them, placing them there.

I couldn't work out how this had started. It felt as though it was more natural to me than breathing. It was vital and dull in equal measure. It was like drinking water.

Deeper in the box, under the toys and the trinkets, a message written in red ink on lined notepaper: *burn the oceans, burn them all, ACCEPT THE CRAW, BASTARDS, BASTARDS. GOD HELP THOSE BABIES TO REST. WINTER BAY 1672.*

I placed the box under my bed and spent the best part of half an hour getting dressed. I had developed a system for pulling on my socks that involved pretty much my feet and nothing else. It was amazing what you could do with your feet when there was no other option. I rested when the clothes were on, eyes closed to the warm throb in the middle of my back.

The vertebrae in the middle of the dorsal region are heart-shaped. Those bearing peculiarities are the first, ninth, tenth, eleventh and twelfth. The way these bones lock together. The way they are designed. Separate, but needy. The faceting. The recesses for the tubercles of the ribs. I'd read the text books when I was able. I wanted to know what was wrong with me, to a tedious degree. I must have said the words, *what does that mean?* to the surgeon and the doctor and the physiotherapist maybe a thousand times in the past three weeks. I knew so much about the damaged parts of my body, and the body in general, that it became too familiar. It became so familiar, it became alien again, like a simple word recited so often that it loses its meaning. I examined the skeleton and saw what the child sees: a grinning, emaciated monster. That these were inside us, wrapped in meat and membrane and mucus, was a horrible thought. Something other than what looked human, but that, maddeningly, also looked human, was trapped in all that wet muscle, its mouth leering behind the visible lips no matter what the owner's expression. The skull was always happy. It knew it would have its day.

I shuffled through to the kitchen and stood for a moment by the island in its centre, enjoying the blocks of amber sunlight on the wall opposite the windows. I opened the pack of pain relief and swallowed a handful of pills and vitamins with a glass of water and headed back to the front of the building, where the books on the shelves waited for fingers that never came to slide them out. Well, they would today, even if it was only temporarily.

Ruth's corner was all set up for her. Blanket over the chair, her favourite cushion. A box of Dr Stuart's herbal teas. A book on the go: Joe Tasker's *Savage Arena*. The till was open, empty. A dish of dry cat food for Vulcan lay on the windowsill. The silence and stillness of the shop seemed somehow wrong. Not because the shop felt like somewhere that ought to be all bustle, but because it didn't seem likely to ever change. It was like being in a mausoleum.

I browsed the stacks for a while, making little appreciative murmurs whenever I saw an author whose work I admired. The books were in good condition, generally, although I thought the prices were on the stiff side.

I made some tea and sat in Ruth's chair. I pinched a couple of biscuits from the pack peeking from the half-opened drawer. I thought about the B&B Tamara and I had bought on the seafront. The keys were in my pocket but I had not been able to bring myself to unlock that door and enter a new stage of my life. It was a shared project; the business was partly Tamara's. It was all there on the legal deeds. Her name. Intractable proof that she existed. Exists. Just in case I needed to be reassured. She had to be here before I could put what was left of my back into making a success of the venture. I needed something to do, I had to get back to some semblance of normality.

I finished my tea and moved to the section on local history. There were half a dozen guide books to the Suffolk coastline, its churches and cathedrals. A couple of tatty histories on the drowned city of Dunwich and some old OS maps that were probably still relevant. There was also a pamphlet, presumably locally written and produced, judging by the poor quality of the paper and printing, about the Battle of Winter Bay in 1672. I didn't plan on reading it, but the coincidence provided an added prickle.

An hour later I'd finished it. The last page was defaced. Somebody had scribbled words: *SUFFER CHILDREN... SUCCOUR TO THE CRAW. THEY WERE TAKEN!* all over it. That word again. *Craw.* I could still make out what the printed words were supposed to be beneath, though. I stretched gingerly, listening to the crackle in my back, and mused about the handwriting. It was different to the other note. What did it mean? I had seen no reference to children in the pamphlet's text.

Southwick had once been a major anchorage for the English naval fleet. Gorton Ness to the north and Dotwich to the south had formed a natural bay – Winter Bay – before erosion sanded it straight. In May 1672, a number of sailors were in Southwick while their ships were being prepared for battle: war with the Dutch was imminent. It was planned that the Allied fleets would form a blockade off Dogger Bank, so that the Dutch fleets could be intercepted if it should make a move to retreat to home ports. The Dutch fleet was anchored off Walcheren Island, biding its time before a strike designed to open a channel in the North Sea for Dutch shipping.

For three days the English fleet lay in the bay, fattening itself with men, provisions and ammunition. The Earl of Sandwich was anxious that the Dutch might attempt a surprise attack but his warnings were unheeded. A French scout ship returned at dawn, the entire Dutch fleet on her foam. By the time the careened flagship had been refloated, and the 90 ships put to sea, the Dutch were charging in from the horizon. Cue bloodbath.

I put the pamphlet back and rubbed my face. I fancied a beer. The thought of that pretty beach turned red with blood, of sunken ships, of burnt, bloated bodies drifting in with the tide for days after the end of fighting, was difficult to stomach. People came here to eat ice cream and get a suntan. They bought premium-priced beach huts and decorated them, gave them twee names, visited them a couple of weeks every year.

They come here to die.

I winced and jerked my head, as if the words had been spoken to me. Yes, they did come here to die, eventually, but that didn't make it into some dark receptacle. It was a village with an aged population, with a reputation for being a winding-down sort of place, a place of rest. I saw old men and women sitting on deckchairs or benches or wheelchairs, staring out to sea as if unpicking a code that could be read by them alone. In the summer they shifted dune-slow across the gravel and wore their best clothes for lunch in the local pubs. They stared straight ahead and chewed and chewed. It was a sort of lethargy, this business of ageing, of dying. It was about slowing right down to a point where your body could begin the business of consuming itself.

Which was pretty much where I was up to. Was I kidding myself? Would I ever run along the beach? Would I ever kick a football again? I could not even bend over to touch my knees. I was here to die too. It was just going to take much longer than it did for most. But it wasn't this, or the ugly graffiti, or Southwick's unpleasant history, that was gnawing at me. I was leafing through books, drinking tea, pinching Ruth's fruit shortcake, and somewhere Tamara was getting on with her life. Perhaps she was wondering about me. Or was pushing me from her mind, thinking me dead. Maybe this was some kind of Ukrainian test. *I go, you find me.* Was I failing her?

Restless, I left the shop, locking the door behind me. Out of season, the streets of the village were invariably empty. All the old people were inside, staring at walls, at televisions, chewing, all Windsor knots and pearls. Waiting for the sun, or the end.

I bit down on that thought, trying to gnaw it off, spit it away. I made my way up to The Fluke and ordered a pint of Broadside. The barman told me to sit down; he'd bring me my drink. I thanked him, to divert the mouthful of abuse I wanted to spill his way. I was no invalid. I could carry my own pint. But then I caught the ghost of myself in the glass of the door as I turned. I was an old man. The skin of my face was tired; it couldn't just be the scars that were doing that. The metal in my back held me upright, but the rest of my body seemed to be railing against it, failing. I was thin and weak. I was wasted.

I sat in the corner of the pub, in shade. There was nobody else, apart from a black Labrador sleeping by the slot machine. The barman put my drink in front of me and I nodded. If Tamara had not left me, what did that mean? My mind wouldn't hold hands with that thought.

I drank half the bitter quickly and asked the barman to change a five-pound note for the phone. I pulled out my address book and flicked through it. I had tried Tamara's mobile phone number a dozen times in the past three weeks. It had not been answered once. I hadn't panicked about this; she didn't like mobiles and rarely used hers. I certainly hadn't seen her receive any calls and she had chosen not to activate an answering service. When I asked her what I would do if I needed to get in touch with her, she had told me she wouldn't be away from me long enough for me to need to call her. I had to assume it was switched off, or shut away in a drawer. It could have run out of juice. She might have lost it.

Nothing of help in the address book. Both her parents were dead. She had no siblings. She had a few friends in the airline business, including one, Catriona, who had been closer than most. They had worked together on a series of flights over the course of a year, shortly before I met her. I called Air France and asked to speak to their personnel department. I was put on hold and then a female voice, in French, asked me how she could be of assistance.

'I'm trying to track down a member of your cabin crew. She might still be working for you, but she was definitely employed by Air France throughout 2010.'

'And you are?'

'Paul Roan. I was a first officer with Lufthansa until last year.'

'Was?'

'I retired.'

'You don't sound so old.'

I laughed. 'I retired for personal reasons.'

'And the person you're looking for?'

'Catriona Beck. She was part of a cabin crew that included my girlfriend, Tamara Dziuba.'

'Ah, yes. I know both of them.'

I felt my heart pitch. 'You do?'

'Yes, Catriona and I are friends. I met Tamara on a number of occasions. Work functions. That sort of thing.'

'Do you know where I can find Tamara?'

There was a hesitation. 'You said she was your girlfriend?'

'That's right. She... We decided on a trial separation. But I haven't seen her for a while.'

'How long is a while?'

'Look, it isn't important,' I snapped. I caught the barman looking up at me in my periphery. I thumbed some more coins into the phone. 'Sorry. It's been six months.'

'I can't help you,' she said, her manner more clipped now. 'If you give me your contact details, I'll pass on your message to Catriona and – '

'Can't you put me through to Catriona now?'

'She's away. Working. She won't be back until Thursday evening.'

I sighed and the sound lingered in the receiver. 'Okay,' I said. 'If you could ask her to call me, as a matter of great urgency, on... '

I gave Ruth's phone number and email address, wishing I had sorted out my own contact details since my recovery rather than plodding around in a daze, owlishly ranging to see if Tamara was anywhere close, carrying a bunch of flowers and a box of chocolates. I imagined Catriona rubbing Tamara's shoulders, saying *It's for the best. You did the right thing.* Tamara nodding. Tamara turning. Tamara seeing some young thing. Tamara falling in love. Christ.

I flicked through the rest of the book and noticed the address of Tamara's old bolthole in Amsterdam. I tried calling that too, but nobody was answering. I couldn't remember the name of the guy who lived next door, and the address book didn't give up any other Amsterdam addresses. *Amsterdam*, I thought. Why would she go there?

I pocketed the rest of the change and drained my pint. I felt better. Positive action. It wasn't much, but I had made the first move; everything from here on in would be easier to decide upon, I thought. I felt a burning low in my chest. Acid reflux. Or my jigsaw ribs making themselves known. I could no longer tell when I was hungry. Too many other sensations jumped the queue. I ate according to the clock now and it was pushing on for noon.

I STAYED AWAY from the beach that morning, despite an ache to return. There was something about the expansive skies that helped me forget myself for a while, stopped me from feeling so limited. But I stayed away because Ruth had asked me to. It wasn't just that she was right, but also because it felt good to do as someone said. Being responsible for an aircraft filled with people blunted your appreciation of a command structure. You took orders that had to do with the process of flying. You requested and were either granted or denied. It wasn't down to personality or reliance. It was mechanical, on any number of levels.

I mooched about. I ate fish and chips. I read the papers. Three weeks after waking up, the world seemed no different to how it had been before my accident. One hundred and eighty nine days of people kicking footballs and arguing and fighting and killing and being rescued. Four thousand five hundred and thirty six hours of people watching TV and fucking and eating curry. Two hundred and seventy two thousand one hundred and sixty minutes of waiting for a bus and shopping at Tesco and wiping your arse. Sixteen million three hundred and twenty nine thousand six hundred seconds of watching somebody wither in Intensive Care.

Ruth came home tired at lunch time. She ate soup and went to bed for a nap. She didn't feel much like talking, beyond: 'Another couple of weeks and that's me done. I can't cope with much more of that or the baby will suffer.'

I welcomed the news. We could sit together on the sofa and watch afternoon films. I could help her eat whatever weird dietary urges her pregnancy demanded of her. It was important to find that groove again, that way of interacting with other people, develop a sense of belonging. I sensed that people brought me secrets to burn because of my detachment. I reeked of loner.

I performed my exercises. Diaphragmatic breathing. Static quadriceps exercises. Pelvic tilting. Transversus abdominus. I bathed. The sky was crowding with clouds, high and thick and grey. A storm was pressing the air into the village. I opened the bathroom window an inch to let the steam escape and sat in my hot, sudsy well, feeling my muscles slowly untie themselves. I soaped my chest gingerly, despite everything there having healed some time ago. I felt fragile, like some wet piece of bone china handled by a butter-fingered child. My ribs felt dog-chewed. They had collapsed under the punch of the radiator grille. One of them had torn into my lung. I recalled some of the literature I'd been given at the hospital from the impressively titled Therapies Directorate. *To be realistic you must give yourself two years to be the best that you can be.*

Cool air eddied through the mist from the bath. The bathroom mirror fluxed in stages of opacity. Ridges of clarity formed. I saw my ribs opened out like the claws of a giant crab. I saw the ruined seagull clatter into the red fist at its centre, beak stabbing and rending. Blood pinked the tip of it and the curled cone of its tongue. Its wingtips raised like the arms of some nightmare conductor priming his orchestra. The squeal of bone grinding against metal. The best that you can be is not the same as the best that you once were.

I came out of this breathless. I had not fallen asleep. My eyes had remained open throughout it. The doctor had warned me about flashbacks. The trauma had been purged, to some extent, from my body, but it would be a while before I felt mentally healed.

I heard footsteps outside, voices murmuring, edged with sharpness in the crisp night air. Two people, returning from the pub. Slightly breathy, a little tipsy. A her and a him. I heard her say *Don't believe the truth.*

Sudden, site specific heat: I lifted my fingers (any number of muscles and nerves jangling as I did so) and dabbled my fingers in the bauble of blood sliding from my left nostril. The footsteps paused, gritted around for a few moments – him kissing her? her kissing him? – before moving on. I suddenly felt exhausted, as if I'd been reading for too long something I didn't quite understand. I wiped and rewiped my nose with my forearm until it had stopped and I looked as though I had tried to open the old Median Basilic and end it all.

I rinsed the blood off and elbowed the lever that opened the plughole. Pink water sank around me, returned to me my weight and discomfort. I dried and applied. I flinched my way into the bathrobe. Sweat greased me; ghosts of copper had settled against my skin: I could have done with another bath. Instead I moved to my bed and lay down, using the hand-held controls to dent the bed so it cradled me just the way I needed.

I closed my eyes and there was Tamara. She was wearing a grey wool duffel coat, floral print top and pale Diesel jeans. Her hood was up and her hair was down and the wind was striping her face with it. I tilted my face to better hear what she was trying to say but the wind was messing with that too. I couldn't read the message on her lips. Hair whipped across the dark red of her mouth.

I heard a sound like a horse's hooves at a gallop on hard earth. I felt it in my bones. But, I realised quickly, there was more than one horse; another was behind it, at distance, catching up. Fast, faster. The percussive sounds tumbled against and over one another, and it reminded me of something I couldn't put into words or pictures. I felt the back of my neck tighten and knew that it wasn't horses. I don't know how, but I knew that it was the worst sound in the world and that if I turned around, whatever it was would destroy me.

I opened my eyes and waited for it to pass.

I COOKED DINNER in Ruth's kitchen, a surprise for her, while she was sorting books downstairs. I marinated some salmon in lemon juice and soy sauce and made mashed potatoes and French beans in garlic. I slapped the fish on a hot griddle as she came up, pushing the scent of old books in before her. She took a glass of wine with only the slightest grimace and I led her into the living room. She was pale. She fidgeted on the armchair, unable to get comfortable.

'Is it kicking?' I asked.

'A little,' she said, with a pained smile. 'Sometimes he gets hiccups. Sometimes I can feel him flinch when a door slams or a car horn sounds.'

'It's a boy, then?'

'I think so, yes.'

'You don't know for sure?'

She shook her head. 'I don't want to know. I want it to be a surprise. But I feel it's a boy. Burly. Throwing his weight around.'

'Can I feel?'

Another shake. 'I don't want be touched,' she said. 'I don't… it just doesn't feel right. No matter how gentle you… it would feel like an assault.'

I digested this, keeping quiet despite wanting to protest. I thought we were friends. She'd saved my life. We were closer than friends because of that. But here she was, putting up a shield. I knew what had happened to her, but it didn't make it easier to deal with. I was a man, but I wasn't a threat.

I said, 'Have you thought of any names?'

Again, a shake of the head. There was something wrong. She was white, glassy. She seemed on the verge of tears, more so than usual. 'I'm sorry,' I said. 'I didn't mean to spoil the mood.'

'It's all right. It's my hormones. I'm all over the

place. And it's also… the baby… whenever I think of it I think of him.'

'We don't have to talk about this. Really. I'm sorry I even started this.'

She took a sip of her wine and it seemed to fortify her. 'It's all right. I mean it. I need to get a grip. And I will.'

We sat in a silence that was far from companionable. I fetched the plates of food and we ate it and put our knives and forks down. I felt like an unwanted, uninvited guest who has overstayed a welcome that had never really been extended. I considered turning in, or going for a walk, but merely the thought of it made my legs burn. I thought of the cockpit of a 777. Right seat. Night flight out of Schiphol, AMS. Velvet sky, deepening. The clean, superbright glimmer of the runway lights. Light wind. Cool, crisp shirt. The power hanging there in the night behind you, as near as dammit one hundred thousand pounds lbf in each engine. The winding up. The knowledge you are flying with a fine captain. Thomas Sheedy, 52. Closing in on 30,000 hours of service. We are confident. We are good. Captain Sheedy says something, but it's all wrong. I turn to him and the top of his head is gone.

'I tried to contact my girlfriend today,' I said.

'Paul,' she said. The nurse voice.

'I have to know,' I said. 'I can't just let things lie as they are.'

'She left you. She went home.'

'Her home is here,' I said. 'With me. She's my girlfriend.' It felt strange referring to Tamara like that. It was beginning to feel as though she was not real, as if she were a dream. Details were softening. One of her breasts was slightly larger than the other; I couldn't remember which one. I couldn't summon the sound of her voice. That she was somewhere else in the world, but still my girlfriend, seemed the most ridiculous idea.

'So,' Ruth said, undercover of a sigh. 'Any luck?'

'A possible lead,' I said. 'Someone who knows someone who worked with her. She's going to call me back.'

'Be careful,' she said.

'I know the risks.'

'Maybe. There might be more than you think. You discover something unpleasant, she's with another man... it might put your convalescence back months.'

'Anything would be better than this... not knowing.'

'I hope you're right. Thanks for dinner.'

She stood up and moved past me, touching my shoulder briefly.

'Ruth,' I said.

'What is it?'

'Does the word... have you heard the word "craw" mentioned around here?'

'What?'

'Craw.'

'As in "stick in the craw"?'

'Maybe, yes. Maybe, no. Anybody use it?'

'Not around me,' she said.

She moved to the bathroom and brushed her teeth. I heard the snick of her bedroom door as it closed.

I cleared away the dinner plates and had another

glass of wine. Ruth wasn't coming back. She'd spent another tough day patching up the walking wounded. Perhaps I was getting her down. How miserable must it be for her to come home just to find another patient?

My things – our things – were stored in Ruth's garage. I went downstairs and into the yard. I pulled open the garage door, switched on the light in there and stared at the boxes. Vulcan made figure-of-eight entreaties at my ankles. I opened a box. I didn't recognise any of the contents. It was only after a while spent picking through books and folders and plastic tubs that familiarity began to sink in. I found a box of Tamara's blouses, individually wrapped in polythene bags. Her smell was in all of them. I found an album of photographs, most of them self-timed ones of us squeezed tight into a 6"x4" frame as if we were unsure that the camera would capture us both in the shot.

I looked hard into her eyes as if the reason for her subsequent abandonment of me could be read. Rubbed the seams and hems of her clothes, searching for splinters of doubt. I closed the boxes and repositioned the packing tape. I could not foresee an occasion when I might unpack all of this again. It was frighteningly easy to imagine taking each box to the beach and setting fire to them under the pier.

I sat and fondled Vulcan's ears for a while, thinking of Tamara, thinking of Ruth. Ruth's own little storage corner seemed pitiful in comparison, but the fruits of her life were surrounding her all the time. She had space to stretch out. She was living. A box contained a first aid kit and a vintage

leather bag, the kind you might have seen a country
doctor pootling around with in the 1950s. There
was a chipped dinner plate with a picture of a duck
in the centre – her own, from childhood? – and a
clutch of old Ladybird books bound together with
elastic bands. There were a few other things. Pencil
cases and egg-cups and dried flowers in polythene
envelopes. Junk or treasure, depending on who was
looking at it.

I closed the door and walked back to my room.
Vulcan followed me, weaving around my ankles. I
gave him some food and patted his head, stared at
my stranger's hand for a while. The scars there didn't
shock me as they had at first. Sometimes I would
reach out for something and flinch, as if someone
else were inhabiting my clothes, a thin imposter
controlled by my mind. I was getting used to the fact
that my appearance had changed. I was coping. Now
it looked as though I would have to come to terms
with Tamara's removal from my life. There would be
no plastic surgery to treat those scars. No bandages
and ointment. My black, scabbed over heart would
just have to chug on with the burden.

Yet I went to bed feeling an uneasy mix of hope and
dread. I had made the first steps to finding Tamara.
At the very least, I would have it from her mouth
what it was she wanted to do. I would not allow
her the comfort of a clean break. *Craw*, I thought. It
made me think of famished black birds. It made me
think of choking to death on splinters of bone.

In the night I was disturbed by the sound of
Ruth moving through the house. It was late, past
two, when I heard the front door open and close.

Some time later, maybe half an hour or so, I heard it open and close again. I dreamed of Tamara's mouth opening and closing too, as she struggled to put into words the nightmare that she had designed for me.

Chapter Four

BLACK LANDINGS

I WEAR THE same clothes nearly every day. Soft, elasticated jogging bottoms. A hooded top with a zipper (I can't pull clothes over my head). Slip-on sandals. I consider it a uniform, just the same as the one I wore at Lufthansa. Maybe a little less glamorous. It's one less thing to worry about. I can move more freely. Sometimes I wish I could climb out of this tight, inflexible skin too. I feel hemmed in, trapped. The pills don't cancel the pain, they just move it out of reach for a while. It's still there, in view, like a dangerous thing put on a high shelf away from the children. And you can't stop glancing at it. You know it will be returned to its normal place before long. *Decide what you reasonably feel that you would like to achieve in your life and think about how using opioids can help you. Set yourself some realistic goals.*

A plastic doll's head with a lazy eye. A Hähnel battery charger. A tube of discoloured Berocca vitamin tablets. A pencil case with a hole in it. An abandoned letter, one sentence long: *I don't know how to say this to you, so I'm writing it instead.*

I take the box to the beach. The sky is porridge. It's unlikely to clear all day, according to the forecast. Dampness in the air, finer than mist. You can't see it, but by the time I reach my little nest of cinders, my skin and clothes are jewelled with moisture. The box too. At first I doubt this will burn, but it's as always: first match. The flame skates slowly along the lip of cardboard, darkening and warping in its wake. It moves fast, dipping into the contents like something hungry chasing down its next meal. The orange curl becomes a bright yellow fan. The smell of smoke as it thickens, turning into a pumping black column, is new, different to the last time. It smells synthetic today, probably because of the plastic. It works hard, this fire, a little industry of obliteration. It won't clock off until everything is gone. Fire is efficient, sometimes horribly so. As a pilot, you don't consider the awful ramifications of a crash. You prepare for an emergency. You do not prepare for your own death.

I toed the remnants into the shingle and stood up. I did some light stretching, trying hard not to think of my new skin separating under the stress. I walked the mile or so between the pier and the harbour wall, looking at the green bite indicators of the nightfishermen hanging above the shoreline like static fireflies. By the time I reached the wall, my top was sodden, clinging unpleasantly to my back. I sat down and pulled the length of yellow string from my pocket. My fingers itched, though I wasn't sure if this was part of their recovery or in anticipation of the task ahead. I didn't practise any of the knots I'd learned, I just played with the string, allowing my fingers to produce their own configuration of bights and falls. The sea was calm, despite the frowning sky. I saw a seal's head break the surface. It watched the beach for a while and then dived down. I looked all over but I didn't see it come back up.

I kept picking at the strands of my life, pre-crash, trying to find some reason for Tamara's departure. But there wasn't one. Not unless she was secretly disgusted by the near miss. If she was, she'd hidden it well. She stood by me all through that summer of meetings, hearings and reports. She stepped between me and the father of a young girl who had been on the flight. He spat at me, tried to punch me, his face turning black with rage as if there had been a crash and she was dead. Tamara talked me down when I was angry and talked me up when I was miserable. At night she held me and kissed me and whispered Ukrainian into my hair. *Ni zhyty, ni vmeraty.* So there was only the hit-and-run that could have driven a wedge between us. Every time I thought of her, the way she behaved prior to her leaving, it would not sit right with events. She had acted out of character.

The ends of the string had disappeared. Somehow I had massaged it into a knot that contained no protrusions. It was folded and dimpled like a navel. I couldn't begin to unpick it. It was seamless. I put it in my pocket, more disturbed than I ought to have been. The fishermen were trudging off the shingle. I never saw anybody catch anything. I was about to follow them, appalled by how the beach seemed to have grown while I was resting, when I noticed a tiny figure at the far end, close to the site where I lighted my fires. I felt a moment of panic, but I knew I never left a fire unattended. I waited until whatever it was had been consumed, and then I put it out and I made sure. If it was a child, it would not be burnt.

The child seemed very small. And naked too. It was a long way away, but although my vision had been affected by the accident, it wasn't so bad as to instil doubt. There didn't seem to be any parents nearby. I shouted at the fishermen, who were much closer, but they didn't hear me. Nor could they see, apparently, what I was seeing, despite their heads occasionally raising to gaze down the beach at the lights on the pier.

But then the figure was gone and already I was questioning what I had seen. Naked babies did not play on the beach, not in winter at any rate. There must have been a guardian nearby who had scooted it back into a buggy. Maybe they had to change its clothes because it had soiled itself.

I thought to go and check, but Charlie was coming down the harbour path, whistling me as if I were a dog. He asked me again if I was up for a fishing trip and this time he wouldn't take no for an answer. When I mentioned the weather, he told me it would clear up within the hour.

'Blue skies and sunglasses 'fore we get to the fishing grounds or I'll buy y'a pint and y'supper when we get back.'

'I saw a child,' I said. 'A baby.'

He gazed back over my shoulder and nodded. 'Yes. We have babies here. They grows up into reg'lar folks an' all, just like you 'n' me. Well, me anyways.'

'I just thought, in light of what happened...' My words tailed off.

'So,' he said. 'Fishin'.'

He wore a happy, expectant look. I'd been putting him off ever since returning from the hospital, citing my weakness, injuries, seasickness, fear of drowning... He was hungry for company, perhaps even seeing me as a surrogate for Gordon, who no doubt would have followed his dad into the fishing business.

'I really have no clue about boats, or fish,' I said, pathetically, as he led the way to the *Gratitude*. 'I'm not even dressed for it.'

He handed me a thick jumper, which he helped me put on, and a pair of boots. 'Now y'are,' he said.

He started the engine and cast off the moorings. I strapped on a lifejacket and sat on a bench to watch him steer the boat out of the harbour. He told me of the Viking rudders that had been dredged up in the fishing nets over the years. He mentioned how the fishing had changed over the fifty years he had lived here. There had been shrimp in abundance once, available the whole summer, but then the beamers would come and hoover the whole lot up in one day. Reduced stocks and punitive EU restrictions meant that the fishing industry was all but dead here; a terrible brake applied to a tradition that had lasted a thousand years. Trawlers were illicitly selling over-quota fish.

Charlie could remember the good times. Fish gold: cod, monkfish and hake, and also dogfish, lemon sole, turbot and lobster. Scallops dredged up from the bed. Exotics such as red mullet and uglies: angler fish, conger eel. Now you could spend a day out on a boat and you'd be lucky to recoup your fuel costs.

There were some still making a living in this line, but not many. Those that did were either escaping from something or had no choice. He'd met a couple of Eastern Europeans who worked on crabbing boats. They were making between thirty and forty thousand pounds a year, but it was breakback work. You lived on board and worked three months before you had a month off. Accommodation and meals were taken out of your pay packet.

Charlie had considered moving on many times – the crabbing boats had attracted him for a short time – but he could never leave the place where he had been born. 'I get headache if I'm away too long,' he said.

He owned a small fish shed from which he sold herring and sprat during the winter ('But only to the older ladies and gents... they're not a fish the young like much'), cod, Dover sole and turbot in the summer. He especially liked selling turbot to Londoners who came out to the village. He could put whatever price he liked on them and they paid without question. And he could still make more money charging the best part of a thousand pounds to groups of fishing buddies that wanted to charter a boat to the wrecks.

'How long before we get to where we're going?' I asked him. The wind was charging the boat, rocking us from side to side. The sea had decided to take up the challenge thrown by the sky and had turned moody. Plenty of chop now. I received an occasional slap of cold spray across the face.

'Just thirty miles or so. We'll drop a net or two and then move on, maybe shoot some lines over a wreck. Bigger fish there. Can't dredge so the bigger boats don't bother.'

I felt as if I was an understudy drafted in to take the place of the lead actor who has suddenly fallen ill. Everything felt unreal, staged. Even our dialogue seemed scripted. It was too mannered, too polite. This wasn't my normal life, and yet it was, now. I had been present, yet absent, and routines had been prescribed without my involvement, and it was all for my benefit, supposedly. I felt as if I were being channelled, though, forced along corridors of behaviour that I wouldn't normally travel. I did not feel free.

This was not just as a result of the restrictions of my injuries, or the exercises I needed to do just to be able to get out of bed in the mornings. It went deeper than that. Southwick might just be a façade, a two-dimensional Hollywood film set. Somehow I needed to get behind the scenes in order to understand fully my role. Or maybe this was how everyone who had once lived a busy, demanding life felt when reverse thrust was engaged and you were forced to be still.

I allowed myself to be pressed and shaped and moulded. I did as Charlie said. I baited hooks. I took the wheel when he wanted to go for a piss. I helped him, after a fashion, to manipulate the heavy nets and their bobbins through the gallows and into the churning, black water. We drank tea laced with rum and watched the restless ocean.

'Y'got y'sea legs yet?' he asked.

'I'm getting there,' I told him. 'Took me long enough to get my air legs.'

'Well, there's a thing. Don't know about flying. Never been up. But I can read the sky a little.'

'You've never been in an aircraft?'

He shook his head. 'Not that odd. Plenty haven't, 'specially my age and older. Never thought to travel.

Got everything I want here. And I don't trust those big bastards anyway. It's not right.'

I said: 'I flew with a captain, Captain Sheedy his name was. He was a very experienced pilot. He'd flown nearly thirty thousand hours on a variety of aircraft. Big ones, in the main. 767s, 747s, you know. He was a good guy. A good pilot to learn from.'

Charlie didn't seem to have a clue what I was talking about. I kept going, if only to stop him from asking me if he flew all those hours without a break. I don't know why I was talking at all. I kept my eyes on the sea; I felt slightly nauseous. I was probably talking to try to stave off seasickness. I really didn't want to vomit on Charlie's boat.

'We had this thing, this agreement, that if we were ever involved in a bad incident, an emergency landing on water, say, or mechanical failure, whatever, we would give the details to the passengers "quick and dirty" style. Tell them straight and tell them fast, albeit couched in polite language, that we were fucked. And then get on with trying to save the plane.

'It went a bit further than that. I had a drink with Joe Sheedy one evening in Singapore. We had one too many vodka martinis and he said that if he was ever in a position where it was really bad, where the likelihood was that there was going to be an unrecoverable spin, or total engine loss, he would look to slam the plane into the ground as soon as possible. Get it over with fast. Better that than getting people's hopes up and filling the cabin with shit and chunder for half an hour before death.'

'Plenty o' death out here too, o' course,' Charlie said.

He was regarding me intensely. I wondered if he was trying to goad a reaction out of me, that this might be his own way of helping with my recovery. Maybe he thought I was too passive, too soft. The accident might well have smacked more than tissue, blood and consciousness from my body. I felt permanently jarred, like something viewed in soft focus, its edges indistinct. A blurred outline that could not recover itself.

'So how did y'get interested in all them big birds?'

The question knocked me back a bit. I was about to tell him that I didn't know, I couldn't remember, but then it was there, as, of course, it had always been there. I just hadn't thought of it in all these years.

'My dad,' I said. I paused, composing myself, trying to put some muscle behind my voice. Speaking of Dad always knocked the breath from me. I didn't often do it, because there was little to remember, and few occasions when it was needed. I missed him, but hardly knew him. I regretted that we'd never had the time to build a relationship. But what there had been was gold. Charlie unfolded his pocket knife and cleaned the blade. I was grateful that he didn't pry, didn't ask my what was wrong. He was old enough to know, to understand. Something to do with his own father, perhaps. Something to do with Gordon.

'We were up north. In Cumbria for some reason. Visiting relatives, maybe. Maybe just a drive to the Lakes. I don't know. It was winter. I was, what? I was maybe four or five years old. There had been a heavy snowfall. On the way back I needed the toilet, so he took me to a park he knew. We were in south Manchester, close to the airport. This park… I can't remember its name. There was a frozen duck pond and a play area. And a café overlooking large gardens with a massive tree in the middle of it. It was misty and sunny at the same time, you know? Weird, but beautiful weather.

'There were kids sledging down the slope towards the tree. My dad must have felt sorry for me – we didn't have a toboggan – so he nipped into the café and came back with a black plastic bin bag. It worked, kind of… but it didn't matter. I was having fun with Dad and it was a great day. But then there was this noise. Big, big noise. I was scared. But I couldn't run to Dad because I was on the bag and I was sliding down the incline. It sounded like the world was shattering. Thunderous. Getting bigger, closer all the time.

'And right at the moment when the bag stopped sliding, I fell back against the snow and looked up at this golden mist, and a shadow passed through it. Huge. Like a shark. And the roar was on top of me. And I remember reaching for it, as if I might be able to just grab it out of the cloud like a toy. Suddenly I wasn't scared any more. I was shaking, but it was from excitement, not fear. Dad thought I was having some kind of panic attack. All I could talk about from then on was aeroplanes. They became my world. I was such a jet nerd after that. All I ever wanted to do was go to air shows or visit the viewing platforms at Heathrow. My bedroom was filled with plastic models.'

Charlie was still inspecting his knife. He seemed unimpressed. And why should he be? It was my thrill, my passion. I probably sounded like a complete arse to him.

'Anyway,' I said, 'flying... it's pretty straightforward. It's just physics. It's just lift and thrust.'

'And crash, far as I can see it.'

I kept my mouth shut. I could have quoted the facts and figures, how, if you had been born on an aeroplane and lived on board 24 hours a day, the likelihood was that it would take over a hundred years before you were involved in a fatal accident. But there was no point with Charlie. There were some who flew their entire lives – the front-seat people, the tea-and-coffee chuckers, the self-loading baggage – and the worst that happened was the occasional hard landing, or a prolonged bout of heavy turbulence. I could tell him we were far more likely to die on his boat, but I didn't want to start a fight.

'These wrecks,' I said. 'From the world wars?'

'Yep. There's about 150 off these shores alone. And from the battle of Winter Bay, y'still get stuff cropping up even now. Y'know, cannonball, and the like.'

'Winter Bay,' I said, nodding. 'Sixteen seventy-two?'

'That'll be the one.'

'I saw something about that the other day. Something about children.'

'Children?'

'Yes. Someone had written in a book. Scribbled on the back pages about children. About suffering. Something took them.'

'Took?'

I waited for a moment, but Charlie was obviously struggling past one-word statements. I said, 'I'll dig it out when we get back. Do you know what it means?'

He shook his head. 'Bit 'fore my time, Winter Bay.'

I wasn't convinced. He knew Southwick inside out, possibly better than anyone living in the village.

'Are you superstitious, Charlie?' I asked.

'O' course,' he said, and for a moment I thought his face might collapse. I wondered if his superstitions were tied up with Gordon. I wondered if he refused to come to sea without a photograph of his little boy in his wallet. Or maybe he murmured a little prayer before he shot the nets. I was about to apologise. I was doing a lot of it and getting sick of having to pussy-foot it everywhere.

He said, 'And so should *you* be, son.'

WE WENT BACK to work. It was time to haul the nets in. I took it easy, but I was enjoying it and I overdid things a little. It was like stretching. You get into a good stretch after a long drive or sleeping in an uncomfortable position, and it feels as though you're rediscovering your body, giving it a freedom it didn't usually enjoy. This was the same. I wanted to haul on the ropes until I felt them burn the skin off my palms and the muscles on my shoulders bulged and sang. I glanced at Charlie's hands and they were like folds of oilskin, the colour of strong tea. He seemed to be palming a million lines: lifelines, love lines, wisdom lines; if he turned his fist over and opened it they might spill out over the deck. I had to rest after a while.

I watched as Charlie pulled in, hand-over-hand, and the silver bulge of the catch glimmered just under the surface, like a furious windsock. It was too heavy for him. He engaged the winch clutches and the bobbins reappeared. Claws, tails and tentacles bulged from the net as it swung over the pound at the centre of the deck. I stared at the dilated lip of the net, drizzling pink water across the boards. I thought I could hear screaming, but it was just the gears of the winch grinding under the weight.

Charlie released the slipknot and it all came slithering out. I reflexively stepped back and slipped on the wash of mucus and blood and brine. I went down hard on my backside as the tide of fish charged into me. Within seconds I was coated in a foam of slime. Charlie was laughing, his hand over his mouth, his shoulders shaking as if he were trying to shrug something off him. But then I saw the knot of confusion tying itself into his forehead. He was staring into the glut of marine life as it arced and shuddered. I stared too.

CHARLIE RADIOED TO shore and the harbour master and a police car and a contingent of forensic experts were there to greet us when we arrived back at the landing stage. We were questioned, but it didn't take long. The police seemed bored. It became obvious that this was something that happened from time to time.

One of the forensic officers said that it was clear without the benefit of carbon dating that the bones we'd dredged up had been in the sea for a long time, maybe centuries. They had been preserved just beneath the seabed until we disturbed them.

Charlie had seemed in shock. He wouldn't talk to me on the way back to the harbour, but turned to the task of sorting the fish, kicking the runts and the exotica and the bad-eaters over the edge. He kept away from the little clutch of skulls and femurs, tossing a tarp over them when he'd finished. Then he went belowdecks to put the haul on ice. I'd stayed by the tarp on the two-hour journey back, cold through to my own bones.

We went for a drink after the remains had been taken away and the statements signed off. It was late. We didn't talk. We sank our pints and our whisky chasers and walked out of the pub. Charlie kept going, down the beach, to his fish shed. The catch had to be taken to market. The excitement of a good haul – a few kilos of big cod in the main – had been blunted. I watched him snatched away by darkness and stared at the sea, or the area where the sea was, for ten minutes. The sigh of it as it collapsed against the beach. It sounded like relief.

It was midnight when I turned the key in the lock. I listened for Ruth but could hear nothing. I went for a hot bath and crept into bed. I couldn't get rid of the cold, even though the heating was on. I felt too tired to sleep. But then I woke up and I was sweltering, the sweat dripping off me. I felt my skeleton clenched within its juicy prison. My grinning incumbent. White skull.

You know, cannonball, and the like.

I rolled over and my heart was beating hard and fast and it was as if the skeleton had somehow got its ribcage to shrink in a bid to press down on what was keeping me alive.

I am within you but you are also within me.

I sat up. Wind cast spits of rain against glass. I knew I'd said the words. Spoken them for my thin, white friend. My blood brother. I suddenly felt claustrophobic and nauseous. I tasted whisky. I felt my stomach rising. I made it to the bathroom before I was sick and I kept my eye on what I was bringing up. Madness: I was looking for splinters of bone. Evidence that he, that *I,* was trying to escape myself.

I got back into bed and lay there shivering for an hour, until I heard the key in the lock. Ruth closed the door gently but there was no sound of her feet on the stairs. I saw a shadow spoil the line of light at the foot of the door and I pretended to be asleep. The door cracked open. I could feel her eyes on me. No doubt she had heard about the skulls. I really didn't want to go over that again just now.

She pushed the smell of the sea in front of her. She was wreathed in a fresh marine tang, as if she had spent all day on the beach, or walking the salt marshes. She smelled cold, but good. She smelled pregnant, I supposed.

She switched off the landing lights and I heard her climb the stairs, the sound of her bed as it took her weight and she diminished into sleep. The house followed suit, creaking and settling around her. I thought, much later, that I heard her cry out, but that could well have been me, or something disturbed in the dunes further down the beach. I listened hard, and she might have been sobbing into her pillow, but the noise might also be the suck of the tide at the shingle, or the fretting of the wind dancing around the village's firebreaks. I might have been dreaming it. I might still be in a coma. This could be death.

9

THIS COULD BE *death*, she thinks, her first thought every morning, before her watch beeps and she thinks hard about how many beeps there must have been since The Man brought her down here, so that she will not forget, so that she can cling to some idea of time.

I breathe, I see, but it's so dark in here, even without blindfold. This is death, anyway. How much longer can you take? How long till he gets bored and decides to end it?

As usual, every morning (this *is* morning, right?), she wakes and it's like not waking, to the extent that she can't quite believe that she has wakened. The dark seems so complete, more so than the shades behind her eyes even, that it's hard to accept. But then her watch beeps, a day has turned, and she can concentrate on getting through this fresh block of time. The next block, with all the things that do and don't happen within it. That can and might happen.

The Man comes every day. Sometimes he does not switch on the light. Despite her fear of the dark, his switching on the light in here – a single bulb covered in ancient fly spots, wreathed in dusty cobwebs – is much, much worse. Like emerging into a nightmare that has been trying to coalesce in a hitherto well-defended mind. The misfire heartbeat. The flutter in the chest.

I read about this in self-help books, talked about it too at classes. Arrhythmia. Can I handle this? Will I give up against my will?

She does not know what the worst thing about the light coming on might be. Perhaps just the sound of his fingers flipping the switch. Perhaps just that. But then she sees – once she's managed the pain of the light's stab at her eyes – The Man, and the curtain in the corner of the room, and both are the worst thing imaginable, in their own way.

The Man brings her hot drinks, or water, or food. He brings good food. Soup and stews and steaming greens. Meat, fish, eggs, cheese. Lots of fruit. He brings her blankets if it is especially cold, and it is always cold. He brings her magazines to read. He allows her one hour every day to read: he unlocks one hand so that she can turn the pages. He switches on a radio that plays calm music – classical or jazz – for one hour before he brushes her teeth, changes her nappy and turns out the light.

I can't look at him. Once was enough. My eyes slid away from him like they could not bear the sight. Like bad dog. One look, maybe a second of him, and it's like he branded me. He is big. Bulky. He reminds me of being kid, a tomboy playing in the street with Yakiv, dressing up in old coat, pillows tied to our waists, pretending to be Mr Shevchuk at the café in

Odessa, fat on his *galushki* and his *nalystniki*. His face. Face of fish. An orange mask (but sometimes I wonder... sometimes I wonder if this might be his real face). He wears big coat with long hood so I can't see back of head or hair. He's keeping his face secret. That's good. That's a good thing, isn't it? That's tick in box. A happy face. Because why would he hide himself if he wasn't going to let me go?

Identifying marks, then. Suck him in. Detail. Anything you can. Wait for the moment he takes off his gloves. Coughs. Try to smell him. Aftershave? Body odours? Cooking aromas? Like grandmother smelling of fried beef and spices after a morning cooking *smazhenyna*. Wiping her hands, like old pieces of blond wood, on her pinafore, over and over, as if she wouldn't be satisfied they were dry until her skin came off. Grandmother with her large black plastic spectacles and the lenses that magnified her eyes. It always used to bother her a little, seeing her *babushka* take those glasses off. Scared her, even, when she was very little. Her eyes would never be as big as she'd expect, and it was like looking at a different person, for a while, until she spoke, until she put her glasses back on.

I can't see his shoes. It's too dark down there, and anyway, he wears long, large jeans and I can't lift my neck up off the bed enough to see. But I can hear him. Hear his shoes catching on the dirt of that floor. He shuffles little bit. Maybe his shoes too big. Maybe he has them by side of door, puts them on, like pair of old gardening boots you never bother to tie up. Something to slip on while you empty bins, or throw ball back over wall to next door kids. A glass of wine in garden with Paul would be nice now. Him with his Cabso, as he calls it. Me with some cold Chardonnay, or cava. The bubbles up the nose make me laugh. Paul stares at me, at my mouth, when I laugh. Like little boy watching magic trick. He likes my laugh. He says it just like bubbles.

Beat the panic. Think of something. Think of anything. Your yoga classes with Miss Regan. It's all so formal and British. Nobody calls each other by their first names. She has no clue what her name is. What could it be? What does she look like? Miss Regan reminds her of a Larysa, but of course, she wouldn't be that. Not here in England. A Penelope, then? A Martha? Mary? Elizabeth? The stretching, the reaching. Sometimes she was so relaxed, so utterly comfortable in her surroundings, in her own skin, that she thought she could stretch beyond what was normal and perhaps open her eyes to find herself in an impossible place, the others staring at her, not knowing whether to try to unknot her or call an ambulance.

The smell of peppermint tea and freshly laundered clothes drying on radiator. Drops of tea tree oil in bowls of hot water. Nicer smells than here. I can't think what it is making them. Rotting fish? Stale earth? Raw sewage? After while, it's like my nose has gone numb. I can't smell anything but stink of whatever it is, and soon, even that is in background. It's not important. What is important is keeping hold of who I am. Track the days. Time is my friend now.

She has been here long enough to not even register the pungent smells that assaulted her so violently on that first day, when she thought she must be sick. The Man had left her immediately, having fastened her hands with a chain to a bolt buried deep into the wall. The bindings around her wrists were padded to prevent chafing. Before closing the door on her, he had adjusted an electric fire so as to keep her warm, and switched on a radio. She had tensed herself to every sound over the following hours, convinced he would return to rape her or shoot her or torture her.

Slow down. Breathe. Try to calm your heart. It is not good for you. You want to end up like your mother? A heart attack at 45? Then relax. Always worrying, she was. Always wringing her hands over some imagined problem or another. Heavy smoker. Drank too much. It's only wine. Wine is good for you. A glass to toast a sunny day. A glass to compensate for a cloudy one. Half a bottle with dinner. Half a bottle without. She slept badly, if at all. Do you want to be like her? Focus. Concentrate. Shift your mind.

Miss Regan, then, with her long legs and her deep frown. She seemed so confident, yet she could never look a person in the face. Always at a point just above, the forehead, as if she were conversing with the third eye, the *ajna*... and being a yoga teacher, perhaps she was. In her bedroom in the pub, with the other women. Not much room. A select bunch were we.

Are they missing me? *She wasn't meant for us. Too aloof. Too... foreign.* There was a waiting list for that class. Someone would have sharked in, as Paul used to say. One out, one in. *Where did she go? She wasn't around for long.* That might have been the extent of it.

Her mind turned to Paul, trying not to imagine him as she had last seen him, scabbed over and spent in his bed, but dynamic, as he had always seemed to her. He was the kind of person who constantly looked as though they were being propelled, that movement was a prerequisite of life, like that of a shark. But it wasn't the kind of energy that made you feel nervous, or exhausted. It inspired you. Even when he was relaxing, there was power in him, and purpose. When he slept, she imagined lifting his eyelids to see a 'standby' icon glimmering soft red where his pupils ought to be.

There was a fraction of her, the most infinitesimal part (awful, unforgivable, disgusting), that found a shred of relief in what had happened to her. It meant she was spared having to watch her boyfriend (and God, wasn't that the weakest way to describe him... no, he was her man, her love, *the* love) curl up like a piece of paper introduced to flame. And if he was in hell, then she was with him now.

She'd read somewhere once, about a mathematician, about how he would find himself some space and time to think, a window of fifteen minutes. The most he could devote to a problem was two or three minutes before his mind wandered. But this was exceptional, apparently. Most people spent less than that. Maybe only a minute or so, before something else impinged. It might feel as though you were dedicated to a task, but only generally. The ordinary mind couldn't cope with that kind of focus.

She tried staying with Paul, but other things snapped their fingers, waved their hands in her face.

That curtain, for example.

It was a shower curtain. Like a shower curtain. White. Or it had been, once. Now it was grey, stained, mottled at its lower edges with mould. It was opaque, but not to the extent that you could not discern that something lay behind it. It was suspended by rusting rings from a rail attached to this low ceiling. So low that the bottom of the curtain was pleated up against the floor. It's bottom hem was filthy, dark with water sucked up by capillary action. It was the only other thing in the room, beyond that pitted lightbulb, to look at. It was so still that she sometimes formed the illusion that it was shivering, pulsing infinitesimally, as if it were touching something that bore a heartbeat and was waiting for her to sleep, or die, so that it could have its way with her.

Not once, in all the days I've been here, has The Man pulled that curtain back. I don't know what's behind it. A bath? But he's only ever washed me with a cloth and a bucket of warm water. If it's a toilet, then why won't he let me sit on it, instead of putting me in those nasty incontinence pants morning and night? What would you need to conceal in a shitty little room like this? It makes me want to scream. I feel this panic build up behind my lips and sometimes its too great for whatever it is to escape. I cry or make this weird sort of sobbing, strangled voice in my throat. What is that? Frustration? Fear? Panic? All of it, and more, probably. I've never made a noise like it before in my life. I'm finding out about myself in here. I'm coming to know me a little better. And I'm not sure I like who I am.

She tried screaming, once. Early. Maybe as early as the first day, although her head was pounding with the dregs of whatever it was he'd bested her with. Chloroform? She remembered the hand and the handkerchief whipping around her face, and then a dream of monkeys linking arms, dancing around a campfire, and she was dancing too. And then waking up with her hands tenderly manacled, and the great, punishing dark, so black she was sure for a while that she was dead. She called out but nobody answered, nobody came. She screamed for help and her voice fell against the walls as if it were constructed from cotton wool.

He came to her later, The Man, and switched on the light and she averted her gaze from the cold, orange plastic of his face, and read the note he pushed in front of her eyes.

Scream all you want. Soundproof. Nobody will hear you.

Why doesn't he speak to me?

Chapter Five

CUR

ON THE BEACH. Nacre sky. Endless stones damp and bright from the retreating surf. I empty the plain polythene bag of its contents and start building the pyre. Milk teeth in an envelope. A mass of clipped hair tied together with rubber bands. A photograph of a man sitting in front of a Mediterranean meal, his eyes scorched out of the paper. I finish him off. First match. The teeth don't burn. I toe them into the stones, hoping that the child that gave them up made a few quid from the tooth fairy. Hoping they fell out naturally. A sweetish smell rises from the burning hair, and it goes with a lilac flame. I see faces in the smoke. Half-recognised. Strangers.

I never wanted children. Or rather, I thought I didn't. I believed I had no time for that, and when my career was over, or at a stage where I had more time, I would be too old to become a father. I thought, post-40, it was a bad idea to procreate. You'd be too tired to play with your offspring when they needed it. You'd be nothing but a mildly interesting fossil to your grandchildren.

I never discussed children with Tamara. She never brought it up so I didn't feel the need. We used contraception when we first started seeing each other and this carried on out of habit. Tamara was very easy around children, and I could see her mothering instinct was coming to the fore. When I left my profession I thought it might be time to discuss family. But then the accident happened. Maybe she left me because she wanted to be a mother and believed that I wasn't interested. Maybe she thought I would be no use now as a father. What good is a dad who can't play football with his son, or swing his daughter around in the park?

I trudged to the bookshop. Ruth was at work, but she'd agreed to let me play shopkeeper. She told me she'd buy me a present if I made more than five pounds in one day. I wasn't seeing her around as much as I hoped. I wanted to talk to her about the boat trip, and I was worried that she was spending too much time doing her job. I suspected it was a way of screening her thoughts from the baby because when her mind turned to the pregnancy she also dwelled upon the events that resulted in it.

Vulcan trotted in after a few minutes and took up his position on the cushion in the window. He paused to look at me while he washed one of his paws, as if he couldn't quite believe someone else was being his underling today. I put out some food and water for him and then I tried to find the booklet about Winter Bay that I had seen the previous day, but I couldn't remember where I had positioned it. I checked my room, in case I had accidentally taken it back with me, but it wasn't there either. Someone must have bought it.

I sat at the desk for an hour, trying to read, but my pain would not allow me to focus. No position was comfortable. Just trying to keep my balance on the rolling ship had caused me agony in muscles that my wasted legs had not used for months. The motion of the sea had stayed inside me, as if it had stolen aboard and was influencing the tides of my blood.

I closed my eyes and thought of one of my first times flying a commercial passenger jet. I had the controls of a 737 and we were flying through heavy cloud, climbing out of Prague. The sun was shining through them, giving everything an otherworldly brightness. It was like flying through glass. We banked left, a steep one, and a couple of minutes after levelling off I suddenly felt certain that the jet was going into a subtle roll. The horizontal situation indicator was dead level though. I closed my eyes and yes, there it was, that feeling of tilt. I compensated with the steering column and the indicators showed we were tilting to the right.

'I think we have an instrument malfunction,' I told the captain. He took over the controls – correcting my manouevre – and checked the display.

'Not that I can see.'

We talked about it and he told me it was spatial disorientation, a fairly common phenomenon that most pilots experienced, even seasoned ones. I'd been made aware of this during my training as a pilot, but until then I'd never experienced it. It was believed to be the cause of an Air India 747 crash in the 1970s.

Now I felt like this all the time. Listing, spinning, a sense of always being about to fall over despite being on an even keel. Nevertheless, thinking back to my days as a pilot had a calming effect. Gone, or at least reduced, was the edge that seemed to harry me all the time. The coldness of or in my bones lessened, and I didn't feel quite so ill-fitted in my skin. It was as if the memory of altitude had nourished me in some way, reminded me of who I was, essentially, rather than what I had become superficially. The breaks and bruises would take time to heal and the scars would be ever-present, but I was coming back. It might take years, but I was still Paul Roan. I still had a part to play in things.

Bolstered by this, and the realisation that I might well make a full recovery given time, I felt the urge once again to connect with Tamara. I was convinced that she would change her mind if she could only see how well I was progressing. And any improvement would surely be accelerated were she to return to me. I couldn't see how she might refuse, despite Ruth's insistence that she would eventually have moved back to her comfortable, certain life even if the accident had been averted.

I dug out the numbers I'd dialled and tried them again. No answer. I tried them again, dialling carefully with the stiff pegs of my fingers, but there was no joy. I felt cheated. My mood upswing had been checked too easily.

I thought of Tamara maybe sitting in a room, dressed for lunch with her old flame, but poring over photographs of me. She'd be chewing her lips as she often did when she was worried or unsure. *I should call him. I should see how he is. How could I just walk out on him like that? At the very least he deserves an explanation, an apology.*

Yes. That's right. Call me.

I closed my eyes and willed it.

Footsteps outside the door.

I opened my eyes, fully expecting to see Tamara's hand reaching out, but it was a bald, heavily-bearded man in a pale grey jumper, bottle-green corduroy trousers and Wellingtons armoured with mud. He was old. He was carrying a box and peering through the glass as if unsure that the shop was open. He seemed uncertain, worried even. I noticed that I'd failed to switch the sign around to read OPEN. I went over and let him in. His expression didn't change.

'Books?' I asked, cocking my head at the box. 'Ruth's not around at the moment, but you can leave them with me if you like.'

'Not books,' he said. And then I saw that his expression was less to do with whether the shop was open and more to do with me. He was assessing me.

'This is… well, let's just say it's a box of things I don't need any more and leave it at that.'

I nodded. I was a little taken aback. Usually I was left items by anonymous donors. This was the first time I'd seen in person someone who wanted to be rid of something. I didn't want to touch the box, so I asked him to leave it outside. He did so, wiping his hands on the back of his trousers. He seemed about to leave when he turned back. Suddenly he was close to tears.

'You're filth,' he said, and it seemed he was having trouble keeping the emotion from his voice. His eyes shone. 'You disgust me. I wish you'd died on that road. Nothing you can do. Nothing we can do. Nothing we've *done*. None of it is any good. Nothing will work.'

I didn't know how to respond. I felt as if he'd kicked me in the guts, despite my feeling the same way sometimes, about my unconventional role within the community. Was this how people saw me? Even as they were leaving me their little piles of guilt to dispose of? I stroked Vulcan's fur and thought about how I had come about this unwanted position. I felt upset: there was a spike in my throat I couldn't swallow around. Sin-eater. Trouble-shooter. Janitor. Eliminator.

I didn't recall seeing the old man around the village before, but then I didn't pay much attention to other people. Maybe he was an out-of-towner come in especially to give the village pariah a box of grief.

I went outside and picked up his offering. It was heavy, and something was seeping through the cardboard, darkening it. There was a faint smell rising from beneath the oily tea-towel that served as a lid, a smell I recognised so well yet could not identify.

I carried the box away from the village, as if it were a bomb that needed to be disposed of in a safe environment. It was heavy. At the pier I hobbled down the concrete steps to the sand and shuffled into the shadows where the ghosts of previous fires waited bitterly for me. The wind hissed around the promontory; slow footsteps moved across the wooden slats of the pier above my head. In the summer this place was thronged with visiting families. Queues in the café for fish and chips snaked out of the door. Out of season I was sometimes the only person in that café for hours.

Blistered, salt-burned supportive columns. An empty beer bottle. The sand gradually losing its toffee colour to the pounds of carbon dust I was adding to the beach. I thought I saw the broken gull being rocked on the curdling tide but it could have been anything. I stared at the box. I knew what was inside. I couldn't understand how he had happened upon it, or why he thought I would be able to destroy it with fire.

I peeled away the tea-towel and gazed at the 'black box' nestled within. Much of it was dented and scratched, the lettering stencilled upon it – FLIGHT RECORDER DO NOT OPEN – partially obliterated by scorch marks. Fire had already tried to have its way with this thing.

'But there was no crash,' I said. 'There was no fire.'

I felt something cold sweep through my bowels, as if I'd suddenly been immersed in the North Sea. I wanted to hurl this thing away. I couldn't understand why the guy had dumped this on me: no beach fire was going to penetrate an exterior capable of withstanding temperatures upwards of 1,000 degrees Celsius. Of course the box was nothing to do with Flight 029, but inexplicably, I knew that if the tape housed inside the thing were retrieved and played, my voice would be on it, monotoning the same mistake that I had made on that night over Madrid.

I lifted the box so that it was level with my face. My slack, sleepy muscles struggled with its weight. I shook it. I smelled it. The tang of metal and a shut-in odour of burned things. Plastic, aluminium, flesh. I closed my eyes and saw jerking passengers belted into their seats trying to scream, but there was no oxygen to feed them because the fire was stealing it from their lungs. I hurled the box as far as I could into the surf, rubbing and re-rubbing my hands on my jeans to get rid of the greasy feel of the thing.

I burned the cardboard and climbed the stone steps back to the promenade, suddenly bone weary. I kept looking back, expecting to see the orange casing tumbling ashore on the filthy brown curl of tide, but I knew it would not surface again without the help of a diver.

I walked around the village for a while, hoping to spot the person who had given the box to me. All I could think when I tried to picture his face was a number and a letter: 34A. I tried to remember if he had said that number in conjunction with the box he had handed over, but the upset of being given the CVR wouldn't let me settle on anything we discussed. By the time I reached Ruth's house, I was convinced the 34A was in my mind for some other, probably trivial, reason. His address, maybe. He must live in a flat. But how could I know that if I'd never seen him before?

I made a cup of tea I didn't want and settled on the sofa, feeling hot and agitated. The room had a feeling of absence. It was a cool room, with little in the way of decoration or ornament. There were no clocks, no pictures, no mirrors. No magazines lying on the floor. No flowers in vases. It felt like a waiting room. It felt like a place that was never meant to be lived in.

I grew impatient. Rest was the only word the doctors ever seemed to toss my way, but the moment I parked myself in a chair it was as if life started to accelerate around me. Tamara was getting older while I sipped tea. Her life, presumably, was thickening with other people, events, excitement, while mine spun like a dead thing caught in a web. Any doubt or regret she might be feeling was being erased every day that went by without my contacting her.

But there was also the possibility that she, like me, was failing to kick on after the breach. There were things to do, there was this old flame of hers trying his best to re-kindle what had existed between them, and she was either going for it, or she wasn't. And here I was wondering whether I ought to give a shit. She didn't stick with me, so who was to say, were she to come back, that she wouldn't hightail it again if some other catastrophe befell me?

The empty room sucked any noise I made into it and shared it around. I placed the tea cup on its saucer and the room filled with brittle echoes. Then I had to move again, to take the cup from the anaesthetic living room and deposit it in the kitchen, which contained a welcome chaos. I stood by the window and looked out at the massive Suffolk sky. There were no aircraft up there just now, but there were plenty of contrails to show where they had been. When there were no jets, it was easy to convince myself that they did not exist, that it was all a mental construct. How could they exist? How could something weighing the same as 800 elephants get off the ground? Lift and thrust. And bollocks. I passed my 'A' level in Physics, I had flown the bastards, but I still couldn't get my head around it. I think, maybe, that part of the accident – the *almost* accident – came about because at base I didn't have faith in these machines. I had trained for years and spent a lot of money following my dream, but that's all it was. A fancy created by an ambitious imagination.

It had been a year since the near miss; I could hardly remember what I needed to do to taxi from the apron to the runway. My hands no longer looked like the kind of things that were capable of the delicate manoeuvring that took a mass of metal up, or brought it down. And now, every time I saw a Trip-7, or a Jumbo, nosing into the blue, there was a frisson of disbelief – as if I was looking at a flying saucer – before the fear descended and rational thought went walkabout.

Rain was rearing up far south of the nuclear reactor at Sizewell. It was at once both a solid black wall and as soft and uncertain as gossamer. I thought of Charlie's nets once they'd been shot, the way they hit the water and then billowed, as if they'd expanded as a result of breath drawn. Black capture, sinking fast.

The other side of the sky towards Great Yarmouth, miles and miles away, but little more than a turn of the head, was as clean as a scrubbed plate. Supertankers spoilt the horizon's line.

There was a piece of paper lying next to the microwave oven. I went to retrieve it, thinking that Ruth had left me some instructions for dinner, but it was just a shopping receipt from the previous day. *Steaks. Broccoli. Orange juice. Folic acid.* I checked the fridge, thinking I might start cooking so that dinner would be ready for Ruth's return, but there were no steaks to be found. The fridge was pretty much empty, bar a bottle of milk, some butter and half a bag of salad. I felt cheated; I really fancied a steak now.

I slung a potato in the microwave and scooped the salad into a bowl. There was a tin of tuna in the cupboard; my fingers were on fire by the time I'd ground the lid off it with the can opener. I ate standing up, wishing there was something to do beyond physio, bathing and the constant dread of things arriving to destroy.

We would have had the B&B, Tam's Place, going six months by now. We wanted to be ready for the Christmas period; this part of the country was a popular place to spend the festive season. Our rubric was a hotel in Hertfordshire where we had retreated for a restful weekend shortly after the hardship of the enquiry. It had a quirkiness about it, despite its luxury. The wall behind the reception desk was covered with ancient keys. There was soft, recessed lighting but only so much as to produce moody pools of blue here and there, and a small bar. It was the subtle touches that we liked, and that we remembered when we started planning the B&B. We wanted to be a cut above. If someone ordered a drink there would always be a little complementary something to go with it. A wafer with a coffee, a small dish of spiced nuts with a beer. Tamara wanted stone-coloured towels rolled up into neat bundles, and sisal baskets in which to store them. There would be something nautical in each room, and each room would be named after a fictional seafaring character. We were going to paint the walls mushroom and have aubergine carpets. A solid oak front door with a bay tree and gravel. Fresh flowers. Fluffy bathrobes. I ached for that time, a promise that seemed to be calling to us from across the years.

I'd finished my meal without tasting it. I scraped the remnants into the bin and fed the plate to the dishwasher. I checked my watch. Ruth's shift had finished an hour ago. It took less than half an hour to drive from the hospital. Coffee with a friend. Loose ends at work that needed tying off. Supermarket trip to fill this refrigerator's belly. So why was I so concerned? Perhaps I was just missing her company. I'd only seen her for a fleeting moment in the past few days.

The rain waded in. It was the kind of weather that tapped politely on the window a few times and then unleashed all hell. I thought of her driving through this, everything – the roads, the windscreen, the black canopy over Bailey's Hollow – turning to oil. I started to shudder. I had to sit down.

I had been out walking that road in a storm like this. Apparently. I have no recollection. I was found twelve metres from the road at the edge of a ploughed field. I'd been hit by a 4x4, at a blind corner. A foot to my right was a ditch filled with water that would have drowned me. A foot to the right there was a gathered pile of dead branches upon which to impale myself. The flesh of my right arm was peeled back from the bone like a thick red sweater sleeve where it had plunged through the windscreen. I was lucky to be found as soon as I was. In all probability I suffered the first of my cardiac arrests out here and Ruth resuscitated me. She called Charlie, and 999. Charlie arrived first. They kept me warm until the ambulance turned up and then he visited me in hospital, with Ruth, a couple of times a week. They both talked to me for hours at a time. They kept me going when my body had forgotten what going meant.

I must have fallen asleep, because suddenly I was staring up at Ruth's face and it was upside down and I felt embarrassed, as if I'd been caught doing something inappropriate. For a few moments we were complete strangers. Ruth's face was inflexible. Maybe the cold had made her stiff. Her eyes were blank, uncomprehending. And then she thawed, or I saw her in a warmer light, or the spell was broken somehow. She smiled and I levered myself carefully upright.

'It's late,' she said.

'I wanted to wait up for you.'

She sat in her favourite armchair. The house ticked around us. There was something about her that I had sensed, without being able to pinpoint, something unusual. Now I had it: she hardly blinked. It was like being with an owl.

Of course, the fact that she had just come off a long shift might have something to do with it. Often, despite being pregnant, Ruth would overload on coffee, which meant that when she got home, although bone tired, she could not rest and had to wind down by watching a film, or reading one of her survival books. But even when she was relaxed, it was there. When you talked to her she would hold a level gaze without blinking. I wondered if she might even be aware of it, whether it was a technique NHS staff were taught to calm down nervous or agitated patients, or disarm troublemakers.

'Did you have a meeting?'

She gave me a blank look.

'After work. It's just, well you were late home.'

'Late home.'

'Yes.'

'I had a few things to do. But not a meeting.'

'How's the baby?'

She shot me a look. Something wasn't right, but I didn't know what to ask, or even if I had, how to couch it.

She didn't answer. Her lips had turned very thin, very white, as if she were about to say something venomous. But then she turned away and I saw the slightest shake of her head.

I was about to say goodnight, not wanting to trigger a rebuke, when she said, more tenderly than her appearance suggested: 'The baby's fine.'

Chapter Six

THE ARCH OF ATLAS

THE TWO JETS jammed together grunt through thin air on an uneven trajectory, a chum of human tissue foaming from the cracked, blistered exhaust nozzles. Fires break out along the fuselage only to be instantly doused by the intense cold. Charred pieces of the aircraft shear away and fall as aluminium rain. Limbs flail through fractures in the widebodies like aborted evolutionary afterthoughts.

Captain Sheedy's hand rests lightly on the stick; the rest of him is crumpled beneath the weight of the collapsed cockpit. Wires and hydraulics whip and thrash in the howl of air pouring through the windows. Captain Sheedy taps First Officer Roan on the forearm and jerks a thumb at the knot of hardware that has killed him. He opens his hand in a *so what now?* gesture.

First Officer Roan unbuckles himself and wriggles out of his seat, careful to not catch his head against the sharp fingers of torn metal pointing down at him. He presses and prods the new configuration of the overhead cockpit while Captain Sheedy drums his fingers against an armrest. He takes down the axe from its fixture and uses the poll to lever away some of the shattered moulding. Eventually a large section breaks clear of the roof. Above the wind's shriek he can hear the squeal of metal as it draws clear of Captain Sheedy's head, or what remains of it. Captain Sheedy has been untidily decapitated. Sheaves of glass and metal must have piled through his mouth as he opened it to scream: everything above his lower jaw is gone.

Captain Sheedy is trying to say something. First Officer Roan stares down at the transverse cross section of Captain Sheedy's head, at the sucking rings of the pharynx and trachea, the coin of white spinal column. His tongue squirms inside the bloody, broken cup of his mouth like some agonised bivalve on a half-shell. He has no hard palate against which to form his words. First Officer Roan wipes and rewipes his palm against his trouser legs and presses it down against the ring of teeth. He feels the dry tongue leap and dance against his skin. He feels the slashed, rubbery underpart of the cheek.

Captain Sheedy says, 'Jethuth Chritht... what have you been eating?'

I FLEW OUT of sleep. The acrid smell of aviation exhaust followed me. I stared at the patterns in the ceiling, wondering if it actually consisted of fissures and swellings or if it was merely the craquelure of my damaged eyes. The smell of burned fuel product disappeared; of course, it might never have been there. I looked down at my hand but could not see the mark of molars and bicuspids beyond the riot of scar tissue. Why should I? I had dreamed. I had wakened. That was all.

Life had become a series of layers. Time was a series of overlapping events, new routines: pills to be swallowed, rungs to be reached for on the ladder to recovery. Injuries were like a callus formed over the skin of what I used to be. Maybe that was what happened to thoughts too, after a serious accident. The brain rewired itself while its swellings and bruises reduced. Areas closed down; others sparked to life. *Some people with persistent pain get inadequate help from mild painkillers. Opioids might help you, but everyone is different.* I thought of the child on the beach, the startling pink of its skin against the hard, grey scab of shoreline. Blond hair like pale flame trying to catch. I wondered what was real and what was not. I thought of reaching out a hand for Ruth and clawing through mist. And Tamara, maybe she was some fanciful construct, made up of smiling models in glossy magazines, memories of other people's features, memories of other people's moods.

I turned to Gray's Anatomy. I had found an old copy propping up a table leg in a forgotten, tarped-over corner of the bookshop's small yard. The boards were warped and mouldy, the pages fat with rain, but I was able to turn them. On one of the endpapers, a figure posed balletically, half its skin flayed to reveal the muscles and bones and blood vessels beneath. Its head was turned away, as if in embarrassment at this super-nudity. It looked as though a tree was growing through the chest and neck, searching fingers into the cavities of the head. Walnut brain. Vertebrae like the fossil of some ancient, impossible sea creature, moving muscularly, peristaltically, through the primordal waves. This is how I saw the body now, as a series of separate, almost independent items. Like the jets in my dream I felt jammed together, ill-fitting. There was no syncopation, no sense of an organic machine working on instinct. I was conscious of every breath I pulled into my torn lungs, every malignant beat of my heart.

Seeing the images of these body parts so dispassionately rendered, described clinically with neutral words, was of help to me. I could bear to consider my physicality if I considered it the same way. I could believe that healing was a process that would lead to a brighter future, rather than a constant reminder that I was something damaged and diminished. I could focus on one particular part of me: the hands, the face, and see how I was getting better. There was no such positivity if I continued to see myself as a whole. I was broken and bent that way. I was a mess. How could I ever come back from that?

I read a little more, dipping into the pages that concerned the sections of my body that had suffered the most. Lots of them. I gorged on Latin names: another buffer between myself and the damage. *Quadratus Lumborum. Tibialis Posticum. Astragalus.* Split. Shredded. Compacted. Shattered. A knock at the door and I loosed a breath I had been holding for too long.

I shuffled over and opened it.

'Charlie, hello.'

Charlie nodded and thrust a white paper parcel into my chest. I almost asked him if he needed it burning, but I caught a fresh marine whiff and realised it was fish.

'Turbot,' he said. 'All gutted, scaled and boned for you. I know how you London types like your clean fillets.' He nodded again. 'You'll eat like a king tonight. And here's a little something for your help.' He passed me an envelope containing three fifty-pound notes.

'I should come fishing with you more often,' I said.

'Y'should. We won't always catch, y'know, th'unusual stuff.'

'Cannonball and the like, hey?'

He laughed, sourly. 'Aye.'

Charlie seemed hesitant, as if unsure of what to do next, whether to say something or make his excuses. I was seeing more and more of him. I wondered if it was because he was concerned about me, or about my proximity to Ruth. Or maybe it was just getting too cold in that old fish shed of his. Even though the sea was in his veins, I imagined that days spent with plastic crates filled with ice and the constant stink of bait could stick in anybody's craw. I felt I should ask him in for a cup of tea, or a whisky even. I was going to ask him about Ruth, what their relationship was, but forming it into a thought made the question seem inappropriate. How could it sound anything other than offensive?

'Well,' he said. His eyes were wreathed in wrinkles and dark hollows, but still seemed young. 'I'll be off.'

'Come and have dinner,' I said. 'I'll cook for the three of us.'

He nodded again and turned away. It was only as I was moving to close the door that I saw the box on the ground.

*   *   *

SECRETS AND DECEPTION. There was a lot of it going on. I thought of every house in Southwick as having a skeleton hanging in the cupboard. Everyone with a dark little corner where things grew that ought never to be allowed to take root. You might feel that you were exorcising them by giving them to me to burn, but it wasn't true. It was like fighting old man's beard. It always comes back. And there was always the memory of it. You couldn't tear those out. No amount of flame would consume them.

I tried to remember how I had come by this peculiar job. I had not asked for it and nobody had suggested it to me. One morning, shortly after I had returned, shakily, to my feet, I found a package outside the door with a note pinned to it. A box of matches too. The note was typed. It read: *Thing unclean.*

I picked the box up, thinking, *Me or it?*

This new box might have come from Charlie, or it might not. It didn't contain anything I'd immediately connect with him, but then I supposed that was the point of secrets. You weren't necessarily meant to be able to trace them back to the source. But he didn't seem the type of person who would need help. He didn't come across as the kind of person who accreted pain, despite his grief regarding Gordon. He was an external kind of person, in every way. I doubted he spent too much time worrying about things. An afternoon out on the sea must dispel as many, if not more, demons than a bottle of whisky, or half an hour on a psychiatrist's lounger.

As I carried the box towards the beach, I wondered if what I was doing helped people at all. Did they feel as though they were handing over the burden to someone else? Could relief be as easy as that? Surely not. Maybe it was all just a plan to keep me active, and to take my thoughts away from Tamara. Well it wasn't working, if that was the case. I thought about her all the time, even when Ruth was around.

I thought of her now, and grew impatient with my task. More of the same. It was fascinating how other people's belongings – collections and clothes and books and letters – could mean absolutely nothing to the person who inherited them, or turned them over with impatient fingers in a junk shop, or burned them on a fire. I wondered if Tamara had discarded the trinkets I had gifted her, or whether she kept them as a secret declaration of a love she could no longer stand. Maybe that was it. She loved me too much to see me suffer. I felt my heart thud with need for her, and my own desperation. I was grasping for every possible salve.

I burned everything in the box, and then I burned the box too. A bra melted around its wire frame. A plastic medicine bottle became so much hot glue. Something caught my eye in the moment it was consumed. I flicked at it with my toe, but it was too late. I peered into the flames and tried to confirm to myself that I'd seen the gold braid of a first officer's cuffs, but it wasn't likely. Just part of a coat, in the end. All I'd seen was the silver trail of a slug, or the sticky remnants of some spilled drink.

But I felt uncomfortable. There was something going on here. There too many odd things going on in my life, all of them since the accident. Patterns and signs. I wondered if someone was playing around with me, trying to put the frighteners on me for some imagined insult. Maybe it was just someone in the village who didn't like the idea of a stranger burying bad secrets, poking his nose in where it wasn't wanted.

The fire was weakening. I gazed at the shrivelled remnants and tried to see a message in them. It occurred to me that I might have put together the box myself.

I kicked sand into the cinders and hobbled away, rubbing my face as I mulled over this fresh theory. If this was true, then was I trying to tell myself something about the near miss? The cockpit voice recorder and the gold braid and the flying charts... were their disposal some subtle method I had for jettisoning that part of my life for good? Maybe once I'd rid myself of the tangible objects, the mental flotsam would follow suit. God knew I had a lot of dark clouds in my head that needed blowing away. I was acutely aware of the fact that psychiatric disorders were the main cause of licence loss among commercial aviation crew after cardiovascular disease. Or maybe I was just looking for a way to distract myself from the crippling loss of Tamara.

Jesus, what a mess. I even felt guilty about not feeling that great still to be alive. I had nipped away from the jaws of death just as they were closing around my neck and all I could do was pule over my woes, and drift around like surface sand scared up by the winter squalls.

I got off the beach and went to the bookshop. I let myself in and switched on Ruth's computer, brought up her music player and got something jazzy on. It improved my mood straight away, as did the warmth from the radiators and the sight of Vulcan as he came trotting up the road. I let him in and he purred so hard he sent vibrations up my arm. He made a beeline for his bed and I put out some food and water for him.

I turned to the bookshelves and thought again about that pamphlet I'd seen. There were other histories of the village and its bloodiest day, but I could find no further references to children, either in the text itself or scribbled in the margins.

I sat down at the desk and let my swollen fingers trace the keys of the vintage cash register Ruth used. The last sale she had made had been a pretty good one: £14.50. But as I read it, there was another little prick to the heart: 1450 HRS had been the time officially logged for the airprox incident.

I almost laughed out loud at the coincidences raining down, or perhaps my knack of flagging everything with a significance that it probably didn't deserve. These thoughts were interrupted by the computer making a little chiming noise; I wouldn't have heard it if I hadn't stopped trying to bend my painful body into positions where I was able to read the titles on the book spines. It took a lot of concentration, forcing the little jars and sprains and aches that lanced into me every time I did so much as arch an eyebrow.

I dithered the mouse on its mat to get rid of the screensaver and there was a new email message in the box. I felt a pang of guilt as I opened up the email application, but Ruth had not said I couldn't use it. I'd given the woman at the airline her email address, after all. What was I supposed to do?

I tried not to look at the list of names in her inbox but my eyes picked up a couple anyway. NHS addresses, colleagues' names I recognised: someone called Penny, someone called Lou, as well as a few standalones I didn't recognise. Funny how a green eye will settle on the male moniker. Who the hell was Danny? Who the hell was Jake? My mouse finger was itching to find out, but I held firm. Ruth was popular. Ruth was kind. She had friends. Many before I was around. Danny and Jake should be worried about *me*.

The new message was from *Beck, Catriona*. Tamara's friend.

Dear Paul, This is Catriona. Elodie Pascal at Air France contacted me about your message. I'm very sorry to hear about your break-up, but there's nothing I can do. I haven't spoken to Tamara for a while. I actually tried to get in touch once I heard of your news, but she isn't picking up. I understand how upset you must be. Maybe she's upset too. If I know Tamara, and she did send me a long letter singing your praises, I think she must be. I hope you can work it out. Sorry I can't be more helpful. Good luck. Cat.

I hovered the cursor over that 'break-up', wishing I could scratch it out. We didn't break up, I wanted to tell the world. It hasn't been confirmed or denied yet. It isn't official. She's still mine.

I dispatched a brief thank you and closed the application. Then I thought about it and opened it again and deleted her email to me, then my reply from the 'sent' folder. Ruth would only be stressed if she found out I was chasing down what would in all probability turn out to be one great, miserable dead end. It was no big deal if she weren't to know about it.

I was suddenly very tired. I'd invested more hope in Catriona than I probably ought, but I felt frustrated. It was easy to dismiss strangers from your life these days, a click of the mouse, a problem forgotten. I was angry that she hadn't bust a gut to do more. I fished out the address book and tried the Amsterdam number again. Constant ring. No answerphone; she didn't like them.

I pushed back from the table smartly and felt my back grind like something trodden under the heel. A young mind in an old body. Death creeping at the edges, looking for some filthy toehold. What were you if you didn't have love? A ghost. Something lighter than you were meant to be, missing an essential part. Always hungry for something food could not assuage.

Disgusted with myself for feeling so uncharitable and morose, I left the shop, tickling the bridge of Vulcan's nose on my way. For the first time, I actively wanted to burn something and I was disappointed not to find some mysterious box awaiting my attention.

I fished the knot out of my pocket and tried to undo it but the edges were gone. There was nowhere to gain purchase and my fingers were too blunt and dumb to do anything beyond scrape around its navel shape.

I watched as a coachload of pensioners parked by the Red Lion came down the steps in a series of arthritic jerks. A couple of ladies, hair carved into frosted sculptures, having already disembarked and huddled into their cardigans, leant back against the wall overlooking the beach and favoured me with sympathetic smiles. *This might have been you one day,* those smiles seemed to say. *But instead, it's you now.*

I trudged past them, past the men with their sprucely knotted ties and brogues, so many bellies ready for cream teas and a cheeky half of Broadside, and angled down the ramp to the sand.

I saw her straight away. There were other people on the beach this afternoon – quite a few, considering how cold and windy it was. There were couples exercising dogs, children leaping off the exposed groynes, elderly men in tracksuits powerwalking. Someone was trying to control a red slash of kite. Other days you could come on to the beach and find it utterly deserted. I preferred it when it was.

She was standing just at the part of the shoreline where the sand became glossy as the frothing tide beat into it. As before, she was still – possibly the trait that attracted my attention – like one of Anthony Gormley's statues in Formby. She was wearing the same clothes, at least it seemed that way to me. If she had changed at all, it was only into another soft, inconspicuous outfit. The kind of colours that would be described in a fashion store as stone, cement, anthracite. She wore a hat and gloves and a scarf was wadded into the gap between her chin and chest. I could gather no clue about what shape she might be under all that padding. I noticed a camera, an expensive-looking DSLR, hanging from her shoulder. When she moved, suddenly, but haltingly, moving up the beach a little way, as if her legs had grown tired, or were beginning to be subsumed by the skirl of sand, it was with a limp, and my blood quickened. She was damaged, like me. But it was not a practised limp: it was fresh pain, a novice limp. The insults to her body were recent.

She seemed startled by some new noise that flew in under everyone else's radar. She turned her head, haltingly – I imagined the splinter and grind of tired, ruined bone – and looked directly at me with fierce, too-white eyes.

Later I realised that she looked like that because of her injuries. She had a scar the colour of raw liver that wormed down the centre of her forehead. It was as if the vein there had escaped from the skin. I was going to leave her alone, but she came shuffling towards me. I might have moved off anyway, but her progress was so pained, so painfully slow, that I felt myself drawn towards her, if only to minimise her discomfort.

'Hi,' I said. I was nodding like a tired child, as if we were sharing some injury wavelength. I stopped immediately.

She nodded too. She didn't say anything. She seemed suspicious of me, or maybe again that was just the cruel repatterning her facial injuries had caused. It looked as though breathing was close to being too much for her.

She moved past me and headed up the beach in the direction of the pier. She hesitated and shot a look back at me. She was wearing that same slightly shocked, slightly quizzical expression. In a surprisingly clear, strong voice she said: 'Come with me.' And then, I don't know if it was the wind that spoilt them or my own gloomy demeanour that twisted her words, but as she turned back into the teeth of the weather, I thought she said, I'm sure she said: *You have death crawling all over you.*

Chapter Seven

DIRECT THERMAL ASSAULT

'I'M A DIVINER,' she said. 'After a fashion. A geomancer. I'm a psychogeographical sympathiser. Empathiser, rather. I'm into stains on time. Bruises in memory.'

Now I was shaking my head. 'I'm sorry. I have absolutely no idea what it is you're talking about.'

'Death, in the main,' she said. 'Death and its echoes.'

'Echoes?'

We were sitting in a booth on the pier, a little wood and plexiglass windbreak. She was drinking sparkling mineral water. I was having a pint. She kept grimacing and I couldn't be sure if it was down to the fizz in her glass, the weather, her pain, or me. After all, how pleasant can it be to sit next to someone who is crawling with death? I'd asked her to confirm that's what she said, but she wouldn't put me out of my misery. 'Don't worry about it,' she said. 'We're all branded by it to some degree or other, anyway.'

She'd said her name was Amy. Amy Slade. She was from a small village in Leicestershire where people drove 4x4s, rode horses and lived next door to international rugby players. 'I haven't been back in twenty years,' she said. 'Once your parents die, there's no pull whatsoever. At least not for me.'

I knew what she meant. My own parents had lived their whole lives, almost bloody-mindedly, in the north-west of England. My dad had been so set in his ways he gradually began to sink into the rut he'd worn away with his slippered feet. When he and my mother died in their late 70s, within months of each other, it was an awkward kind of relief to know that the drive up the M6 to the funerals would be my last.

'Do you visit their graves?' I asked. I wasn't circumspect in any way. I sensed she wouldn't appreciate it.

'No. They're dead. It's just all just stones and bones and brown flowers now. You keep them alive in your head, don't you?'

I agreed, although I hadn't told her that my own parents had passed away. It spooked me a bit, that, as if she already knew. I suppose, when you reach a certain age, you won't be too far wrong. But people were getting older, these days. I cringed inside at that. Another forty or fifty years of wearing this knackered body did not appeal one jot.

I looked down at my hand. She'd slid a card between my fingers and I hadn't even noticed. It was pale, eggshell blue, and contained only her name and telephone number and a small icon, an embossed skull in off-white. I copied the number into my phone's memory – I lose paper for fun – and raised my head to thank her.

The sun was behind her so it was difficult to scrutinise her face too closely, but I could see that, like me, she'd been through the wards. Even without my beloved *Gray's* to hand I could see that her face had been rebuilt. Her speech was slightly slurred, its edges blunted, as if she suffered from a cold. The scar that wormed down the centre of her forehead was thick and proud, following the path of the remains of the frontal suture, just above the nasal eminence. Not that she had much of that either. Her nose looked as though it had been broken and re-broken. If she had modelled for *Gray's Anatomy*, H.V. Carver would have had to get his eraser out and re-draw the whole section on the skull. Her eyes might well have been affected by whatever incident or accident ruined her, but I could picture her as being naturally wide-eyed. It was pretty intense, that stare of hers. Her irises were the kind of blue you see in the sky on frosty, pastoral mornings. So pale as to almost be another colour entirely, or no colour at all. I doubted she could express pity or sadness, especially as her eyebrows had that knitted, oblique look of someone perpetually angry. Maybe she had reason.

'Tell me,' she said. And how wrong could I be? There was a sudden softness to her face that almost slapped the breath from me. I saw how, before damage, she would have been beautiful, in her way. As beautiful as someone with piercing, werewolf eyes could be. It was obvious what she was digging for; there was no call for playing it coy.

I told her about the hit-and-run and part of that segued, rightly or wrongly, into my fears for Tamara. She showed no surprise, and maybe she was incapable: enough nerves had been severed in my own face to show me the expressions I would never pull again.

She took a sip of her drink and said: 'For me, it was fire.'

She had been working. Her pre-accident job. Interior design. She'd been working on a hotel refurbishment project in the east end of London. Hoxton's allure was on the rise and the surrounding areas were keen to get their snouts in the trough. The hotel wanted a spruce up, wanted to lean towards the boutique look. Neutral colours. Monsoon showers. As many throws and rugs and as much Egyptian cotton as possible. She had been flipping through a colour samples catalogue with the hotel manager in his office, pages of buttercream and oatmeal, when the fire alarm went off. The manager had checked his watch and assured her there was no drill planned for that time of day and asked her to show him the cobalt tiles again. It was what killed him, she reckoned.

By the time they could smell smoke, yells and shouts were already coming at them from the corridor. Both ends were blocked by flame; the fire escape was maddeningly just beyond one wall of it. The manager left it too late, bolting for the door when the fire had really started to intensify. Amy watched him become a twisting, howling fireball and calmly went back inside his office and closed the door. She drenched his coat with bottled water and wadded it against the threshold. She went to the window and opened it the inch or two that it would allow her. The streets were clogged with afternoon traffic; the rush hour was just beginning. She could hear sirens but they were a way off. The paint on the door was blistering. She would be dead before they got here.

She remembered being very calm as she lifted the heavy desk chair and rammed it through the window. She tore down a curtain and wound it around her wrist then punched out the remaining jags of glass, not wanting to tear her skin open before she jumped to her death.

She had thought about Vesna Vulovic, the flight attendant who famously survived a 33,000 foot fall after a bomb went off in the Yugoslav Airways DC-9 in which she was working. Other names. Others who fell and survived. Chisov, 22,000 feet. Magee, 20,000 feet. Alkemade, 18,000 feet. Amy had read that if you fall 2000 feet, or above, you reach a terminal velocity of 120 mph. You couldn't fall faster than that. Seven stories up. What was that? Seventy feet? It would be over before she drew breath to scream. She wouldn't reach fifty miles an hour. Piece of piss. Her father had fallen down the stairs once. A couple of flights. He was getting on, by then, but he simply got up and walked away. Not a bruise. 'I just relaxed,' he explained, when she asked him how he was. 'Tense up and you do yourself a nasty injury.'

She went to the minibar and twisted the caps off all the miniatures. She didn't stop necking spirits until they were all finished. Flames were piling through the firecheck door by now. Thick smoke was making lazy, deadly, beautiful patterns across the ceiling. She clambered up onto the windowsill, closed her eyes, slackened her body and 'just let myself go'.

'Jesus Christ,' I said. My glass was in my hand; I jerked as if shoved when she finished with that line. Beer slopped on to my leg; the wind was so cold that the liquid felt warm.

'I landed on the roof of a parked car. I don't remember a thing, of course, but apparently it's better than landing on concrete. What saved me, other than being completely relaxed, was that it didn't have a sun roof. I don't need to tell you the rest. You know it all. Operations. I had to have my pancreas removed. I'm a full-time diabetic now. Depression. Coming back. Hopefully coming back. Physio. Blah.'

'How could you be completely relaxed?' I asked. 'You could have died.'

'I would definitely have died if I'd tensed up. Impact forces transfer directly to the internal organs in such circumstances. I'd have been a sack of jelly. And anyway, in the moment before I left the building, I wasn't afraid of death. This just seemed like the most desirable way to check out. Better than choking, being torched to a cinder in the corner of a hotel room. For a few moments, I was flying.'

She'd moved away from London as soon as she was able. She couldn't deal with the high rises and the traffic any more. Hotel work was out for good. Getting in a lift caused her to sweat and grey out.

'So why here?'

She gave me a look. I'd seen it before. It was the look a stranger gives you that says: *Do I trust this person? Are we going to be friends? Am I about to make a big mistake?*

'I'm working,' she said, at last.

'But I thought you said — '

'This is a new job. A hobby, really. But it keeps me busy. It gets my mind off other things.'

'Like what?'

'Dreams of falling. Of being pushed.'

I swallowed hard. 'This business, what was it you said, divining?'

She nodded. It was an unpleasant movement. Her hair twitched as if she were being manoeuvred, a poorly produced glove puppet. I wasn't enjoying my beer. The scar on her forehead made her look as if her face had been turned inside out. I had a crazed urge to pull off her beanie but knew, somehow, that to do so would mean tearing the flesh from her scalp at the same time.

I wasn't sure I wanted to know what it was, but she took a sip of her water and pointed out to sea.

'There's death shot through those tides,' she said. 'Things that happened across the centuries that have left their mark. It doesn't matter how long ago, how big a gap between then and now, you can always pull the lips of the wound together and stitch it shut. Study the scar for clues.'

'You lost me at "There's",' I said. I was fidgeting. I was overdue some pain relief and my pills were back in my room. I didn't want to invite Amy back because there might be a box waiting for me and I didn't want to have to explain it. And I didn't like where this conversation was heading. She was clearly some kind of nut; an afterlife groupie or an emo who had overdone it on goths and self-harm. But then if that was true, what was I? She was a mirror. You didn't cheat death without it getting some of the filth from under its nails into your skin.

'And how do you do that?'

She shrugged, made a bow of her lips. 'I don't know. I couldn't do it before the accident... or rather, I wasn't aware of being able to do it before the accident. Now I can.'

'Do what?'

'Have you been listening to me?'

'Yes,' I said, exasperated. 'I'm trying to understand, but –'

'It's all over you,' she hissed.

'What is?' People were turning around to look though I hadn't realised I'd raised my voice.

'Death,' she said, her voice collapsing, her face collapsing, tears in her eyes. 'Death.'

I LEFT HER then. I didn't mean to be so abrupt, but it was either leave or faint or scream my head off. Pain's spiked glove was squeezing my spine at its base, lazily, recreationally, like one of those power clamp wrist-exercisers. She made to follow me, and for a while it was the world's most pathetic chase sequence; two close-to-crippled people trying to top three miles per hour on the slanting road back up to the centre of the village. But when, after a while, I checked back, she'd given up to resume her usual posture, boots planted firmly in the sand, staring straight out to sea. I thought of skulls in fishing nets, polished white by the dab and suck of pan-eyed fish and prawns, those good old sea maggots. I wondered what those eyes, surrounded by so much chaos, could see.

Up on Cannon Point, the culverins – six Elizabethan siege guns pointing out to sea – gleamed under a sky of dirty milk. Birds' nests in nude trees were shadows in a lung X-ray. I heard the distant breath of engines, a long exhalation, but did not look up.

I got back to the shop – no boxes waiting for me – locked the door and stumbled through the narrow hall of books to my room. It felt like a black corridor narrowing around me. I felt water on the back of my hand as I lifted it to jerk open the door, and I frowned at the ceiling, but then I remembered it had not rained for days. It was sweat drizzling off my forehead. That sound, like an old boiler overworking, was my breath. Everything at the base of my back felt loose and disordered, like the bottom of a canvas bag of individual iron tools.

I made it to the bed and kind of collapsed against it; I resembled some old punter at a bar who's had far too much to drink but is trying to maintain some semblance of sobriety. I said 'Thank You' to Tamara as she handed over the plastic wallet in which I kept all my drugs and then swore at her because she hadn't unzipped it for me. I took some pills, dry-swallowing them because I couldn't turn the tap, and then tried to find a position that was bearable while I waited for the bastard things to take hold.

'Where are you?' I asked her, but she wasn't falling for that one. I looked up to the spot where she had been standing and tried to make her re-materialise there, but she was just memory dust clogging up my mind. I couldn't picture her without that lovely, cheeky half-smile. She seemed so close sometimes that I could smell her.

I must have fallen asleep, although it seemed only seconds later that I opened my eyes to find the light gone and the sounds of female footsteps scratching and clacking on the road outside the window. I very carefully got myself upright, pausing every now and then for the lances and jags and bolts, but they never came. The worst ache was in my chest; I must have pulled a muscle breathing so harshly. I checked my watch. Early evening. I'd been asleep for four hours.

I shuffled through to the bathroom and now I had no trouble getting the taps on. Steam leapt up. The mirror fogged instantly. I cracked open the window and started the long, arduous chore that was undressing. I pushed my focus back, purposefully blurred my eyes and thought of something else – Tamara, of course – to prevent myself from sucking up the detail of all these bruises and bumps and snakes of scar tissue. I turned off the taps and silence came rushing back. I could still hear footsteps, but they were far away, maybe not even those made by the same person. Unreliable echoes. Just the muffled, tricksy sounds of night time, now.

I got in the bath. Closed my eyes. Too hot in here. I could feel my heartbeat assaulting my insides. The surface tension, if I checked, would be shivering, as if something unspeakably large were closing in. Heat. I thought of what Amy had told me. I tried to put myself in her position. An impossible position. I tried to imagine what was worse, smothering and burning, or falling from a great height. Both were horribly violent deaths, and the irony was not lost on me that I had spend fifteen years poking a stick into the eye of both possibilities. It was amazing now to think that I had never given a moment's thought to an aeroplane disintegrating at 30,000 feet, or an engine catching fire, or the inferno following a crash. But then I supposed if we all succumbed to fear of occupational hazards, little would get done every day.

I soaked a flannel and draped it over my face. It moulded quickly to my features and the air I sucked in was hot and tasted faintly of soap. A brief dance of cold air came through the gap in the window. I felt drowsy with the temperature and the morphine in my bloodstream. At such moments I felt as near as I was likely to being comfortable. I could consider Tamara, and her actions, with a detachment that simply was not there during the hourly struggle to cope with this new body and the itinerary of pains, fresh and old, that it brought with it.

I put myself behind her eyes. I imagined her getting the phone call and imagining her putting down her book, or her cup of tea, and calling a taxi (she didn't drive) to take her to the hospital. She was gregarious, but I imagined she'd repel any chatty overtures from the cab driver. Rain on the windows, maybe. She rubbed her hands together when she was anxious. *Were you anxious? Did you come to the hospital? Or did you decide to start packing straight away?*

I stayed with the loyal Tamara. I saw her hurrying through the rain to the A&E entrance. *Pol*, she'd say. *Where's Pol?*

The confusion. Ukrainian words slipping through. The receptionist stoically asking her to calm down. Gradually making herself understood. Close to tears. Hysteria. *Will he… is he all right? Can I see him?*

The long wait sitting in a plastic moulded chair in a room where everyone wants to be a million miles away. Blistering coffee that tastes nothing like coffee, but nobody cares. A TV on with the sound turned down and everyone watching and nobody seeing. The edges of the waiting room blacking out and everyone falling into the gap without a sound. I couldn't hold up the foundations of a reconstruction of something that had not happened. Loyal Tamara? No such character was listed in the credits. The whole scenario turned to ash.

The bath had cooled slightly. I reached out and wrenched the tap, hurting my finger on the handle. I swore. It felt good. I swore some more. Heat surged through the water. If it hadn't happened like that, then what? The phone call. *We're sorry to inform you… he's in the operating theatre now… he's critical…* Putting the receiver down. Calling the taxi. *Where did you go?*

I opened my eyes and turned off the tap. What I thought was the trickle of water was more echoes from the road outside; a very young child's laughter. Late, wasn't it, for babies? But what did I know? It didn't matter.

I'd been fretting so much over the why of Tamara's actions that I'd neglected the where. And both avenues of thought had offered me an in: taxis. How else would she leave the village, especially if she had a few cases with her?

Quarter of an hour later I was on the phone, a list of the taxi firms – three of them – in the immediate vicinity. I knew it might be a long shot that any of them would still have a log of the actual phone call Tamara would have made, but there was a chance the drivers themselves would remember picking her up, especially if she was distraught. A handsome woman going to pieces. People remembered that.

The first number produced a dead tone. Maybe they'd gone out of business. The second firm I called, contrary to my suspicion, had a log that went back as long as a year; neither Tamara's mobile number, nor the B&B's, were on their records. I considered the possibility that she had called from somewhere else, a restaurant for example, but she only ever went out to restaurants with me, and anyway, it would have been difficult for the hospital to contact her beyond the numbers that existed on my person at the time of the accident. Despite my fears that she had abandoned me straight away, logically it didn't wash. She would have come to see me, if only to gauge how destroyed I was before bailing out. I stuck with the date of the hit-and-run.

The third taxi firm had no records at all. 'I'm just a one-man outfit,' he said. 'One man, one car, one phone.'

I tried to describe Tamara to him but it was piss in the wind.

'Look, mate,' he said. 'I'm busy. They say we're coming out of recession, but it feels to me like I'm still up to my neck in it. So if you don't mind, I've got to clear the line for all those punters who aren't about to call.'

I was about to put the phone down but had a thought. 'Okay, I'll book a taxi,' I said. 'Now, if you would. Take me to the A&E in Ipswich.'

HE WAS A hefty guy in his mid-forties. I knew he was hefty before I even saw him, because he sounded his horn three times from the cab before coming to the door and giving it a weighty knock. He was back in his driver's seat by the time I'd hobbled to the door and he wouldn't look me in the eye then. Guilt at rushing an invalid along. Guilt at not being there to help him into his seat. He wore a glossy moustache and a side-parting. Little white pinch marks on the bridge of his nose showed me he'd just taken his glasses off. You become a regular Sherlock Holmes when you've little else left in life beyond observation.

'Please,' I said, as he threw the gearstick into first. 'Hang on a sec.'

'You do want to go to the A&E, don't you?'

'Yes, but it's no rush. I'm not having an emergency.'

'You look as if you have, and not that long ago.'

Another Sherlock Holmes. We could have opened a practice. 'Never mind about that,' I said, and I took out my wallet. Already his expression was of mild regret at accepting this job.

'This is the woman I was telling you about on the phone,' I said. 'I really need to find her. It would help me enormously, more than you can imagine, if you could tell me if you picked her up.'

He sighed and held his hand out for the picture. I felt a momentary pang when I handed it over, as if in doing so I was somehow casting Tamara away. I fidgeted nervously, wanting the photograph back all the while he was wiping the grease off his mitts all over her.

'This is like in the movies, isn't it?' he said. His piggy eyes sucked her in. Tamara had been wearing a tight white T-shirt on a cold day when I took the picture. I swallowed it down and waited.

'You know, it's difficult. I pick up attractive girls like this all the time. Friday, Saturday nights, you know?'

Yeah, I thought. *Yeah, right. Here we go.*

'But this one, this one I'm not sure about. I can't quite remember…' He was rubbing his chin now. I saw black hoops of sweat in the hollow beneath his bingo wings.

'This *is* just like the films, isn't it?' I said.

He thinned his lips into a sheepish *what can you do?* kind of smile. I took out my wallet and withdrew ten pounds.

'She's ten pounds important to you, is she?'

I took out a twenty as well. He pocketed the notes and went back to the photograph, frowning, rubbing his chin.

'For fuck's sake,' I said.

'There's no need for that.' He presented the photograph back to me, flicked out between two fingers. 'Yes, I remember her. Of course I remember her. She was in tears.'

My tongue thickened; my throat narrowed. I wanted to pull him near to me, see if I could smell her perfume on him. She had sat in this car. Tamara might have been sitting where I sat now. I pressed my hand against the upholstery.

'Where did you take her?' I managed.

'The hospital. Same one you're going to now. I take it she was coming to see you? This was months ago.'

'Over six months,' I said. I placed the photograph back in my wallet and tucked it safely away from him. He kept his eyes on my pocket, as if he could still see the outline of her through my jeans. I knew how he felt; she was like that. She left an impression. 'And then what?'

'And then what, exactly? I don't know. I went off and had a pie, read the papers, took a guy to the airport. You know. Same old, same old.'

'I mean, you didn't wait for her? You didn't take her back?'

'Didn't take her back, no. But then, by the looks of you, it wasn't likely to be a quick visit. No grapes and chocs for you, I'd imagine.'

'You didn't take her back at all? Later? I mean, hours later? Days?'

'Nope.'

'I don't have any more money, other than enough to pay for this trip. We could stop at the bank...'

He held up his hand, nervous now. Perhaps he realised that what he'd done was less than chivalrous. 'It's all right. I don't want any money...'

Any more, you mean.

'... I didn't take her back, no. Not that day, not ever. I haven't seen her since. There are other cab firms, you know. I'd remember having her in the car. She's a handsome woman, that one. A special catch. You lucky swine.'

I could have punched him, but I would have set my rehabilitation back weeks. Instead, I pulled on the door lever.

'Hey, what about my fare?'

I unfolded myself, gritting teeth, clenching fists. 'Like you said,' I grunted. 'There are other cab firms.'

He stepped on the gas and gave me the Vs as he tore away. Any satisfaction I had in wasting his time was short-lived: I was wasting my time too.

I waited another twenty minutes for a different taxi firm to send a driver round. I showed him the

photograph too, before we set off, but drew a blank.
No bribe needed this time. We travelled the 35 miles
or so to Ipswich in silence. I was glad he preferred
quiet, although I could have done without the smell
of stale cigarette smoke. At the A&E entrance he
wished me well and I grabbed hold of that, guarded
it hard and fast against the suspicion that this was
already a wild goose chase and that Tamara had
simply called a different cab firm, or thumbed a ride,
or simply vanished into thin air like the vapour from
an open bottle of the perfume she liked to wear.

Inside the hospital, I was rapidly shunted from the
counter when it was clear that there was nothing
freshly wrong with me – *Can't you see there are sick
people waiting to be treated?* – and told to talk to
someone at the main reception. Once I was there, a
security guard with thighs for arms and industrial
chimney stacks for legs peered down at me from the
shadow beneath his security guard's visor as I tried
to make myself understood to the receptionist.

Eventually she suggested I go to the ward where
I had lived for half a year. I had to ask her where
it was. In the end, one of the porters, perhaps
taking pity on me, bustled me into a wheelchair
and pushed me what seemed like miles through a
bland chemical-smelling labyrinth. He helped me
out of my chair when we'd reached a far outpost
of the hospital. This was Death Alley. This was the
place where plugs were pulled. For the first time it
occurred to me that I should perhaps be grateful for
Tamara's leaving when she did. Otherwise I might
not be here now. She could have said the word if
the doctors believed there was no way back for me.

I'd have been a flatline. A black mark on a chart no longer needed.

I shuffled to the ward, suddenly feeling worse than I had since I emerged from the coma. Was that hospitals, exerting their malign presence, or just fatigue? It had been a long day. I'd done more travelling around today than in many, many months.

Another desk. Another sour-faced woman behind it pushing a pen, filing a document, wishing she was anywhere but here, having to talk to this denuded old-before-his-time wreck of a man who looked as though he should be given a permanent bed in this place.

I was about to ask her I don't know what... I thought this would be easy before I'd realised what 'this' was, and I was fumbling again for the photograph of Tamara when she said, her voice flat, her face somehow even sourer: 'Hello Paul. It's lovely to see you.'

BARBARA TOOK ME through to the lounge area and made me tea. She'd built up a head of steam now and there was no point in trying to make myself understood. I was now, at least, in the company of someone who had looked in on me while I... slept, probably most days. It was a relief of sorts, though I desperately wanted to find out what had happened to Tamara. I felt closer to some kind of resolution than I had in ages.

She handed me the tea. She was talking about Angela and Catriona and Fay, nurses I did not know, who had brushed my hair and wiped my arse and chatted to me while I withered on the vine. I took the cup. It rattled in its saucer. I cried.

I LIKED THE sour face, I decided. It did not let up. Even when she was trying to bring me round, coax a smile out of me. The tea was hot and sweet and it reminded me that I hadn't eaten anything since breakfast. Toast was offered. I gobbled it down. I was *this* close to asking if I could move back in.

'What's the trouble with you?' she asked me. 'Why haven't you been back before now to say thank you for everything we did for you?'

I blew out my cheeks and ummed and ahhed, but she punched my knee. 'I'm kidding with you, you silly badger,' she said. 'I could tell, even when you were lying on that bed, yawning and dribbling away, that you were soft in the head. And a pilot. Why would I want to get on one of those massive planes knowing that they might have soft shites like you up front flying the buggers?'

It worked. I managed a little chuckle and felt better for it. I stared into the remnants of my tea and said, 'I'm trying to find my girlfriend.'

'Your girlfriend?' Barbara said, as if she couldn't believe I'd have such a thing. 'Tall girl. Dark hair. Olive skin.'

'Yes,' I said, and I was so excited the cup started rattling again. 'Do you know where she is?'

She shook her head. She seemed confused. 'We were all waiting for an invitation to the wedding.'

'What? You've lost me.'

'While you were in your coma, the girl… what was

her name, now? Right, Tamara, well she wouldn't stay away from this place. We ended up putting you in a different bed, one with a pull-out cot underneath it so that she could stay with you through the night.'

'But she's gone. She left me. I'm trying to track her down.'

Barbara suddenly looked as though she wanted to be back at her desk, doing things with paper clips, fielding calls, calling for a crash team. 'Oh, God, Paul. I'm sorry. Sometimes, you know... the pressure. The day-to-day grind. The not knowing. It can wear you out. I've seen people in this hospital turned into emotional wrecks. What's the word? Wraiths. They come in all hopeful and determined and in no time at all they're grey and hopeless, and I'm talking about visitors here. Especially coma patient visitors. You're waiting for something that might never happen.'

'How long did she visit for?'

'You were in here from the April to the October. She was a fitting in your room for maybe a whole month. We just thought she'd drained her batteries. Not for a moment did we suspect... Look, she showed real devotion. You don't often find it, even in long-married couples. She was a puppy by your side. She talked to you. She held your hand.'

The pain of tears that could not come. I shook my head, trying to force it away. 'But then she left me,' I said. 'She left me.'

'I don't know what to say,' she said, spreading her hands. The sour face was gone now. I caught a hint of what she must look like when she was off duty, with friends, family. She was kind and I was grateful to her for looking after me. 'We talked about it. It seemed... unlike her. She didn't seem the quitting type. But, circumstances change. People change. I don't know what I can do.'

My mind was full of ideas. Maybe security had footage of her on the CCTV. Maybe someone talked to her about the futility of it all and she had let slip where she was going, who she was turning to. But Barbara told me to stop it.

'Maybe she just needs time,' she said. 'You've been gone for six months. She thought she was going to lose you. To all intents and purposes, you went to sleep and then woke up again. It might have felt like moments to you. But you've carved a great hole in that woman. She needs to mend, just like you. Give her a chance. Give her time. A girl like that, the way she behaved at the start... people like that don't just turn off. She'll get in touch.'

She might have said all of that, or I might have imagined much of it. It was everything I'd hoped and feared she might say, but it was what was expected of her. She was in the mending business. I still didn't feel better about things.

I said hello to other faces, people who knew me better than I knew them, made empty promises to keep in touch and let them know how things were going. They and I were forgotten as soon as we turned our backs on each other. I made my way back to the exit. Shortly before I reached it, I heard footsteps behind me.

'Need a lift home?'

*　　*　　*

Ruth always put the heating on in her car for longer than was necessary. After twenty minutes it was stifling. I wanted to open the window, but the electric control on my side was busted. She had all the power and I didn't want to ask her; although it was hot, there was frost in this car too.

We got back on the A-road and she let me have it.

'What do you think you're playing at, Paul?' she demanded. Her eyes alternated between the road in front and, via the rearview mirror, the road behind. There was a weird, concomitant feeling that nothing in this car therefore existed; she didn't look at me once. It was as if she were rehearsing lines from a play. It kind of helped. I didn't say anything.

'I'm trying to help you. We're all trying to help you. Why don't you believe me?'

'I do believe you.'

'About Tamara, I mean.'

'I doesn't matter what I believe. I have to find out for myself. I have to hear it from her. We sold our flat to be here. You don't just walk away from that kind of commitment. At the very least she'd want her share of the money.'

'You'd be best to just let her go and get on with your life. How much happiness could you have with her if she comes back to you? She left you. You wouldn't be able to bear her nipping out to the shops for fear of never seeing her again.'

I turned away to watch the traffic. 'That's not it,' I said. 'You obviously don't understand.'

'I'm not sure there's anything *to* understand, Paul.' A sigh. A tut. 'Look... I'm being unfair to you. I'm being selfish. I thought... I hoped...'

I turned back to her. The intensity was gone. She no longer shot looks at what was behind us. Now she was concentrating on what was ahead. Her look had softened. She seemed more like a lost girl. It was fascinating the way her emotions swept her, physically, from one end of the female spectrum to the other.

'You hoped what?' I asked, but I knew.

'I thought something might come of us.' Her voice changed completely. It might have been someone else now, in the car, magicked into her driving seat while I was looking the other way. She was all soft curves, her angles and arches and teeth concealed.

She'd been in to collect some of her things. She was now, officially, on maternity leave. Not seeing her in her uniform was unusual. So was seeing her without her hair pinned up. A lot of those lines around her eyes were down to me.

'That's good to know,' I said. 'Really. I just need to put this to bed. I can't function.'

'It's not just me, either, although you've come to mean a lot to me. It's others in the village. They need you too.'

'To dispose of their dirty little secrets?'

'That's one way of putting it. But not every secret is dirty. There are some desperate people around, Paul. They can't organise their own lives. They can't… you know… forge a path.'

'They can't build their own bonfires? They can't lift their own bin lids?'

'Maybe not. Maybe it's about distancing yourself from something. Not getting your hands dirty with what's been soiling your mind for so long. You're a symbol, don't you think? A white knight.'

'I'm a sin eater,' I said. 'Do you really think burning Percy Filth's porn collection is going to cure him of his habit? No. He'll be back in the newsagent's tomorrow replenishing his stock. You know, I do this shitty thing for them, not for any recognition, but because it's there, it's something to do. You say they need me, but they don't give a fuck about me, about who is doing this for them. And I can tell you, the feeling's mutual.'

I saw her wince. She breathed deeply. Her face paled a little.

'You all right?' I asked.

'A little pain,' she said. 'It's fine. It's sitting in this position for too long. Junior is making it known that he's not happy.'

'That makes two of us,' I said, and regretted it. I saw her slump a little.

'I'm sorry,' I said. 'That was uncalled for. And it's not true. I was just being a smart-mouth.'

'It's all right,' she said. 'You've been through a lot. You feel free to speak your mind. I'm a nurse, you seem to forget. I can take all that and more. I've got skin thicker than a hippo's.'

'I've got a head thicker than a hippo's,' I said. 'Really, I mean it, I'm sorry. I am happy. I'm lucky to have you as a friend. You're saving me in any number of ways.'

Her grip on the steering wheel changed, became lighter. She shuffled herself upright and sighed. 'Well okay then. Let's not talk about negatives any more.

You'll thrash it out with Tamara and one way or another we'll all find where we're at.'

Her voice was soothing now. All of her anger had dissipated. Perhaps she was calmer because she'd broached a subject we'd been skirting for a while. Perhaps it was because she had left work and could look forward to preparing for her baby. I felt encouraged too, and not just because I'd engineered some positive action for a change. I'd been too passive, allowed my life to follow a course it instinctively railed against, deep inside. I knew what I had to do and I was doing it, regardless of Ruth's warnings. This felt right and so it *was* right.

She was talking about painting a room for the baby, now, but I was losing focus. It really was warm in the car now, and it wasn't too bad after all. You could see how cold it was outside: the wind shearing through the trees, the sudden barrage of rain as it was turned against the windscreen. All grey and dreary. I closed my eyes for a second and the heat followed me down. The engine in the car changed its tune. It became deeper, more powerful, misfiring, making the song of metal fatigue. The heat shimmered as I grew accustomed to my surroundings. I placed a hand against the window. Windows punched along the side of a cabin. The serge of my uniform, itchy, uncomfortable. Half a dozen passengers sitting next to the wing were trapped in their seats, thrashing around, deep in fire.

PART TWO

LONG HAUL

Flight Z
DEAD RECKONING

I SIT NEXT to a ruined marionette in the bulkhead seat and cast glances over my shoulder at the fry-up the rest of the plane is turning into. A comber of thick, black smoke clings to the ceiling, uncoiling swiftly towards us like a roll of carpet kicked out across a floor. At the bulkheads it curls down and, almost tenderly, blankets us utterly. A hand finds mine, undercover of this lethal fog. All bone, hot as something left for too long on a barbecue.

You breathe and the smoke gathers in your lungs like something solid: crumbled Oxo cubes massing in the back of the throat. The heat threatens to seal your airways shut. The jet lumbers on despite the fuselage cindering. Grinds and explosions cause misfires in the engines. A body from the 747 hanging through the cabin roof of the triple-7 looks like a baby reaching out to be held; its fingers are smouldering. I ask the woman next to me where she's headed and she says Burnley, which gets her laughing but it's too harsh, hijacked by coughs. She hangs over the edge of the seat, mouth open, a thin rope of black sputum spinning from the back of her throat, black tears smudging the grey flesh of her face. Her eyes have frosted over from the chemical effects of the smoke.

On the other side of me is a fat man whose clothes are shredding away from his skin in sheaves of carbon. His skin is tight and shiny where the flames have scorched the detail from him, like sausages blistering in a pan. A tiny rupture in his flesh as he jerks in agony sends geysers of boiling fat sputtering against the plastic controls melting in the cabin ceiling.

'I was a lonely child,' he says, and I have to incline my head towards him, the smoke is smothering all sound. 'I was cripplingly shy. I never had what you'd call a healthy circle of friends. I had a stammer and I was so self-conscious of it I would sit in the corner of the playground every day and cover my mouth with my hands. And here I am. Middle-aged and nothing has changed. I'm flying home to my studio flat, regretting not saying this and not doing that every second of the day. I could have had a house full of laughing children and a wife by now. But I was too busy blushing and checking my teeth for spinach.'

His eyes burn with a violet flame.

A woman comes seething out of the smoke, hands outstretched. Her lungs have been seared dry. The dead-match remains of her feet drag sooty marks along the aisle. She's trying to say something to me but I can't tell what it is. Her vocal cords are so much incinerated tissue. She's imploring, beseeching. Her hands ask questions but also assume the aspect of somebody holding something fragile. All she is cradling is the restless curls and curves of the thing that is killing us all. The starboard fire flashes out for a second and one crisp figure, fused with the chemical syrup that is its seat back, rasps what was once the ball of its thumb over a beef jerky tongue and turns the page of a duty free catalogue long-turned to ash in its lap. People look up, querulously, as the PA softly chimes and the captain screams in agony.

An old, bearded man waves at me from seat 34A. His hand is a burning orange glove. He shouts over to me: 'Nothing you can do. Nothing we can do. Nothing we've done. None of it is any good. Nothing will work. Where is our sacrificial lamb? Where is our meat for the beast?'

The woman getting closer to me now. She's alternating between outstretching her hands and drawing them in close to her tummy. What does she want? Food? I look around for the flight attendant but she's busy trying to pat out with fiery hands the inferno twisting about her body.

The woman reaches out one of those black, famished claws for me. Burned tendons hang from her like loose horsehair on a violinist's bow. I turn away from her and ask the ruined marionette next to me if she's enjoying the in-flight film.

The hand on my shoulder, hell-hot, manic grip. She leans in close and though the smell of smoke is all around and inside us, I get a flavour of what's in her.

She exhales: 'Where's my fucking baby?'

Chapter Eight

THE WRECKS

I woke up with a taste in my mouth that I couldn't identify but that I knew very well. It was maddening. I sat there playing around with it on my tongue, wondering where it had come from. I was uncomfortable and hot. Sense came to me. I was sitting in a cold car, my forehead against the window. I was covered with three or four thick blankets. The glass was all misted up. Rain hammered the other side of it. The car's engine had been silent a long time. I peered at the clock in the dashboard. Gone three in the morning.

I struggled out of the position I'd been sleeping in, swearing and gnashing at the pain. I hooked a claw around the door release and tumbled out into the frozen, teeming night. Blind moon, tonight. A ton of cloud. There was a childhood spike of fear and panic when I realised I did not know where I was. The road beneath my feet had some give in it; it felt like packed soil, hardened only by the fierce cold. I reached back inside the car and pulled a couple of the blankets out and around my shoulders.

'Ruth?'

Shapes materialising. Near black, on black. Water nearby: plaited dark iron. Fields stretching away like so much barren scree at the end of the world. I noticed the impossible knot was in my hand and I was fiddling with it, trying to find its edges. Something to distract me; a pacifier. Though I knew we'd been here a while, I put my hand on the car's bonnet. Dead cold. I checked the back seat in case Ruth was in there, asleep. The car was empty. I tried contacting her on the phone, but she wasn't answering. What the fuck was she playing at?

I turned through 360 degrees. Pale stain of orange light on the horizon. How far away was that? I turned back to the opposite skyline and there was utter dark. I blinked and squinted. Another shape emerging. Deepest grey. Like a pepper pot. Okay. Okay. That was the ruined mill in its lonely field. I knew that. I'd often used it as a marker when I was trudging around, trying to bring the muscles in my legs back to life. A bolt pinning the landscape and my mind into place. Sails long gone. The mill was still and cold and broken. I knew how it felt.

So the light behind me was Southwick. Which meant, by dint of amateur triangulation, I must be on the harbour path. It would make sense. I swore, casting a final glance around me just in case she might suddenly reappear and save me from this, then started moving in the direction of the mill.

I kept my eye on the mill, or where it ought to be under all that darkness and wet. There was nothing. I could hardly see the path and had to rely on the occasional forks of lightning to help confirm I was on the right course. I was loath to switch on my torch and give away my position in case there was danger up ahead. The mill stood away from the path, down an incline. I could see water glimmering around the necks of the reeds. I had to climb over a fence and

pick a route through a jungle of dead electric wire that
had once penned in animals long gone from this field.
My feet grew sodden as I slipped into freezing cold,
ankle-deep water. I could see it sluicing over the sides
of the riverbank now. At the same moment, just before
it was snatched away by the dervish wind, I smelled
food. Soup, maybe. Or a beefy stew of some kind. I
felt the storm fall away slightly as I came under the
shade of the mill. Lightning showed me the skeletal
remains of the sails. There was a tight, creaking sound
as if the wind was trying to turn the seized gears of
something that would never turn again. I heard a
crack, and stopped, wondering if one of the sails was
about to come free, but then I felt something in my
mouth – a piece of tooth; I'd been clenching my jaw
so hard I'd broken one of my molars. I spat it out and
edged around the mill to the entrance. Any kind of
door was long gone. There was one piece of timber,
jammed obliquely into it as a token signal barring
entry. It was hellish black in there. Now I switched
on the torch and the pitted brickwork sprang into
horrible relief. Kids had been here, but long ago.
Graffiti spray-painted on to the walls was faded to
the point of illegibility. There were Coke cans and foil
takeaway cartons lying around, worn paper thin from
time and corrosion. There was recent activity too,
though. The reeds had all been mashed into the floor
from the constant comings and goings of someone
or something. There wasn't the stink of animal, but I
couldn't trust my senses in this downpour. I got closer
and the beam from the torch picked out candle stumps
melted into pieces of shattered crockery. A paperback
book was a puffball of mould.

There was a sleeping bag on the floor, but it was soaked through and filthy with mud. There was a plate encrusted with ancient food and a spoon glued into it on an upturned crate. The aroma of food I'd caught must have been flung to me on the wind from somewhere else, because this place was dead. But no. I could smell something oily and burned now. Like tallow. There was fresh rope, its cut end had recently been rewhipped, trimmed and dipped in wax. Someone had been working here. Some shelter. The wind came bullying in through the open windows and the holes in the brickwork. I couldn't stay here. I moved off in the direction of the sea.

What had Ruth brought me out here for? And why had she abandoned me? She knew the woman who ran the breakfasts at the café, but that wouldn't be open for another three hours or so. Charlie's fish hut was nearby, but he didn't sleep there. He'd be mad if he did in this weather. No, he lived in Breydon, the village between Southwick and the dual carriageway, about a ten-minute drive from here.

I felt my stomach lurch when I thought that Ruth might have committed suicide and actually edged along one of the slipways to look into the blank mirror of the water. But like mine, her 'incident' lay many months in the past. It had defined her, in the way that mine had not, or had yet to. She was managing to heal with time, and maybe the baby growing inside her was acting as some kind of marvellous balm, despite its origins. She was forcing through that separation, trying to detach the rape from its result, and becoming stronger for it. I suppose she had to, if she was going to forge any kind of successful relationship with the baby. Who knew if it would work? Scars were still present – how could they not be – in the way she could not bear any physical contact, but I was still wrestling with the time issue. In my mind, the impact had occurred only recently. In real time, half a year had drifted by.

I stared into the sea but I knew she had not done this. Her commitment to other people was too great, almost to the point where she failed to protect herself. I made a vow to try to give back some of the care she had afforded me, no matter how angry I was at her now for abandoning me. She deserved it and it would do me good as well to stop teasing open my bandages and mewling about how damaged I was all the time. I had to get a grip and accept that this was what my life involved now. There was no going back. Pain waited for everyone at some point or another. I was just unfortunate that it was climbing all over me at this moment. How you dealt with it when it was upon you was what mattered most.

I moved back on to the main harbour path and felt more confident in my location. The masts of sea boats were just discernible now: perspective showed me a corridor between them down which to travel. The curious, massive space above the ocean was different, I don't know how or why, to that above land. It seemed more reverent, cowed by the great mass of water; maybe this was how the world appeared when elements collided. I tugged the blankets more tidily around me and shuffled on, resigned to a drenching. At least my physiotherapy would be done early today, I thought to myself.

Twenty minutes later I reached the end of the path and bore left on to an area of dunes. I trod on the blackened remains of a beach fire and shuddered at the recent memory of my dream, unable to prevent myself from casting a suspicious eye to the heavens for a glimpse of nightmare, of something that would never be capable of rising from an airstrip.

I kept going. There was nobody about, not even a nightfisherman in a glowing orange tent to give me some beacon to aim towards. The cold found its way under the flapping hem of the blanket, through my sodden jeans and into my legs. I thought scar tissue might offer more resistance, but no; less, it seemed. There were more cracks to get through. I imagined the cold steeling in while I was having operations to mend my shattered limbs. It lay alongside the marrow, now, and would be with me always, even on the hottest summer afternoon.

I was sweating, though, by the time I reached the bookshop. There was no sign of Ruth here either. What was going on? I wondered if she was at Charlie's house, but that didn't square with her leaving me on my own at the harbour.

I felt as if I'd just woken up from another coma, with another puzzle to solve. And here was more shit: the keys to the bookshop weren't in my pocket. They must have fallen out while I was in the car, or perhaps Ruth had taken them while I was sleeping.

I was about to call a taxi to take me to Breydon – walking would wipe me out – and had opened my wallet to check how much cash I had, when I felt a key in the zip-up compartment. It was the key to Tam's Place.

What decided it was the rain, which was intensifying. Sheets of it were hurling themselves in from the sea. I hobbled as fast as I could along Surt Road to North Parade and fumbled the key into the lock of this dark building, in a street of dark buildings. It felt darker, somehow: the curse of a place that has not been lived in for some time. The breath of air that came at me once I'd forced the door in against the hill of circulars and free newspapers reminded me of the first time I'd been to see it, with Tamara. A much more different day to this you couldn't expect. Hard sunshine. The sea glittering, difficult to look at. I had a belly full of fish and chips and my hand was on her arse as we were led over the threshold by the obsequious estate agent who had an irritating way of talking that we couldn't stop giggling about. He kept referring to us in the third person, as if we weren't there.

'And there's plenty of private space should Mr Roan and Ms Dziuba think of having a Master... Roan? Roan-Dziuba? There's a mouthful, hahaha.'

'Your private space,' I'd kept asking Tamara on the way back to London. 'How much of it is there?'

'Enough to accommodate you,' she replied. 'Easily.'

Rain hissed against the glass panels in the door as I shut out the night. The smell of damp approaching like someone unsure of what was ahead. Dim shapes in the gloom. I rubbed my wet hair with the blanket and tried a light switch. No joy. I struggled to remember the layout of the building from the tour we'd been given. It was hard to believe that this place was mine now. I felt as though I was walking through a house I'd never visited before. I suppose my mind hadn't been on it at the time. Tamara's arse had felt good under that sheer wrapping of knitted merino. I was thinking, I remember, yes, we'll have this and make a go of it and it will be great and who cares that there's a lot of work it just feels right and yes and yes and yes.

Remnants of that good feeling had stuck around. I wouldn't be able to be as pro-active as I had planned, but I could still plan and budget and co-ordinate. Get busy and keep busy. Keep my mind off things by focusing on others. If I could prove to myself, through this project, that I had some use, that I wasn't a vegetable likely to languish in a wheelchair for the rest of my life, Tamara might come back.

Five rooms on the ground floor. Dining room. Lounge. Private lounge. Kitchen. Office. The office was a small room, half a room, really, with a space for a desk and a chair and a safe and little else; my torch cast weak, fragmenting light against the walls. Bare bright patches showed where pictures had once hung. The only other thing in the room was a lever-arch file filled with plastic wallets containing invoices with faint, illegible type on them.

I poked my head into each room, trying to suck in some of the positive ambience I'd felt the previous summer. Now, in the dark and the cold, the work that was needed seemed insurmountable. The kitchen units needed replacing; God knew how long the old ones had been in place. Some of the doors were hanging off the carcases. The linoleum was peeling away from the floor. Every wall needed a fresh lick of pain. The toilet needed replacing; the old one was a gutter of stains and cracks. The cost of refurbishment kept kerchinging in my mind. I had a good amount of money saved up, and an inheritance to draw upon, but it was still going to be a steep outlay.

I eased up the stairs, hoping there might be a bed and a mattress so I could lie down. It didn't matter how dirty the damned thing would be; I needed to work away a few hours and although I'd slept in the car – and Christ, more than enough over the past six months – I still felt tired. The doctors had urged me to rest. The body repaired itself best when I was unconscious.

I decided to move on past the first floor to the top of the house and start there. Two double bedrooms. One single bedroom. And then the largest bedroom, a private section with its own sizeable bathroom and shower. It boasted the best views too. The previous owners had clearly decided that their own happiness was more important than the premium price they could have demanded for such decadence. There was a bed frame in here but nothing to rest upon. There was a very cheap-looking wardrobe in one of the other rooms too, that looked as if it was still standing, albeit in a vaguely upright position, by dint of wishful thinking. No other furniture. Another shower room that needed totally replacing. I descended to the first floor thinking that the best way to clean the whole place out would be to torch it, but the thought of flames made me feel sick, and I knew that there'd be something else waiting for me in the morning when I got back, no matter the ugly weather. Skeletons came out to dance rain or shine.

First floor. Four double bedrooms, two en suite. One single bedroom. Wallpaper touching its toes. One shower room. A mirror with a crack in it. A toothbrush lying on the floor, bristles thick with mould. A copy of *Mojo* magazine partially obscured by dust. A dead beetle.

A noise from upstairs.

I've just been up there, I sighed to myself, trying to rationalise it, trying to keep my heart calm. Maybe it was just my physical presence, after months of absence, or empty space, causing a greater-than-normal level of subsidence. Some animal trapped in the attic, making a final bid for freedom.

I came out on to the landing and stared up into a blackness that my feeble torch could not pierce. Darkness made an oblique across the staircase like the diagonal of a guillotine blade.

There it was again. It was a kind of slumping noise, as if a heavy person was trying to get comfortable on a bed never known for it. I stood on the landing and felt my heart fraying, bit by bruised, gnarly bit. I didn't know what to do. I had seen nobody up there, but I hadn't exactly stuck my face to the floor to check under that old bed or pulled open the wardrobe door to see if my own private Narnia waited inside for me. I hadn't taken a peek through the loft hatch. I hadn't checked to see what state the fire escape was in, or the flat lower-level roof.

'Hello?' I called up the stairs, but I couldn't generate much volume. My mouth felt drum dry. The door to the master bedroom creaked. Weird acoustics: I could hear the weather all over the house – especially at the landing window behind my back

– but it was shut off from that particular corner as that door closed. And it wasn't a draught closing it. There was a pause, and then it was pressed into the doorway. I heard the click of the latch bolt snap home. I heard a ferocious cry. I had no idea what it was; undercover of the storm it sounded like metal tearing, cats copulating, the lusty railings of a distressed baby.

Ten minutes later I was in the alleyway outside the house, staring up at the windows and not knowing what it was I was expecting to see. I had gone up to the top floor somehow, found the steel from somewhere. Call it pilot's nerve – maybe that kind of thing does not leave you, really – but I got up there and placed my hand against the door as if I might feel something, some hideous vibration through the flesh to confirm what my ears thought they'd heard. I couldn't bring myself to turn the door handle. The prospect of seeing the room as I had initially left it was far worse, somehow, than any yawning terror my imagination could throw at me.

Outside, in the rain, I thought I saw the lazy shift of low-spectrum colour from one side of the pane to the other. But my eyes weren't what they were. Nothing was as it was.

I guessed it to be another three hours till sun-up. The rain was showing no signs of dropping off. It looped and swirled like sheer silver dresses on a washing line. The cold was affecting my movement. It had sunk so deep into my legs that they were shivering even when firmly planted on the ground.

I was fiddling with my phone, trying to stab some sense out of it in order to find a taxi number, when I saw Amy's number. I checked the time. It was four in the morning. Christ. I couldn't. I couldn't.

I did.

She answered on the first ring. She didn't sound tired at all. 'Airman,' she said.

'You remembered.'

'I kind of knew you'd call. I just didn't think it would be in the middle of the night.'

'You weren't sleeping?'

'I cat nap. During the day, mostly. I prefer not to sleep at night. Psychological. And anyway, I do my best work round about now.'

'Could I come to you? I'm locked out. Nowhere to go. And I'm freezing my nuts off.'

'Only if you'll agree to help me,' she said. But she didn't wait for me to agree. She gave me her address; she was renting a flat above a sweet shop in the centre of the village, opposite the main hotel. I shuffled and snuffled for another fifteen minutes and thought, maybe, that the sky was just showing the first dirty green-grey streaks of dawn by the time I reached the triangular lay-out of shops.

A figure was standing in the narrow ginnel between the sweet shop and the post office. It had to be her, although I was made uneasy by how still she was, like a dressmaker's dummy in a window. That's what damage did for you, I thought. The rest of a life marked out in yards achieved, rather than miles. The moment when life changed for us involved lots of movement, critical movement: my monumental collision with a car; the flail of limbs as she fell seventy feet. More animation than we would ever know again.

'Inside,' she said. 'I have a hot shower. Something hot to drink.' She flapped a silver cape from out of a bag. It looked like something NASA might use to panel its lunar landers. 'It's for hypothermia,' she said. 'Runners use them all the time. You see them flapping around at the end of marathons. Like a super-hero convention.'

I'd been out in the cold for two hours, more or less. Being inside the B&B didn't really count; it had been colder in there than on the beach.

She held my hand as we ascended the stairs. At the top, she got my shoes off and handed me a mug of steaming soup. She watched me spoon it down. It was bad stuff, rehydrated packet 'broth', but the heat of it and the sugars in it instantly perked me up.

'Better?' she asked.

I nodded, handing the mug back. The shakes in my hand were lessening.

'Shower next,' she said. 'Take as long as you want.'

I made sure the water temperature was tepid to begin with; I didn't want to scald my new flesh. But after I'd grown accustomed to it, and the greyness in my toes and fingers had turned to pink, I whacked the heat up until there were billows of steam obscuring the rest of the bathroom. I stood under the jet, letting the water pound the back of my head, and wondered what help it was that Amy had been referring to. I'd not taken much notice of her flat before shutting myself up in the bathroom, but a single pool of light above a desk had shown me that her life was one disorganised mess of papers.

She'd left a large, ratty-looking but clean towelling bathrobe for me to wear and I gratefully wrapped myself in it. As soon as it was on, I felt my eyelids droop. Warmth was pressing in from all sides. Like the winter wind, it was almost an assault, but this was one I could live with.

She was sitting at her desk when I came out, on one of those ergonomic chairs without a back to force your posture erect. A glass of whisky sat by her arm. She flapped her hand at the coffee table behind her without looking around. Another glass for me.

'Some more cockle-warming material,' she said. 'I won't be a minute.'

I sat down on the sofa. There were papers not just on her desk but in every available space. On the floor under the windowsill was a rank of grey box-files. Most of the fresher spine labels listed road names – A3, A49, M56 – but there were place names too, punched out on faded and cracked Dymo red tape: Dunblane, Warrington, Morecambe, Hungerford. Other, less recognisable names not readily associated with tragedy. A new file, marked Southwick, lay next to the whisky. My hand brushed against it as I picked up the glass.

'I've got the accident and disaster and tragedy sites of the last hundred years documented in these folders,' she said. 'Photos of motorway pile-ups. Zeebrugge. Paddington. The rescue operations. Other stuff. The Chinese cocklers. The sky looks fantastic in the background. Air crashes. Manchester. Lockerbie. Kegworth...'

'But why are you here?'

'I'm a ghoul. I'm here for the death.'

'What death?'

You've got death crawling all over you. I took a stiff pull on the whisky to calm my nerves. Being around this woman set my teeth on edge. She was like tin foil on a filling.

'That's something I'd like your help with,' she said.

I wasn't ready to hear it. I asked her if this business of disasters, of geomancy, was how she made her living.

'Kind of,' she said, 'but it's not, like, officially my real job. My real job involves designing websites for small businesses who've realised the hard way that nobody wants flashy, flash-based pages any more. Just simple stuff. Simple stuff rules. I do it all on my MacBook. It pays for the petrol for my Mini and it means I can be mobile. All I need, wherever I land, is a socket to recharge my gadgets. But I make most of my money sending photographs of disasters – the wreckage, bodies if possible, the aftermath, cleaning up, that kind of thing – to a handful of clients over in the States.'

'Sounds dodgy,' I said. 'Sounds like you're whoring yourself out to questionable people with unappetising appetites.'

'It's not like that,' she said. 'These people are researchers.'

'How long have you been doing it?'

'Since my accident,' she said.

'Are the two linked?'

'I expect so. It's hard to say, because I couldn't be sure if I was able to do what I do before I jumped out of that hotel room.'

I finished the whisky and put down the glass. 'I'm sorry, you lost me there. Do? Do what? Take photographs of death locations?'

'No,' she said. 'Remember what I told you about echoes?'

I did, but I thought I must have dreamed it. 'You hear echoes?'

'Kind of. Kind of feel them too. Tremors.'

'Through time.'

'Through time.'

'Ever since your accident?'

'Yep. Maybe, I don't know… maybe a switch was thrown in me because I was so very close to death. Maybe I have an affinity for it, without really knowing what it is. Maybe some deep, unmineable part of me does know, but I won't ever be conscious of it. Not till the moment I check out, I suppose.'

She was looking at me in a strange way, and this time it wasn't that ferocious cast of her eyebrows, her dark grey eyes, or the scar carving through her forehead.

'Not me,' I said, twigging. 'I'm sorry, but I don't think so.'

'Maybe not,' she said. 'Maybe you need to open yourself to it.'

'To death? I was about as open to it as it's possible to be without actually being dead. I didn't like that place. I don't want to wallow in it, thanks.'

Books on photography were stacked by her bed: Alfred Stieglitz, Paul Strand, Eugène Atget. A wide-angle and a telephoto lens sat on a table next to a scuffed Nikon DSLR and an iBook plastered with *Finding Nemo* stickers. I thought of what might be on the memory card inside the camera and wished I had another drink.

She reached out a hand and placed it on my own. Her fingers traced the route of the scar tissue. 'The scars are the worst part, for me,' she said. 'I don't mean in any pathetic oh-I've-lost-my-beauty shit. But they bother me more than anything else. More than memories of the fall itself, and trying to make the decision that went before it.'

'Why?' I asked.

'I look at myself sometimes, when I'm naked, and I don't recognise myself any more. I know I'm me – I know my eyes have not changed although much around them has, and, bar the new aches and pains, I feel the same, but... I feel like an impostor. I feel like someone came to me while I was in my hospital bed, comatose, and covered the real me with this... this full body mask.'

'Can I have some more whisky, please?'

While she refreshed our glasses I tried to think of something to say that might make her feel better. But I understood, and sympathised, with her for what she'd revealed about herself. We were strangers to ourselves. Our shapes had changed. Things were gone. Things were added. It would take a long time to become comfortable with our physicality again, if we ever would.

I moved, an involuntary shudder. I imagined my skeleton, white, basted in my juices, grinning. Trying out its new moves.

'I read somewhere that, roughly every seven years, our bodies replace their own skeletons. You know, the equivalent in new calcium. Bones and marrow and so on.'

'That doesn't exactly help with my identity crisis,' she said, but not without some degree of humour.

'Maybe it does,' I said. 'If you accept that we're changing all the time anyway. It's not like we're lizards, or anything, but we still shed our skins over time. You're not who you were ten years ago. Mentally, physically. All that remains the same is how you see the world and maybe not even that.'

'Eyes,' she said, and I had to look down into my glass because she'd said it hungrily, desperately, as if she were anxious for any buoy to hold on to, to keep her afloat.

'What is it you want me to do?' I asked. 'Why are you here, in Southwick? Is it the baby?'

She nodded. 'That, and other things. Kieran Love, from Ely. Seven months old. A weekend trip to the seaside with his parents. He was found broken over one of the wooden groynes on the beach. Stiff with cold and rigor. It was as if someone had tried to use him as a hammer to bash the groyne deeper into the sand.'

'Spare me the details,' I said and took another deep swallow of whisky. 'Jesus. Is it any wonder I never wanted children? How can you want children when there are people out there who will do this to them if they get even a moment's chance?'

She was watching me, waiting for me. I could almost hear her say it: *Go on, get it out of your system. And then we'll crack on. Then we'll get down to business. We have plenty of time.*

'I'm sorry,' I said.

'It's okay. This is unpleasant stuff. I'm not looking for you to be Mr Ice.'

'What are you looking for? Why do you need my help anyway?'

'Because I've been watching you. I've seen you on the beach in the morning, burning those boxes. I've seen you in the bookshop, reading stuff.'

'You took that pamphlet.'

'I bought that pamphlet. What I'm interested in is tied up with Winter Bay and the battle that took place there on that one day.'

'That one day three hundred years ago.'

'This isn't like a stain on a rug. It doesn't wash out over time.'

I glanced around me as if I'd see the pamphlet among the pounds of loose paper lying on every available surface. There were maps and charts and grids drawn on tracing paper, broken-backed notebooks stuffed with co-ordinates and colour-coded diagrams and print-outs and clippings from newspapers yellowed with time. Two hefty external hard drives were plugged into the laptop and they blinked acid green colour across her desk, chuckling away softly in the background over the secrets that vibrated inside.

'You read it?' I asked.

'I read it, yes.'

'Someone had defaced it. Scribbled on the pages in pen. Something about children.'

'Would you like another drink?'

'I've had enough,' I said. I knew straight away that she hadn't seen what I'd seen. I hoped she'd simply taken no notice of it, or been so wrapped up in the prose that it hadn't even impinged on her consciousness, but it was unlikely. 'Can I show you?'

'I didn't see the words,' she said.

'Can I have –'

'Which doesn't mean that they aren't there,' she said.

We sat in silence for a short while. We both knew what she meant. She hadn't seen them because there were no words. But she believed that I'd seen them. Which meant that either I was crazy, or she was crazy. The likelihood was that we were both mad, our minds decayed after the long recovery from our respective accidents. Bits of us still lay on the roadside and on the car roof outside that hotel. Molecules shifted, torn away, re-positioned. The tiniest bits of the roadside were impacted into me. Minuscule flecks of cellulose from the car were under Amy's skin. We were composites. We were not merely of ourselves any more. We were less and more than what we once were.

God, I was pissed.

'Show me the pamphlet,' I said.

She pushed herself out of her chair and picked her way around various reference books on the floor to a box filed with the word CURRENT written on the spine. She extracted the pamphlet and, without checking for herself first, handed it over to me.

I flipped through the pages, hoping now that she was right, that there were no added words and that the pamphlet was just an ordinary, slightly dry account of a lethal coming together between Dutch and English ships in the North Sea. But there it was again. And my breath caught in my throat because it was written so hard into the paper that the point of the pen had gone through the page. How could she not see this?

I held it open and showed her, placed my fingernail beneath it.

'See?' I breathed. 'SUFFER CHILDREN... THEY WERE TAKEN! Can't you see?'

'It's not there,' she said, and paused, and smiled and said: 'For me, at least.'

'But I can see it.'

'You can see it. Have you seen anything else?'

I told her about the child I'd seen, alone, seemingly naked, at the end of the beach.

'The spot where you have your little fires?'

'You think that's significant?'

'Maybe,' she said. 'What else?'

I told her about the fishing trip I'd taken with Charlie, and the nasty little haul we'd landed.

'Where are the skulls now?' she asked.

'I don't know. Morgue? I don't know what the procedures are. They were old skulls. Hundreds of years old, they said. Maybe they're being carbon dated, or filed away in a museum cupboard.'

'I doubt it. I'd like to see those skulls.'

'I wouldn't know how to help you. We could go to the police, but I can't see them happily ushering you through to the room where they keep all the dead things, can you?'

'Take me to the place where you found them.'

'What, now?'

'It's light enough.'

'I don't have a boat.'

'Let's worry about that later.'

THE RAIN HAD stopped when we went outside, the wind's threat receded. I was still mumbling and grumbling to put her off – it was warm and cosy in her flat, despite all the grim scribblings – but she seemed to be one of those people who lock on to an idea and refuse to let go, like the jaws of a pit bull. Light scored the sky; great streaks of ochre parting the night, widening, pulling it apart. The sea was flat. Massive oil tankers on the horizon looked like tiny cardboard cut-outs on a child's picture.

I was bone tired. The cold had not entirely been massaged out of my legs by the radiators in Amy's flat; now it raced back as if invited. There was movement down on the beach as we reached the stone steps above the promenade café and began to gingerly descend. An early-morning jogger perhaps, a brief flash of white, lumbering and stuttering over the uneven beach? A plastic bag blown by the wind? By the time we'd made it down to the sand, it was gone. A tree branch skinned of bark, polished and nude, was a limb pointing back to the marshes, as if it were trying to get me to return to the car, urge me back to sleep so that I might wake up to find everything was good again, how it should be.

'Who's Charlie?' she asked.

'He's a fisherman. He's lived here all his life. He sat with me a lot in hospital after I was found. Talked to me. I owe him my life.'

'Did you go out far?'

'Pretty far, yeah. Although you could still see the lighthouse. What about this boat? We're going to have to charter a trip. Not cheap.'

'We don't need a boat.'

We made our way along the sand until the light from the lighthouse was flaring periodically above our heads. She got me to stand with my back to the sea, looking up at the large, brilliant lens under the dome.

'Look at the lighthouse for a few seconds. Then I want you to close your eyes and think about what you saw out there, on the water. Let whatever it is that's in the dark make itself known to you.'

I didn't like the sound of that. She had her back to me, to the lighthouse, but the reflected shots of light from the sea, and the paling sky, turned her eyes into something inhuman. It was like watching something failed but dangerous trying to learn the skill of mimicry to better its chances at getting close to its prey.

To avoid this, I did as she asked and closed my eyes, even though it left me exposed to her. *She isn't the threat here,* I chided myself, although in answering that question, I'd posed myself another. I'd admitted to myself that there *was* a threat. I just didn't know what shape it had assumed.

I was back on the water but I wasn't aware of Charlie behind me – it was as if he was an actor awaiting his cue in the wings – or even the boat beneath my feet. I might have been little more than a disembodied eye, hovering above the waves, a camera filming a dramatic documentary.

I thought of the sea giving up its secrets. The bulging net. The little cluster of clean white skulls like a clutch of hideous eggs at the centre of all those scales and tentacles and slime. I heard again, impossibly, the distant thunder of horses' hooves. The same pattern as before: a strong, insistent canter and a ghost at its heels, much weaker, yet faster. I looked around but there was nothing but water. It must be thunder, then; weird, syncopated thunder. But there were no great stairs of cloud: only clear sky stretching to the horizon.

I heard the sound of those skulls skittering across the boards, saw the gleaming spheres and opened my eyes to see them represented in Amy's eyes, which were rolled back in their sockets. She was clutching the lapels of my coat. Her mouth was open and I saw the ring of her throat relax and contract as if she were about to gag. She was as exposed and as intimate as at the moment of an orgasm or a death rattle. I tried to shake her out of it but she was lost to whatever had unwrapped itself in her mind, or that I had passed on.

Then she returned, her eyes dropping back into the sockets of her face like ghastly slot machine windows.

'Are you all right?' I asked.

She turned and spat into the sand. Black blood.

'Christ,' I said. And then, again, with more urgency: 'Are you all right?'

She nodded, although such a movement in her seemed anything but positive. 'Give me a minute.'

I slowly coaxed her back to the stone revetment and sat her down on its cold, hard edge. She didn't seem to mind.

'What was all that about?'

'There were deaths here,' she said. 'Many, many deaths.'

Her face was threatening to collapse. There was deep woe underpinning her voice. Not the melodramatic stuff you see in attention-seekers bemoaning their crap marriages or crap jobs, but the kind of near panic that people can find themselves in when hit by bad news that they can do absolutely nothing about.

'We already know this,' I said. 'There was a huge naval battle out there. Heavy losses on both sides. Bodies were washing up on the beaches for days afterwards.'

She gripped my hand so forcibly I cried out.

'There were others,' she said. 'Others that suffered that day. All of the children were taken. Their parents watched them die.'

37

PAUL... HE IS considerate lover. He takes time with me, because I find it hard to reach orgasm. Just like reaching. Stretching out arms. Tip-toe. Trying to get hand into cookie jar. I don't always get there, and he is upset by this, but I tell him not to be. I get as much pleasure out of seeing him climax as coming myself. I knew he would be gentle with me. He has good control of himself, unlike some lovers, selfish, racing to be finished. It's like he holds reins, can steady himself if it looks as though he is about to lose himself to the moment. His hands are soft, they were soft. He had beautiful hands, before. His nails always clean. I used to hate the boys in Odessa, home from the factory, and they were clean, they smelled of soap, but their fingernails were disgusting.

Paul. I wonder if he is still able to love me. He was so ruined. The doctors, they reassure me that everything is in full working order. Even if he ends up in wheelchair. We can still build family. Build family? Is that right? Like wall. Like house. And why not? Something secure and comforting. Somewhere to retreat to. Bosom of family. The heart, the hearth. Warm and safe. I remember in kitchen back home in Odessa, with my father, my dear *Tato*, just before he died. I don't remember face much, but I remember his arms around me as we sat by the logs burning in the stove. I remember the colour of his skin, and the hair poking out under the cuffs of his shirt. I remember his smell, and above all how comfortable he was. My tiny body was like last piece of the jigsaw puzzle that was him. I fit him. I press my ear against his chest and hear his heart trotting along, strong and healthy, like horses on the beach at Tenderovskiy Isla

Yak vas zvaty?

Mene zvaty Tamara.

My name is Tamara.

I am learning English, thanks to Paul. Better English, not so formal as I remember at school. He has funny ways of saying things. I used to think everything was funny, every English person, when I first come here. All their words seem so stiff. It's like they ought to have lips like closed purse to be able to say anything. Paul used to pretend to be very posh English gent. He make me laugh. He said things like actors in black and white films. Terry-Thomas. George Sanders. Ralph Richardson. Received pronunciation. Queen's English. Plum in mouth. He used to copy this, pretend to twiddle waxed moustache. *Oh, I say. You sir, are a cad and a bounder and I shall have satisfaction. What-what!*

Is that the door? Is he coming again? Will it be this time? Will it be fast?

My father died when I was very little. He suffered a huge stroke while he was asleep in bed. Everyone said how this was good thing. Best way to go. But it bothered me throughout my childhood. I had terrible nightmares. How could they be sure he didn't suffer? Someone told me that you were doomed to spend the rest of eternity experiencing the moment of your death over and over again. I dreamed of him asleep, trapped in sleep, while his brain betrayed him. I thought of him with his eyes sealed shut, his mouth sealed shut, unable to scream for help because the darkness and sleep held him prisoner. If only he had been awake, he might have been able to survive. I haven't slept well since then. I still don't. I found out there is a name for the fear of sleep. Somniphobia. That's me. I'm frightened to go to sleep. But now I'm frightened to be awake. I used to think that being asleep would bring me closer to my father, but it's unbearable. All I can dream of is his struggle against this invader that killed him, and I think, me too, *Tato*. I'm in same boat. I'm so tired, so stressed… I wonder if it will have… what is word? Detriment effect? I wonder if… but no, I won't think about that. I won't let it happen. Move on. Think of other things.

Mene zvaty Tamara.

I remember learning English at school. The teachers thought I was very good, a quick learner. But the only reason I concentrated so hard was because of one of the English teachers. I don't remember his name, but he had this awful mouth. It was like chopped liver. Purple and wet and big. His lips slid against each other, like worms mating, and his teeth didn't seem to be as fixed as ought to be in his gums. Maybe he had denture. But it was like he was self-conscious of this horror mouth, this horrible pit of teeth and spit, so he had grown large moustache to either try to hide it, or draw attention from it. But it was like big banner. People stared at him. It didn't help that his other features were so tiny and non-descript. He had little brown eyes and button nose. Really, if it wasn't for his mouth, hungry thing, like something wet and red you find in man's magazine, you'd think he was pixie.

I learned English fast from him because I wanted to be anywhere but in his class. I did good homework because I didn't want him questioning me alone in his office. Sometimes he was near enough for me to be able to smell his mouth if I wanted to, but I breathed through my own mouth then, scared to smell something that made me feel sick, or scared.

Feet on the steps.

I imagine this man, The Man, I imagine his mouth is like that. Like a fox's. Wild and wide and meant for only terrible things. The Man has never whispered I love you. He has never kissed a cheek. He has never smiled.

Chapter Nine

SIGNALS OF DISTRESS

WE HUDDLED TOGETHER on the stone for hours, it seemed, too scared, too cold to do anything else. By the time we unfolded ourselves, limbs cracking like so much kindling, the sun was bleeding over the edge of the planet and there were people on the beach. Joggers, beachcombers, fishermen. Old people. No children. It was as if there were no children left anywhere, as if they were a fanciful dream.

We made our way back up to the village hub. There was a café open early for the fishermen. You could buy pints if you wanted, and I was sorely tempted, but I bought us hot, strong, sweet tea and we sipped it in the window, blasted hands wrapped around the chipped mugs, skin slowly changing colour from blue to livid white.

I struggled to get any more out of Amy. She had had a shock. Her chin was glazed with blood, I didn't want to try to wipe it away in case I only worsened her predicament. Some job to be involved in, I thought, if you were squeamish like that. I thought again of how she had spat that red oyster from her lungs and wondered if she might have something more serious than slowly knitting bones and diabetes. She seemed unfazed by that, as if it were a common occurrence. Maybe it was some reaction to the things she was connecting with, a heaving-ho of bad stuff, like vomit from a belly writhing with bacteria.

'What did you see?' I asked her. And then, thinking, maybe, she hadn't actually seen anything, I asked: 'What were they like? The ripples? The echoes?'

But she only sipped her tea, or turned away to look out of the window at the whitened, fragile dawn. In profile it was easier to see her tears, clinging to her eyes like soft contact lenses, threatening to spill, but never quite making it that far. Her lip trembled whenever she opened her mouth to take in some more of the tea. *This was over three hundred years ago,* I wanted to say to her. How can it hit you so hard?

'Something's not right,' she said. 'It's like finding fresh blood on a fossil. There's something not... sitting quite right.'

I tried to pry, but she was closing down, withdrawing, a tapped barnacle on a ship's hull. I said I was leaving and offered to escort her home, but she ignored me, dabbing instead at a fresh trickle of blood from her nose. I didn't want to leave; I didn't like the idea of abandoning Amy in this state, but it was getting late. I had pills to take. I needed sleep. But first I was anxious to find out what had happened to Ruth.

I walked the hundred yards or so to the bookshop. Vulcan was in the window, but the door was locked. I rang the bell. Nothing. I tried her on the phone. No answer. I tried Charlie's number. It rang and rang. I wondered how long I should leave it before calling the police. I thought of the car on the harbour path, imagined two bodies cooling in the boot and my fingerprints all over the doors. I suddenly wished I was back in the cockpit, many thousands of feet above the clouds, living my dream day upon day.

I went back to the café but Amy was gone from the window. By the time I'd made it to the main road, I could not see her, but it didn't necessarily follow that she'd returned home.

I stood for a moment, waiting for sense to land. I could try Tamara's old work colleague again, but our last conversation had presented me with a dead end. If she was covering for Tamara then I would not be able to get past her door. The only thing to do was go to Amsterdam. Try her at the apartment, even though there had been no response. Where else was there for her to go?

I was walking, as if determined to get over there straight away. It felt right. If she was there, she would see for herself the lengths to which I was prepared to fight for her. I could see it on the news: *Severely injured man risks paralysis to be with the one he loves.* "When I saw him, I realised I'd made a mistake in leaving him like that. I never stopped loving him. He's shown me what a fool I was. I won't ever leave his side again."

I made a few calls and, giddily, found myself booked on the overnight ferry from Hull to Rotterdam two nights hence. It was done. It had been so long since I'd been master of my own plight that I felt slightly guilty about it, as if I'd stolen a piece of chocolate from a child's birthday hoard. I didn't know whether to tell Ruth. Part of me dreaded the lecture I would get. More of the same about being cuckolded, about not being physically or mentally prepared for such a trip. But part of me relished it. I was taking back my life, scarred handful at a time. It was time to stop burning other peoples' secrets and start revealing some of my own.

I found myself outside the Sailor's Reading Room, a museum that opened to the public for a limited time each day. There was a private reading room at the back where old sailors and fishermen were allowed to come and go as they pleased. An old boys' club. I suddenly wished I'd been a seaman more than an airman. It would be fascinating to sit in among those men and listen to their stories about terrifying storms, record-breaking hauls, superstitions. I rattled the handle; the museum was closed. But I could see movement in the back, beyond the public gallery of ancient manuscripts, diary entries, photographs and ships' logs; the arcane yet beautiful display of maritime gear: old sextants, porthole frames, divers' helmets. The room gleamed with a thick haze of dull brass and iron. The colour was almost heavy enough to touch; you might have to actually wade through the museum in order to see anything.

There was a face against the glass in that back room. Heavily bearded, shaded by a dark cap. Inscrutable.

I waved. The man held up a finger. *Wait.*

He disappeared for a moment and then I sensed someone behind me. He was smiling, his beard split to reveal brown teeth studded in a mouth like tiny coconuts at a fairground shy.

'Room's closed,' he said. He smelled of rum and tobacco and oil.

'I was just checking the opening times,' I said.

'Back later,' he said, and widened his eyes at me as if he'd passed on some great, secret knowledge.

'But it's not open again today,' I said.

'Got keys,' he said. 'In charge.'

I didn't want to come back if it meant being given a private tour by a smelly man who couldn't train his tongue beyond two words at a time, but since that morning, and the events shared with Amy, I'd grown more and more curious about the village's history. There were secrets in that water, or at the least, misdirections. I wanted to dive in.

'Seven?' I asked.

'Seven good,' he said.

'What's your name?'

'Name's Jake,' he said. He gave me another brown smile and backed off as if I was holding him at gunpoint. His odour was equally reluctant to leave me too. I carried it around with me for the rest of the afternoon.

I was in two minds as to whether to head off to the junk shop to waste another hour or catch the bus to Breydon and Charlie's house, which struck me as being just one more dead end to smack my face against, when I noticed that the bookshop door was now open. Movement in the back room. It was Ruth. I changed tack and headed towards her, called her name. She made her way through the bookshop and stood at the threshold, barring my way.

'Where have you been?' she asked.

'Where have *I* been? What about you? You left me in the freezing cold in the middle of nowhere.'

'You were in the car. At the harbour.'

'I know where I was,' I said, and it was all I could do to keep the anger from my voice.

'Hardly the middle of nowhere.'

'It might as well have been. I had to walk back.'

'No you didn't. If you'd waited I would have driven you home. Where did you spend the night?'

I moved past her, confusion and annoyance causing a headache to start pulsing just behind my eyes. I snatched up my pills from the bedside table and poured some water. I took them all at once and we stared at each other while I worked them down my throat.

'I was asking the questions,' I said. 'Now you tell me where you'd gone. I couldn't find you anywhere.'

'I was at Charlie's fish hut,' she said.

'Doing what? Anyway, I didn't see you there.'

'Did you knock? Did you go in?'

I shook my head. 'It was quiet as the grave. There were no lights on anywhere.'

'What can I say? I was in Charlie's fish hut. I was checking up on him, taking him some food.'

'But he lives in Breydon.' This was getting more and more perplexing. I felt like an alien being introduced to complex rituals. I didn't understand.

'There was a last-minute charter, a firm of accountants from London booked a fishing trip. They wanted to push off at first light and Charlie needed to prepare. He'd been rushed off his feet all day. He's still out there now, and will be till dusk. Would have appreciated some help if you hadn't gone haring off across the county.'

I had no comeback. I hadn't knocked, but there had been no sounds coming from the fish hut. Yet

Ruth's car was there. What more proof did she need? Maybe they were both asleep, Ruth choosing not to get back into the car and risk waking me by starting the engine. I don't know. It seemed, suddenly, of no importance whatsoever. I felt foolish.

'Now you,' she said. 'Where did you run off to? It'll be the ward again for you if you don't slow down.'

Amy's name was on my lips, but at the last moment I chose not to tell Ruth about her. I didn't want to tell her I'd been to the B&B either. I don't know why. It seemed crucial I keep some secrets for myself.

'The café on the pier. The back window was loose. I climbed in and went to sleep on one of the banquettes.'

'You did *what*? You couldn't climb a pebble with a set of portable steps, never mind hoist yourself through the café windows.'

'It's amazing, the lengths you'll go to, when you're desperate.'

She gazed at me levelly and seemed on the verge of saying something. But then she softened, the nurse face gone, the arms unfolded.

'You look like the shitty sheets we take off the beds,' she said.

'That good, hey?'

'Bath. Pyjamas. Sleep. I'll bring you something to eat.'

I DID AS I was told. There were no little adventures. No footsteps outside the bathroom window. No voices. No box on the doorstep, no shattered seagull spreading its wings, all the better to reveal its magisterial injuries. By the time I was in bed I couldn't work out how I'd got there. I seemed to be moving much more easily these days. Only the previous week I'd needed assistance to get in or out of the bath, and into or out of my clothes, but I was managing okay now. Perhaps it was because I was overdoing things. My muscles were getting a workout, being stretched and flexed so much that everything attached to them had no choice but to follow suit. There were the inevitable aches and pains, the cricked neck, the jarred back, but things were getting better. This rushing to be mobile again might mean that somewhere down the line there would be cataclysmic payback, but I couldn't take a retrograde step now. There was always the chance that I was a good healer, a fast healer, and that I was merely ahead of what the doctors predicted.

I closed my eyes and listened for the pain. It was all over me, dulled by analgesics, like concentric circles tattooed deep into my flesh. My skeleton shook and sat up, grinned down at me and said: 'If I had some eyelids I'd give you a wink, old friend.'

I opened my eyes and five hours had gone by. A tray next to the bed contained a plate with cold ham, cheese, a chicken leg, a bottle of water. There was a note. *Eat this when you wake up. I'll be in my room if you need company. Rx*

I managed to eat some of it. Your stomach shrinks when you're in a coma. Liquid feeds just don't keep your gut at the shape at which it's happiest. And it's got other things on its mind, like slowly consuming you, from the inside out. More IV juice? No thanks,

I'll tuck into some of this slow-cooked belly of Paul.

The meal re-energised me to some degree, but now I really fancied a drink before I went to the reading room. I don't know why. I didn't want any nasty shocks and I thought the best way to combat them was to be slightly numb. The 22 pills a day I was popping just didn't seem to be enough. The synthetic morphine when mixed with a whisky and beer chaser would soften the edges of whatever horrors lurked in the back of the museum. Or maybe I was being paranoid and all I'd find would be a few twee letters home from sailors missing Mum.

I went to The Fluke, ordered my drinks and sat in the window seat. Ruth would have heard me moving about – unless she was asleep – and might be wondering why I hadn't gone to see her. I got the feeling she wanted to talk. I wasn't all that sure I wanted to any more.

No boxes for three days now. I didn't miss the grim little job of burning them, but I was concerned about the timing. Why now? I couldn't shake the suspicion that the boxes, and what they contained, were clues, like the strange items I'd found on the beach, or the way the seagulls all stood facing in the same direction. Rationalising it, I might have pointed out that the seagulls were merely facing into the wind, the better for taking off, but the fact was there was no wind that day. There was an explanation for everything, but it did not satisfy. Nothing would stick.

I swallowed the whisky – a harsh, cheap blend – and washed away the taste with a swig of beer. I felt a rush of alcohol meet the prescription drugs in my head and everything went warm and fuzzy. I gazed around me at my fellow boozers and felt a strong wave of affection for them all.

For Ruth too, and I was tempted to finish my drink and go to her, fix the tension that had developed between us. But I couldn't, not now that I had booked my trip to Amsterdam and not let her know about it. She was patently appalled by what she saw as a futile search that was going on largely behind her back. How could I account for my movements when she always presented a negative face? I knew, and appreciated, that she felt responsible for me and was looking out for me with a tenderness I frankly did not deserve, but I couldn't understand how she could not grasp – refused to grasp, it seemed – my need to discover the truth.

Don't believe the truth.

Where did that come from? I stared into my beer as if there might be an answer forthcoming in the pattern of bubbles. A female voice, something I'd overheard somewhere, once upon a time. I'd invested it with an adornment all my own, given the words Tamara's voice for some reason. Now I remembered: one of the passers-by on Surt Road, chatting outside my open bathroom window while I soaked. Footsteps, snatches of dialogue. Why remember that particular snippet? Why remember anything? The coma part of my head, still coming back, ejecting nonsense. The drugs unlocking strange little chambers of thought. The beer talking.

My drink finished, I resisted the temptation to have another, and hauled myself to my feet.

Jake was standing outside the pub as if he'd known I would be emerging from it at that moment. He was carrying a white plastic bag and my heart sank, but he didn't try to hand it over to me, or beg me to get rid of its contents. It turned out to be a packed lunch. I hoped it contained something with raw onions, but I guessed it didn't. He shared his odours around like the open throat of a binman's lorry.

'You work here?' I asked.

He nodded. 'Work here. And harbour. Sell fish. Got hut.'

'Doesn't everyone?'

He shrugged and led me around to the front of the museum and, checking both ways that the coast was clear, unlocked the door and shooed me inside.

'That was a bit *Smiley's People*, wasn't it?' I asked.

'Shouldn't open,' he said. 'Bit naughty.'

'Why are you doing this?'

He gazed up at me shyly while he knelt to bolt the door shut. 'Helped us. Burned shit.'

I closed my eyes and nodded. I wished I hadn't asked. I wished I'd simply waited until the normal opening hours were in play. I wanted him to leave it at that, but of course, he didn't.

'Abusive parents. Not happy. Long time. Prison Dad. Mum died. Dad wrote. And wrote. And wrote. Thousand letters. Kept all. Never read. Couldn't chuck. Fucking bastard. Dead now. Burn them. Burn all. Never read. Wouldn't read. No guts. No willpower. Thanks mate. Thanks tons.'

'Don't mention it,' I said. I thought he had an accent at first, maybe something Baltic, but it was a combination of shyness and a breathing difficulty that made him hitch in breath after every couple of words. He'd somehow adapted the way he spoke so that he could get his meaning across in spasmodic phrases. 'Do you live here? In Southwick?'

He shook his head. 'In Breydon. Little house.'

'You know Charlie Finglass?'

'Doesn't everyone?'

He gestured to the back of the museum. We went through. The inner sanctum. Normal punters were only allowed to use the front of the building, where the photographs of heavily bearded men in ganseys and oilskins stared into ancient cameras as though willing their plates to break, and the ships' logs were locked behind glass and left open at a page to show what was little more than a shopping list of supplies taken on board before a voyage. Hardtack. Dried apples. A nanny goat for fresh milk.

He saw my assessment of one of these and frowned, as if he couldn't understand why I was choosing to stay in here when there were obviously greater treasures to enjoy in the forbidden zone. 'Hardtack yum,' he said. 'Flour water. Baked hours. Last years.'

'The cornerstone of any nutritious breakfast,' I said. He laughed and a tension I had not known was there fell away slightly. I was nervous as hell and could not understand why. It must have something to do with the room I was about to be led into, I thought, with Jake all the while scampering ahead of me, pulling curtains or shuttering windows to prevent anybody seeing that a mere civilian was being admitted to the secret chambers. A fusty darkness fell, reminding me of my grandparents' houses: antimacassars and gimcrackery and stale nicotine. Every colour you could think of in the range between café au lait and bitter chocolate. Beige predominating.

'Hot drink? Cold drink?'

'I've just had one.'

'You mind?' he asked, brandishing his thin plastic bag. I saw something that looked like an eye bulging against a bottom corner.

'Not at all.'

We stood awkwardly while he opened the lips of his bag and delved in. I was waiting for a cue, although we were where we had intended to be; a silly British trait. The need for hand-holding at every step. In the end, although he told me to 'go mad', it was the sight of his eating that turned me away.

I couldn't escape the sound nor the smell of it, though. And the image of him wadding his white bread triangles into the corners of his cheeks, like a dentist packing a mouth with cotton wool, would not be dismissed. I didn't know how to proceed. There were ledgers, maybe hundreds of years old, left lying on coffee tables as if they were disposable magazines about celebrity TV stars. Yellowed and curled photographs stacked in a plant pot. Ancient maritime pieces, arcane stuff I couldn't put a name to, worth hundreds if not thousands of pounds, lay about like things discarded in a mechanic's garage.

'Why isn't this in the museum?' I asked, and made the mistake of glancing at him.

He was doing things to a pie that I'd last seen in a porn film as a teenager. He extracted himself from it long enough to spray crumbs at me, along with the words: 'No room. Too dear. Robbers around.'

'And this place is Fort Knox, isn't it?' I said.

He shrugged, rolled his eyes, nodded, went back to noshing his pie.

I flicked through one of the ledgers but it was full of more of the kind of stuff that was on permanent display out front: passenger lists, receipts from ships' suppliers, letters from one captain to another. It was interesting in the way that all old documents, written on stout paper in sepia copperplate, are interesting, but once you've ploughed through three or four pages, you kind of get the gist. I was getting deflated. There was nothing here. No secret stash of mind-blowing material. Nothing that would help me, at least – not that I knew what help I needed, or what I was meant to be looking for.

'Kid stuff,' Jake said.

'What?'

'Kid stuff. Broken chest.'

My mouth was open. I closed it. His mouth was open. He didn't close his. Broken chest? Was he talking about Kieran Love? He let me watch what was rolling around with his tongue and I tried to decipher what he'd said. How could he have known that children were occupying my thoughts of late? Maybe he didn't know, but there was that thing about Nietzsche and the abyss. He obviously walked the dark side of the canal, like me. We understood each other.

He was nodding towards a corner of the room. Every time he did so, titbits fell from the corners of his mouth and a fine dusting of dandruff from his hair.

'Okay,' I said, but could not bring myself to thank him. At the back of the room there was an old chest, a domed trunk, with a broken lock and latches, but otherwise restored. It seemed to have once been covered in leather, but only small sections of it remained. The wood – cherry it looked like – had been hand-sanded. Some of the oak straps had been buckled or snapped and were now fixed, after a fashion, and I thought of poor Kieran's greenstick ribs pulverised over the groyne on the beach. I thought of the tatty cardboard boxes that were brought to me and thought I'd enjoy the job of burning stuff much more if it was transported in handsome containers such as this.

I opened the lid. Inside there were old pieces of paper, many of them fragile and sleeved in protective Mylar. There were pictures drawn by childish hands. Letters. Some of them to parents, some of them to God. All of them were asking for the same thing.

'How old are these?' I asked Jake.

He swallowed. His throat rippled. 'Dates on,' he said. 'Can't remember.'

I checked. Some of them *were* dated. Letters from the 1800s. Letters from the 1700s. Maybe some that were even older, but the paper was so deteriorated, the ink so faint or illegible that it was difficult to tell.

Dear Father, Please don't let this happen.

Mother, I will miss you so. God's willing, after this you'll be safe.

Help me help me help me help me help me help

Dear God. Almighty God. Tell my family I love them.

'What is this?' I asked, looking up. The light, such as it was, bled around Jake so I could only see him in silhouette. Motes sprang away from him as if the dust was repulsed by his odour. He kept chewing, kept smacking away at his endless lunch. Kept speaking wetly, haltingly, around whatever it was he was consuming as if it was too hot for his mouth.

'Kid stuff,' he said. 'Letters home. Bad place.'

'What place?'

'Can't say. Not child. Not selected.'

'Selected?' One of those long, slow shudders was rolling along my back. Some fiendish knitter was binding the strands of my muscles tighter and tighter with needles like meat-hooks. I was finding it hard to breathe in this room filled with dead things and the smell of Jake, just as I had all those years before as a child in my grandparents' tiny, stifling living room. The black and white television and the assault of furniture polish. I felt the kick of my blackened heart and thought I would throw up. I had to get out, but I had to know what had happened here.

'Mothers' talk. Myths, legends. Maybe true. Maybe not. Foreign lands. Unknowable places.'

'Jake… I don't understand. Tell me straight, would you? Where were these letters from?'

He stopped eating and licked his lips. He tucked his chin in against his chest. His voice and his breathing changed. It was as if he were channelling someone else through him, and in this room, this madness that was flying around us, it would not have surprised me.

'These letters came in on the tide from the children that were taken from our village and those who continue to be taken they wash up on the shore in bottles and the letters sometimes come with other things fingers and blood still wet and teeth and other things I can't bring myself to think about and nobody can do anything about it because nobody knows where they went and every hundred years or so it comes again and the cycle continues and we should be grateful after all that it is but once every century or so now I must ask you to leave.'

His face had turned blacker within the ring of shadow he had created for himself. Now the breath I recognised in him returned, but it was shallower, weaker. He had tired himself out. Were there any healthy souls in this forsaken place?

I put down the letters – I had absolutely no wish to look at any of them again – and slowly stood up, listening to the stirrings in the joints of my back like a technician will listen to the valves in an old radio. I was convinced that I was dead. That I was an impossible memory of myself. The near-miss had been nothing of the sort. The Trip-7 had ploughed through the Jumbo and everyone had died, including me. This was what happened when death arrived. You took what had killed you, or it took you, and you were formed and led and possessed by it for the rest of eternity. My existence was about injury and child-snatchers and fire and a sea that threw up nasty little secrets every so often, like a wolf regurgitating something unholy and indigestible.

'I'm sorry,' I said to Jake, without knowing what I was really apologising for. It was second nature these days, it seemed.

'No hope,' he said, and he was strangled again, a Morse code voice. I didn't know if he was referring to me or the children or the village or himself. All of us, probably.

At the door I paused. Something he'd said.

'Jake. Every hundred years or so, you said. Every hundred years or so it comes again. What is this 'it'? Do you think there's some kind of, I don't know, a cabal that has a grudge against your people? Your village? A blood libel running down the years?'

He was shaking his head.

'It is. The Craw.'

He wouldn't say anything else, no matter how often I asked him to repeat himself or explain himself. *It is. The Craw.*

I went out looking for children.

Chapter Ten
QUICK AND DIRTY

SHE WAS LYING in bed, blankets wrapped around her, reading a book bearing the title *Alive*.

'Shouldn't you be reading magazines telling you how to breastfeed?' I asked.

'Crap,' she said. 'How many thousands of years did we get by without that?'

'How's the book?' I asked. 'Rugby-playing cannibals going down well with junior?'

'He's fine,' she said. 'But I've got indigestion.'

We both laughed. The air felt instantly clearer, freer of the unpleasant electricity that seemed to have been arcing between us of late. That and the awful, smothering feeling I'd had at the museum, and the fruitless search afterwards.

'Where have you been?' she asked, as if she could read my mind. But I knew how I looked. My fingers were grey with cold, my shoes wet. I could find no position in which to get comfortable. My back felt like a thin bag filled with rusting, useless ironmongery.

'Out walking,' I said. I didn't tell her that I'd covered the entire beach, nor that I had patrolled every street in the village, spying through kitchen windows, trying to spot a child frowning over a plate of greens, or playing on a video game, or reading *The Beano*. I gave up when I felt myself becoming so agitated I wanted to rap on the doors and ask the people where the children were. Why don't you have any children? *Where are the fucking children?*

Here they were, or one of them, at least. I was with Ruth and I was calming down and it was a warm room and she was going to have a child, soon, and my God was I frightened for her. I was trying to find a way of bringing it up, this business of a childless beach – who had ever heard of such a thing? – and trying to understand the things I'd seen already that seemed to give a lie to my suspicions and fears. The naked toddler by the pier. An infant's romper suit washed up on the tide. But I couldn't be sure. Nothing was certain. Everything was riddled with meaning.

'Pour us a drink,' she said.

'Water?'

A brief shake of the head. 'There's a bottle of Talisker in the cupboard. Fetch us a scant millimetre.'

'What about the baby?' I asked.

'He'll have a double. Go on, panic-boy. A coating for the tongue is all I'm after. What do you think's going to happen? Junior's going to drop out trying to bum a fiver for a rock of crack? It's probably more dangerous for you, anyway.'

I got us both drinks. A dribble for her and a large one for me.

'Scant millimetre,' I said when I got back. 'Sounds like a French private detective.'

'In a science fiction novel.'

'Yeah. I feel as if I'm in a science fiction novel sometimes.'

She took the tiniest of sips, a mere dampening of her lips. They glistened in the caramel light. 'There's science fiction *in* you, for God's sake. You're the bionic man.'

'It's not just that,' I said. 'Don't you feel that this place is a bit... detached, sometimes? It's so far away from the main road. It's totally cut off. It's forgotten. It's like a different world. Like something out of Verne, or Haggard, or Doyle.'

I looked down at my glass. It was empty. I didn't remember drinking it, but the oily, hot taste was there at the back of my throat. I poured myself another.

'I suppose so,' she said. 'And there's also the sea. All of this will be gone one day. As happened to Dunwich.'

I'd read about Dunwich. Capital of East Anglia. A rival to London, centuries ago. Coastal erosion had meant that much of it had fallen into the waves over the past eight hundred years. Southwick had suffered a sea surge, or a *seich,* of equal proportions in the 1950s. Erosion, plus the sinking of East Anglia and global warming in general, meant this entire coastal region, the county itself, was at risk. In another eight hundred years the landlocked cities of today, such as Norwich and Ipswich, might well be coastal towns.

'You ever heard the bells?' At midnight, it was said that you could hear the bells of the eight lost churches ringing beneath the waves.

'Sometimes, although I can't help thinking that's just me, hungering after ghosts.'

A different sort of tension was unwinding between us. The heat of the room and the spirit in my belly were conspiring to make me feel drowsy, but in a pleasant way. The pills I'd taken that morning were enjoying one last hurrah, jazzed up by the Tallisker. My throat felt thick with something. Desire, maybe. It had been so long that I forgot what it felt like. She had put the book down. The blankets had shifted while she was sipping her whisky. She was wearing a chocolate brown blouse. It was drawn very cosily over the mound of her belly. She was tight as a tick. A slipped button allowed me to see the ice-white edge of her bra. I returned my attention to her face to find that she had been watching me watching her. I didn't look away. She didn't look away. She kept talking, as if there was nothing wrong; I hoped there wasn't. It took a moment or two to realise what it was she was talking about, and then I froze, barely breathing. I poured another drink. For her as well as me. The baby would survive. I just wanted to get tanked as quickly as possible now.

'It was a cold night. Much colder than this. Or maybe I'm twisting the memory. It was in the middle of summer, after all. I'd been drinking in The Fluke all afternoon, first day of my holidays. He said his name was Jimmy and he was looking for work. He was nice, in a kind of rough and ready way. Clean grime, if you know what I mean. Posh grunge... I don't know. Long hair and a bit of stubble going on. Biker jacket. Jeans. Old grey T-shirt. But he smelled good. Scrubbed.

'We talked for a long time. He showed me his motorbike. At one point he picked me up and sat me on it. I liked that. He was strong. There's something about being whisked off your feet that's pretty giddy. It doesn't happen when you're an adult. He did plenty of that later on.'

The hand that wasn't holding her glass snaked out of the blankets and wrapped itself around mine.

'He bought me drinks. Said he was travelling up from Dover. He'd been on the Continent, driving around Germany, Switzerland, Italy, France. Labouring on construction sites. Waiting tables. *Sucking in life,* he said. *Sucking hard, like a vampire without teeth.* He wanted to drain as much experience from everywhere he visited, whether it was Prague or Plymouth. He said he wanted to suck some life out of Southwick. And he did. He did that all right.

'But what I don't understand, Paul, is that we were getting on so well, we were flirting with each other like crazy. Too much cider. The excitement of meeting a new person you find attractive. That madness, summer madness in the air. I'd have, you know... oh God, no time for being prudish now. I'd have fucked him that night. No sweat. I'd have gone with him down to the beach and had him all ways if he wanted. But either he didn't get my signals, or he chose to ignore them. Maybe he could only take what he wanted. Didn't like submissive women. Christ, I think about how many of us there are, strung across the world, staring after his bike tracks with bites and bruises and dislocations. Babies growing inside.

'At closing time he walked me home. I asked if he wanted tea and he said no. He hung back, he said good night. When I said good night too, when I was closing the door, he kicked it in and knocked me off my feet. And then it all happened, so fast I couldn't keep up with it. He was punching me and kicking me and throwing me around. So fast I didn't have chance to take in breath let alone scream for help. He moved like he was used to it. He'd done this before. We ended up in the kitchen. He tore the trousers from me with such force that he almost skinned my thighs. He raped me while he had a kitchen knife pressed against the back of my neck. I daredn't try to lift myself up, he was too heavy anyway, in case it just slid right into me and killed me, or worse, severed my spinal cord and left me paralysed.

'He got off me, cleaned himself up, pulled his jeans on and left. I didn't see him again.'

Her fingernails were lightly scoring the tender flesh of my inner arm, becoming almost unbearably gentle when they encountered a fold or fissure of scar tissue.

'Come here,' she said. She was crying. I went to hold her and she held her hand against mine, a barrier. She reached for my neck and drew me down. She kissed me deeply and confidently. Whisky fumes. Vanilla shampoo.

I lost myself to it. Her mouth was soft and firm at the same time, maddening. Blades of black hair swung into my face, bobbing with the ebb and flow of the kiss. Again my hands went to her, touching her lightly on her back. She jerked up and slapped my hands away. A silver wire of spittle looped between our mouths.

'Don't touch me,' she said. 'Don't you fucking touch me.'

She raised herself, tears threatening, and leaned over on one hip. 'Sorry,' she said. She supported her head with her hand and leaned in to kiss me once more. Her other hand slid between the buttons on my shirt and scored a line between my nipples. I felt the skin on my scalp tighten so swiftly I thought it might just peel away from my skull. There was something both carnal and lazy about the way she kissed. She kept her eyes closed. Our mouths, yoked together, worked separate orbits. Sometimes they lost contact, but she didn't mind, she just kissed what was there and slowly worked her way back. When I went to touch her again, the third time, her eyes snapped open and her hand gripped my wrist. She didn't say anything. She drew me on to the bed. My back was screaming, but the kiss provided a salve. I wouldn't allow pain to ruin this. She pressed me down on to the mattress and swung one leg over both of mine. I felt her belly press and graze against my cock and I drew in breath. I felt dizzy with need. It had been so long. Tamara came into my thoughts and I forced her away, with bitter relish.

Ruth broke the kiss. I felt my face flush under her scrutiny. I had not seen her like this; I had not believed her capable of such behaviour. She wore a sleepy, sly expression. She kept her hand on the centre of my chest. She leaned over to her bedside cabinet and threw open the door. She withdrew two lengths of thin rope.

'Put your hands against the rails,' she said.

'Ruth, I — '

'Do it, or go back to your room. You won't touch me. I won't be touched.'

'I won't touch you.'

'You will. You say that, but you will. You all do. Go on, put your hands against the rail. Now.'

'This is unnecessary, Ruth.'

'I'll decide that. This is a big fucking step for me. If I'm not in control, nobody is. It's me in the left-hand seat, Mr Pilot. Okay?'

She tied both my wrists to the headboard. She tied them well. I wasn't the only one learning knots at the foot of a master. The knots were secure, but not so tight as to cause me discomfort. Once I was fastened down, she took off her pyjama bottoms, but left her top on. Light caught in the glossy tangle of her bush. She unfastened my jeans and tugged them down my legs. She gave up with one leg off, and made a sort of 'oofing' noise as my penis sprang free of my briefs. It was pretty much the only part of me that had escaped injury, but it didn't seem to be at that moment. I was swollen and red and throbbing. I felt close to tears with anticipation and worry and pleasure.

'The baby,' I said, and couldn't find a way to finish the sentence.

'The baby will be fine,' she said. 'I'm getting it back for all the kicks it's been giving me lately.'

She paused as she reached for my penis. I saw her face harden.

'We don't have to do this,' I said.

'It looks to me as if we do,' she said. 'I can't leave you like this. You might explode.'

We laughed, but it was a slightly desperate, manic moment. She took me into her mouth and the moment changed into something else, no less manic, no less desperate, but different. Only seconds went by before I felt the familiar tightening in my balls, a gathering of sensation.

'Ruth,' I said. My voice was strangled. I fought

against my bindings but there was nothing I could do. 'Ruth!'

She didn't stop. She recognised what was happening, but she didn't pull away. I came for what seemed like minutes and she kept her mouth on me. When it was over, she leaned over and discreetly spat my seed into an empty tea cup. She lay alongside me in the bed and kissed my shoulder. Her hand stroked my belly. She didn't move to release me and I didn't ask her to. My head was a thick jungle of dark greens, blues, purples.

Neither of us spoke. She kept stroking and caressing, pressing her breasts against me. Her hand kept returning to my penis; her hand did not remain still. I was hardening again. I felt both spent and fecund. She touched herself and her fingers came away shining. She raised herself and held my penis at an angle where she could impale herself upon it. She held herself open and slid down on to me. A deep, animal noise at the base of her throat. She moved slowly at first, finding how we fit each other. When she was comfortable with the arrangement, she increased the pace, finding a position and a rhythm that she seemed to lock on to, as if it might serve her the swiftest, most intense release. She fucked me harder and faster than I liked, but I had no way to calm her or alter the pace. I felt the firm weight of the baby denting my abdomen. I couldn't stop myself from imagining the body inside her, curled into itself like a leaf, being jolted and bounced against the soft womb walls. The pale swell of eyes. Hands held together as if in prayer. I heard the slosh of her insides and bit my lip. I felt the awful conviction that she was using me as a tool to terminate her pregnancy. She was surely moving too quickly, driving too deeply, for this to be anything other than an abortion attempt. Her face was a stiff mask of concentration, but this was no prelude to climax. She was not hunting the tail of her orgasm; there was no rising expression of ecstasy coming through. But I couldn't get through to her. I couldn't pull back. The ropes chewed at my wrists. And now I could hear a baby crying somewhere, a lusty shriek fuelled by hunger or pain.

Another button had slipped free on Ruth's blouse. She clutched the gap closed with her left hand, swept the lamp from the table with her right. Darkness rushed in like a guest at a sex show. I couldn't square her modesty with the almost violent way that she was fucking me. I couldn't take in the breath I needed to ask, not that she would have paid me any attention. She was focused beyond reason. She seemed to have forgotten my physical state, or chose to ignore it. Any tenderness was being erased with each stroke. There were more than two people in that bedroom now. It was as if she were using me to reenact the assault she had suffered. This was no confirmation of love, no act of passion. This was an exorcism.

And yet.

The sweat was flying off her. I felt drops of it hit my torso. Noise was building inside her, like something trapped, chipping its way free. In between, little mewls of contentment and arousal. She came with a long moan of exultation, which tapered off into deep gasps, as if she were in the delivery room already, the baby being coaxed from her. *Come on, you can do it. One last push. Breathe... breathe...*

My own climax, seconds later, was lost beneath the weight of her and her moment. Secondary, weak, forgotten. I felt dirty. Regretted taking even a second or two of sour pleasure from this. It was not right. She pushed herself away from me and swept to the bathroom, leaving me locked to the bed.

I don't know when she came back because, miraculously, I'd drifted off to sleep. But when I awoke, minutes or hours later, I was clean and dressed and freed and she was sleeping beside me, wrapped in a thick towelling bathrobe and the protective circle of her own arms. Or that's how I should have seen it. All I took from that was that the barrier was back up. Keep out, those arms said. No entry.

'Pregnancy suits you,' I whispered to her.

Chapter Eleven

ERROR CHAIN

THE NIGHT CHANGED, became a different kind of blue. Riven. Unstable. Spastic flashes of electric light shivered and skidded across the walls of my room. I lay there, coming out of sleep, my fingers idling in the dried juices of lovemaking on my belly and pubes, trying to remember if it really happened, despite this physical evidence. It was unbearably hot in here. I got up, wincing at the twinge of muscles I'd forgotten how to use, and, rubbing my wrists, shuffled over to the window. The glass was opaque with condensation. Bursts of radio static from outside. Car doors slamming. Not good at any time of day, and certainly not now, at a couple of minutes shy of four in the morning. I wondered how long it would be before I slept through till dawn.

I opened the window and it was as if the words were waiting just beyond the frame for a chance to slip through and assault me.

I think she was trying to find her way home.

A police voice. Impersonal, male, tired. Who wouldn't be, doing this thankless job? Bodies in winter. I thought of Ruth and the guy who had raped her. Maybe he had returned for more fun and gone too far this time. And then I thought of Tamara and I was lashing out in the dark, trying to find something to wear, my heartbeat so strong and hard that I could taste it at the back of my throat: burned and broken and rank with old blood. I imagined her thumbing rides, trying to get down to me, her head full of apologies and hope, and I would kiss all that sorry away because I had plenty of my own now and together we'd sit and talk and thrash this out and move on together, stronger.

The blue light and the radios were nothing to do with Tamara, they couldn't be, so why was I stumbling out of the door, barely dressed, shoeless, tears standing in the wings, waiting for their cue? It wouldn't take much. They knew their lines back to front.

I was stopped almost immediately by a police cordon on North Parade. Yellow tape. Squad cars parked at jazzy angles to the road, doors open, the full-on disco lighting effect. A police constable took me to one side and asked me my name. I told him I owned one of the B&Bs on that stretch of road and asked him what had happened.

'Which B&B?'

'Tam's Place,' I said.

He referred to a sheaf of notes on a clipboard. 'Say again?'

'It's not called that now,' I said, feeling clot-headed. 'But it will be.'

He stared at me in that way the police do, endlessly patient, patronising. Waiting for a slip up, the tongue to wag too much.

'Seventy-eight North Parade,' I said.

He didn't glance back at his notes. He kept his gaze on me. I put my remaining nude arm into its shirt sleeve and did what I could about my corkscrew hair.

'Come with me please, sir.'

We moved beyond the cordon to a knot of men and women dressed in long coats. Beyond them, a white tent shivered under the smack of wind coming in from the north. I felt a nauseous little belt when I saw the members of a white-clothed, masked forensic team dashing in and out of the front door of my B&B.

Without seeing it happen, I had been passed on to this new group. One of them grinned expansively at me like a shark that has somehow learned the ability to dress itself in human clothing.

'Mr Roan?'

'Yes?' My voice was betraying me. I sounded weak and crumbly, right at the edge of things. All he had done was speak to confirm my name.

'I'm Detective Inspector Liam Keble.'

He pronounced it 'key-bull'. And then gave me another deep smile. I found myself looking at his teeth, checking for morsels of human flesh. His eyes spoilt this look. Instead of being flat and black and dead, they were animated, a pretty shade of blue. His hair was blonde, long enough to tickle the collar of his shirt. Surfer hair trapped under a fedora. He seemed a bizarre mash-up of *Dragnet* and *Point Break*.

'Aren't you cold, Mr Roan?'

'I don't feel it,' I lied. 'Scar tissue has its uses.'

'I see. Can we get you a hot drink? Would you like to sit down?'

'What happened here?'

The smile lessened; this was his smile of sympathy, it was conspiratorial, it drew you in. He was a master of that mouth, I realised. He acted with it constantly, I could tell. And despite the prettiness of his eyes, they didn't sparkle after all. He was dead, north of his cheeks. Sharks' eyes after all.

'A body was discovered on the premises of this bed and breakfast establishment about an hour and a half ago.' He said 'establishment' with relish, or irony, as if he was toying with the supra-formal speech that was common to his ilk. The smile returned. He reminded me of an actor. I scratched my head, internally, while he played with me, digging for a name. It helped to combat my nerves.

'Where were you...' he said, clapping his hands together, then steepling the fingers, bringing them to his mouth. His forefingers rested against his bottom lip. He had large, thick fingers. Killers' fingers. The nails were shaped and polished. He must have had them professionally manicured. I liked the guy, no matter that he was trying to get me on the sharp tines of his fork.

'... Oh, let's say, an hour and a half ago?'

'I was in bed.' Better. My voice had found its muscle again. He noticed it too. His eyes widened a little, the humour leapt about the corners of his mouth like electricity. I could tell he'd seen this before. The liar returning to the script. Confidence in his own lines.

He lowered his chin, and the shadow from the brim of his hat concealed the top half of his face. Just the teeth now. Jesus, he was good at this. I thought: *William Devane*, that's it.

'And where would bed be?'

'Bed would be in the rear room of the Vulcan book shop, just around the corner from here. On Surt Road.'

'And you're up and about. Why?'

'It's a free country,' I said, lamely. 'And anyway, I told your friend over there,' I pointed at the PC who had taken me over to him. 'I told him I own a property on this road.'

'Many people own a property on this road, Mr Roan.' He spread his arms and looked around him in mock surprise. He gasped. 'Where are they?' He gasped again. 'Oh no, there's a party on the promenade and everyone is missing out.' He put his hands together and pointed his forefingers at me. A child pretending to aim a gun. He said: 'Except you.'

'I don't sleep too well,' I said. 'The lights disturbed me.'

He nodded. There might have been an expression of concern on his face, or sympathy, even. 'I'll tell you what disturbs me,' he said, and gently clapped me on the shoulder, propelling me forward in the direction of the B&B. 'Skeletons in the cupboard,' he whispered.

I flinched from his touch. I glanced at his hands as if I might see some evidence of his putting sordid little boxes of bad secrets together for me to burn.

He leaned in to me, conspiratorial. 'I don't mean figurative skeletons, in case you were wondering,' he said. 'Not the panties and Dear Johns and death threats. Yeah, I've heard of you, what you get up to. You get paid for doing any of that shit? No? Christ. One of those people who's doing their bit for the community, hey? Otherwise known as a cunt. Anyway, you want to be that to those people and there's no skin off my nose, et cetera. But I'm talking about real skeletons. Dem bones, dem bones. El bonio. Calcium cowboy. Real. And guess where we found him?'

'I've no idea.'

'Yeah you do. You've saved us an hour or two's work, you know. We'd have tracked you down before breakfast but it's difficult at that B&B. Nothing there to link it with you at the moment. It's a bit, what's the word? Quiet? Business a bit slow?'

'I had an accident.'

'That's quite an alibi.'

'It's no alibi. I wasn't aware that I needed to provide an alibi for anything. Are you arresting me? Charging me with something?'

'It might happen.'

'Well until it does,' I said, not knowing how angry I should allow myself to be, or how angry I would be allowed to get, 'you can dispense with all the tough cop routine. I've done nothing. I was explaining why the business hasn't taken off. There is no business. Not yet. I'd like to see you get any work done lying six months in a coma.'

We were standing outside the B&B. It seemed diminished somehow, sunken. It looked as if the buildings on either side of it were helping to keep it up. I thought of the figure I'd seen in the window, or thought I'd seen. Now it appeared that there had been someone in the building. A vagrant, perhaps. A squatter. He or she had found something unpleasant in there.

'Who was in there, anyway?' I asked. 'Who found this so-called skeleton?'

'We got a phone call,' he said. 'A concerned neighbour. Saw someone mooching about the property.'

'And the body?'

'A child,' DI Keble said. 'A little boy or a little girl. We don't know yet. But it doesn't really matter because... hell, a *child*, Paul. You don't mind me calling you Paul, do you, Mr Roan?'

'So what happens now?'

'When were you last here?' he asked.

'Yesterday,' I said.

'Yesterday? So, it was you doing the mooching about?'

'Possibly,' I said. 'Probably.'

'This body, this skeleton, has been in situ for... according to my forensic labrats...' He made a great play of pulling out his notebook and moistening his thumb and flipping pages. '... At least two weeks. Maybe more. And you didn't see anything?'

'It's the first time I've been back since accident. My girlfriend —'

'Your girlfriend? Who would that be?'

'That would be Tamara Dziuba. Can I finish?'

'Tamara Dziuba. There's exotic. How do you spell it? What is she? Model? Actress?'

'She's done some modelling. When she was younger. She worked as a flight attendant.'

'Too much make-up, don't you think?' he asked. 'I mean, I'm not saying Tamara wore too much, but it tends to be the case, wouldn't you say?'

'I don't have an opinion on the matter.'

'How did you meet her? I met my wife on a rollercoaster ride. No kidding. I almost threw up in her lap. She took pity. She sells expensive jewellery in a shop where you have to be buzzed in. There's nothing in the window displays. How confident is that? You and I would have to re-mortgage our houses three times over just to be able to buy a share in a watch strap. Très exclusif.'

'I met her at work. Is this part of your questioning?'

'It is, yes, if I say so. So you were an air steward?'

'I was a pilot.'

'No way,' he gripped my arm to anchor himself as he took a step away from me, another theatrical play at surprise. 'A pilot. How exciting.'

'Not really,' I said. 'It can be a grind. Boring even. It's all routine.'

'Well I think it is exciting. Especially if things go wrong. Although I understand some pilots can go through their career without ever suffering an engine failure. Is that common?'

'Yes,' I said. And wished I'd told him I was a school janitor. 'I'm not a pilot any more.'

'Is this related to your accident?'

'No. Although, yes. I can't fly any more. My eyes aren't good now. I left the job.'

He was looking at me as if expecting me to explain. When I didn't he remained quiet, but I wasn't going to fall for that psychology again. It's only an awkward silence when at least one person is upset by it.

'Where's your girlfriend now?'

'I don't know.'

'Okay,' he said, and he seemed suddenly tired. The creases in his clothes, a faint food stain on his tie, suggested he'd been on the go for a long time. 'Shall we go in?'

For a moment I thought of trying a joke, asking if he had made a booking, but I didn't think it would go down too well. He followed me through the door.

'I need hardly say this, but don't touch anything.'

'Where are we going?' I asked, irritated that he should be ordering me around on my own property, regardless of the situation. The place seemed utterly different now that there were remote lighting systems dotted around. Their intense LEDs scoured every corner of every shadow. It was like walking through a film set.

'Top floor bedroom,' he said. I felt a jolt at this. My legs met the stairs and I began to ascend. I was faltering, exhausted by the time I met the first landing.

'I'm sorry,' he said. 'I shouldn't be putting you through this.' But he didn't offer me the chance of a rest, or the opportunity not to make the journey. I didn't tell him that I'd made the same journey the previous night, or what I'd seen, or thought I'd seen. What I'd heard.

At the top of the building I held on the banister and waited for him to move past me into the bedroom. But he paused behind me, wanting me to enter ahead of him. Plastic sheeting lay on the ground. More LEDs spotlit the room. Men and women in white gowns and masks and covered shoes padded softly around, carrying small briefcases or cameras on tripods. The chatter of radio static volleyed up and down the stairs as if we were in an enclosure at some science-fiction zoo where something made from electricity stalked.

The wardrobe was open, its door having finally fallen off, or been torn free by the shocked hand of whomever had found it. Inside, lying on an uncovered pillow, was a small skeleton, positioned (it seemed, sacrilegiously) in the shape of a foetus, although this body was much older than that; five or six years old, I'd have guessed.

'Do you have anything to say?' Keble asked.

'No,' I said. And then: 'How long did you say this has been here?'

'We're not exactly sure, but we reckon maybe three weeks.' He rubbed his forehead, trying to remember something, trying to figure something out. I wondered if he'd watched *Columbo* as a kid. 'Tell me,' he said, 'when did you wake up from your coma, just out of interest?'

He knew very well. I got a sense of him knowing more about me than I did. 'About three weeks ago,' I said. 'Of course, the first thing I did – weak as a foal, barely able to walk more than two steps – was kill a child, bone it and stuff the remains in a top-floor wardrobe.'

'I'm not accusing you of anything,' Keble said. 'But you'll agree it would be seriously remiss of me not to at least question you, the hotel owner, about this?'

It was a question that didn't require a response. Instead I watched the forensics team work around us, effusively irritated by our presence.

'We'll talk again,' Keble said. 'In the mean time, I need hardly say this, but I'd strongly advise you not to leave town any time soon.'

'I'm going nowhere,' I lied.

Chapter Twelve

THE CRAW

GETTING OUT OF Suffolk is difficult, if you don't have a car. I caught an early morning bus to Darsham. I was looking at a five-hour journey, with three changes, before I reached Hull. The train to Ipswich was old and cold and noisy. One of the windows was broken, its hinge bent, incapable of being closed. Frigid air rushed in and swirled around the carriage; I couldn't be bothered to move to another. Shooting pains in my legs and hips and back kept me nailed to the seat. Delayed muscle aches from the supposedly tender act I'd shared with Ruth.

I was alone for that first leg, apart from a huffing attendant who clipped my ticket while his huge gut tried to pour out over the top of his poor, failing waistband. I ate the breakfast I'd packed for myself. A handful of raisins, a pot of yogurt, a dozen pills.

I had crept from my room like a thief in the night. Outside, in the unholy bleach-blue of dawn, I had listened to the kiss of the sea on the beach and felt drawn to it. I wanted to sit in the sand, feel the cold mask one type of pain in my legs with another, watch something burn and produce alien colours. But there were no boxes. The village was pure, or its folk had found someone even more damaged and blasted than me to turn to for redemption.

I smelled something burning. Acrid, chemical. A bonfire flickered in a back garden abutting the embankment. A man in a thick grey jumper throwing black parcels on to the flames. Things wrapped in bin bags. Now gone, swallowed up by the fences and hedges and trees. Back gardens shot by like slightly different scenes from a flicker book. Well maintained lawns dotted with the gaudy colours of children's toys. A trampoline. An inflatable paddling pool. A barbecue, a pergola, a pagoda. Now and then they would be punctuated by something unusual. A yard without grass. An old car in the middle of a lawn.

The backs of these houses stared blindly on to the tracks, most of their curtains drawn. In one or two windows, though, bodies shifted slowly under bleak yellow light, like lizards in a vivarium. I saw fragments of lives before the position of the train altered, cutting me off from them. A man with his arms raised, stretching or surrendering. A woman folding clothes, her face a sunken pit of misery. Children cowering from something real or imagined.

I turned away and stared at the patterns in the worn seats. How many people had travelled on this dinosaur? It felt and sounded like the last journey anybody would take. The brakes were applied. When the train stopped I would open the doors on a locomotive's graveyard and find the driver taking an axe to our ride. But it was just Ipswich, and I had six minutes to get to another platform in order to catch the next train to London.

In little over an hour I was at Liverpool Street and I felt as though I had come thousands of miles. The speed at which everyone operated was frightening. It frightened me too to think that I had once moved like this; faster, even. Southwick was like a village trapped in aspic. I found myself wanting to turn on my heel and get back on the train and simply bury myself back there in the slow and the sure and the uncomplicated. But that was only the surface of things, I reminded myself. That was not me. I was a hive of worry and uncertainty. Everywhere I went that would remain, no matter how sedate my surroundings. I was taking action. I had to keep at it. I had to find out.

I took a Circle Line tube train to King's Cross, keeping my eyes closed as often as I could, unwilling to meet the gaze of my fellow travellers for fear of what I might see there. By the time I'd found the correct platform at St Pancras I was starting to flag. I bought a coffee and washed down some more pills. I stared at my legs and almost saw the pain vanish from them, the shake of discomfort slowly extinguished by the mask of analgesics. I used to hate painkillers. Pain was a necessity, I thought. It was the body's alarm system. Now I was disabling it, or some of it. When you're in pain all the time, it didn't seem to matter any more. It was like a fire alarm going off in a house that has been reduced to ash.

I tried to relax despite the constant blur of people thrashing around me. They moved so fast that I thought someone must get hurt. A collision, a torn muscle. I was grateful when it was time to board the

train. I found my seat and collapsed into it. Weeks of
nervous exhaustion that had piled up in my muscles
came pouring free. I was asleep before the doors
were sealed shut.

I slept all the way and when I woke up, it was
lunchtime and the light was different, like something
refracted through a seashell polished almost to
translucency. Everything was different, despite the
sea being the same flat expanse of mud grey. The
wind bit harder and tasted of salt and oil. The
clouds seemed heavier. The people were tougher,
more solid than those I had left behind back home
and in London. They, like trees growing up in the
teeth of ocean gales, appeared more anchored.

Now I had eight hours to kill before the ferry
left. I spent them eating and reading and writing a
letter to Ruth that I would not post. I had twelve
pages of it done by the time I took my seat for
dinner in a pizza restaurant set back from the
coast. Flags in a car showroom shook as if they
were trying to free themselves from their masts.
The wind was so strong it seemed to dimple
the glass in the window frames. I drank half a
bottle of Chardonnay and raged and pleaded and
begged. The ink seemed to turn darker as I let it
all come. *You should have let me die*, I told her.
You should have let me drain away into the soil.
Everything that had once been me was gone. I was
starting again and I didn't want to. I tore into her
about the way she had treated me during what
should have been a watershed moment in our
relationship. *I hated you a little bit, when I ought
to have been falling in love.*

I ought to have been writing to Tamara, but doing that might jinx what I hoped would be happening within 24 hours, that I would be able to speak my mind directly to her.

I finished off the wine, paid and limped out into a gale. I caught a taxi to the ferry where I suffered a harrowing moment when I thought I'd left my passport back in Southwick.

But it was there, at the bottom of my rucksack, showing the face of a man I no longer was. That caused its own problem, and I argued and pleaded for ten minutes until I was able to persuade the guard on control that it was me. I was waved through, and I hobbled on board the great ferry. It took a while to find my way to the cabin decks, and then to pinpoint my room. It was tiny, no window. One of the pursers asked if everything was all right, and he actually winced when I turned to face him. We chatted for a while about the room and about prison cells and although I was only joking, he took it all seriously.

'Give me a moment,' he said, and he went away.

He came back having scored me an upgrade, explaining that it would be a quiet crossing; the ship was far from full. He led me to a family-sized room with a porthole view. It was surprisingly spacious, and comfortable, like being in a budget hotel that made an effort. I gave him a tip, although he tried to refuse it and explained that his mother had been in a motorbike accident when she was much younger, and that she was still struggling with the after-effects now, many years on. I don't know if he meant to make me feel better, but the pleasure of the upgrade was dented a little.

After he'd gone I showered and changed my clothes, then went looking for dinner. The buffet-style service was pretty grim, but it was quiet and I was in and out quickly. I had a stroll around and found a bar. Just outside it was a children's activity area, comprising a ball pit and a small area where DVDs could be watched and pictures coloured in with the help of a kids' entertainer. But the entertainer was currently sitting on his own with his arms folded, staring into space. I was walking by the ball pit when a child emerged from it, making me jump. She smiled at me; her mouth filled with gaps. She might have been any age between five and ten; I had no idea. She scooped up one of the balls and threw it in my direction. It pinged off the plastic surround, but I flinched anyway. She laughed and dived back into the sea of plastic. I watched her making her own entertainment for a few minutes, trying to understand why I was so fascinated by this everyday display. But that was it. It *wasn't* everyday, not for me. Not for anyone living on my tiny curve of England. Watching this child juggle and jump and thrash around was like being at the zoo and stumbling upon a thylacine.

A prickle of threat. I was newly aware of my clothes, hot and vaguely uncomfortable. Sweat sprang up into the fissures of my scar tissue that weren't for ever sealed shut. I was being watched. Two adults – the child's parents, no doubt – were observing me observe their daughter with this mix of incredulity and pleasure etched on my ravaged features. I knew straight away what I must look like. I tried a smile that must have horrified them further and moved away to the bar where I spent a nervy hour winding down over a long beer waiting for the security guards to come and take me away for questioning.

There were occasional PA invitations to join Steve in the casino lounge, or Anna for Bingo or Dave and Dave for comedy. I forgot, for a little while, that I was sitting in a bar on a big boat. Eventually there was the suggestion of motion, the slightly queasy feel of movement beyond your control, a subtle pitch and yaw that I knew so well from flying, but that felt different, more unpleasant, in water. I went up to the bar at the uppermost deck – the ball pit was empty now, the kids' entertainer gone – and stared through the window as we departed from Hull. Quays and cranes and containers. Spotlights bleached the landing bays and turned the water into so many chips of white ice. You could see the deck from another window, glossy with rain, empty of people, all the way to the sleek, black control tower where I imagined a pilot sitting in a huge chair, steering this beast with a joystick the size of a matchstick. I suddenly missed that sense of control and power, the responsibility that comes with managing hundreds of people and millions of pounds worth of gear. After twenty minutes we reached wide water and the lights, having grown less powerful, stopped reaching out alongside us.

The lift doors opened and half a dozen women came into the bar dressed as though they were on their way to the Oscars ceremony. I decided it was time to turn in.

Somehow I found my way back to my room, despite a series of missteps. I opened the door with

my flimsy paper keycard and shut away all the rough
coffee and bad food and cheesy entertainment. I sat
on the edge of my bed and pulled from my rucksack
the copy of *Gray's Anatomy* I'd liberated from the
bookshop yard. I felt my muscles and bones tense
in anticipation about what they'd learn about their
uneasy marriage this evening. I made myself a cup of
tea and lay back on the bed. There were three other
beds folded into the wall, waiting for a family that
I would never produce. If I'd wanted children, how
could I be a dad to them now? It was uncomfortable
for me to rest this book on my knee, let alone eight
or so pounds of squirming flesh. I was fit for nothing
but a long wait for the grave.

*The lachrymal are the smallest and most fragile
bones of the face. They are situated at the front
part of the inner wall of the orbit, and resemble
somewhat in form, thinness, and size, a fingernail.*

The bones of my face had been shattered that night.
I hadn't been able to cry since, though I'd wished
heartily for the chance. I rubbed my eyes now, trying
to work out if the bumps and hard little edges around
the orbit that I could feel through the skin were mis-
matched burrs of bone, or whether they had always
been there. I could imagine my fleshless skull looking
all wrong, cracked and warped like a model made out
of broken pieces of pottery. I thought of the edges of
my eye sockets and how they were more like the sharp
rings of hard little calcified mouths, like those of fish
pecking and chewing at coral reefs. I thought of how
Ruth looked at me with real hunger sometimes, and
had done, even in the dark, the other night when we
fucked, *when she fucked me*, on her bed.

I read about the Canal of Petit in the eye. I read about the sinuses of Valsalva in the heart. I read about changes in the vascular system at birth; how, at that first shriek and gasp of air, parts of the heart and lungs change, shut down, fire up.

I felt the tremor of horses in the sand. That doubling up of hooves. One strong, coming on hard, the other fainter, yet faster. A slant-rhyme. A fracturing echo. The words at the edge of the page threatened to lose their shape and become a black border that I would not be able to escape. I tried to tear my gaze away, but the text held me fast. The skeleton in the wardrobe uncurled its body, the bones crackling. It reached out its hand for me. The tiny skull full of a grin.

Something wet, with density, hit the porthole window, releasing me from the tyranny of the page. I glanced that way, but the angle was too narrow to confirm what it was. A shadow writhed on the carpet. I pushed myself upright. I was thinking of sharks and morays and the crazed, alien beasts found at unknowable fathoms. Whales the size of airports. Kraken. Sea serpents.

There was dark matter on the glass, some awful footprint left by a thing bleeding, it seemed. Something smashed behind me and I heard muffled laughter in the corridors. I checked my watch. It was coming on for two in the morning. I had been reading for four hours. Another smash from the corridors, coming closer. I heard raised voices. Kids on the piss who couldn't take their booze, giving in to anger. It all seemed to kick off outside my door. Volleys of rage. Incoherent threats and counter-threats. Women chipping in, shrill, goading. That hard-on people got for impending violence. The thrill of it, seconds away.

I heard a clear, female voice cut through the noise: 'There are children asleep. Cut it out. Take it elsewhere.'

That seemed to take the sting from the moment. More blather, hot air, posturing. But going away now, the testosterone dissipating, although not without a last roar of outrage from that rogue male. I left it a while before limping to the door and peering out. I heard a click as another door shut simultaneously, but I couldn't tell which one. Probably the woman who had shouted down the group of revellers.

Splinters of glass were strewn across the carpet; here and there an ugly ring of glittering teeth where the jagged base of a pint pot lay like a hunter's trap. I called out but there was nobody nearby. Not wanting to invite the wrath of my vigilante neighbour, I decided against calling out again and instead grabbed my key card and headed for the stairs. There was no staff in the cubby holes from where they conducted their operations. The upper deck was similarly silent. There was a cloud of oppressive odours though: dead alcoholic drinks, perfume that had turned sour on tired host skin; it was something like an assault.

The bar was empty, though far from clean. Empty glasses crowded the counter; spilled beer filmed the table-tops. It was so still, I could hear the splash of drips from the beer spigots landing in the overflow trays. I moved past the children's ball pit once more, pausing to stare into it. It appeared a weird construct now, without anybody to play in it. And it seemed inconceivable that those hundreds of coloured plastic balls should not begin to shiver, just prior to the emergence of some grinning head.

I was willing it to happen, tricking my eyes into thinking that it *was* happening, and I spooked myself. I moved on; I didn't want to see what might rise, what was buried. Too much time had passed.

I was dreaming, I thought, as I heard the cascade of plastic behind me, dry rain falling. Just a natural realignment of spheres, I thought. Just maths, working itself out.

I checked out the buffet. Nobody there. I glanced again out of the windows, in case we had somehow arrived and I had not been roused from sleep, but there was just the endless soft grey of the North Sea. The lifts were not answering my call. The doors at the top of the stairs were locked. I descended. Where the doors to the cars ought also to have been locked, one was swinging open. I went through into the hold. Exhaust ghosts. The gleam of cellulose. I thought I might find a yellow-jacketed staff member helping someone retrieve something from their car, but I could see nobody. There was the thrum of engines beyond these walls, and nothing else.

I was about to head back to my room, thinking that running away by going to sleep might fix things, when I heard a long, slow scratching noise, as of the tines of a fork being dragged along a plate. Only this was a harsher, more raw sound. Its edges were jagged and they caught on my nerves like a duff chord played on a badly tuned guitar. I saw my face reflected in a car window and it was all drawn back, my teeth gritted, eyes wide. If I'd been able, my ears would have been pricked, like a startled cat's.

The sound had come from aft and starboard. I heard something wet and fast; it was like the smack and slither of something – a crippled dog, maybe – that wasn't too concerned about rebounding and ricocheting off hard things in its desperation to be away. Or, I thought, checking behind me where the doors were, to be nearer.

I heard the sound of heavy tools dropped on hollow steel. I heard someone swear once: bleak and brutal. I heard a child cry. As if in response to this sound, above all others, the slither and smack repeated, more frantic this time. I wondered if someone had been assaulted down here, a serious assault; someone left for dead. A parent. That would explain the frantic movements at the sound of a crying child. He, or she, was trying to get back to their children, to protect them against whatever had done this to them.

But I knew that was all just hope on my part. I knew that what was making that noise was something to do with me. I'd brought something with me from the beach. I was introducing the infections within me to every corner I walked around.

I started edging back towards the stairs. I would go back to my room and sleep until we had docked. Don't leave the room. No need to leave the room.

I got to the door and slipped through, trying to ignore the way that my shadow moved, or that of the thing that was rising up behind me. I moved up the stairs as quickly as I was able and caught a whiff of the rising tide of oil and sea water and the filth and detritus that shivers at the bottom of the ocean. I saw bloodied children's handprints on the walls and gouges in the carpet formed by something that ought to exist nowhere other than between the covers of a book of fairy-tales.

I heard Jake's voice, stilted and stalled, beyond the battering of metal as something came closer, bouncing off the cars, heading straight for me. He was trying to tell me something, but the words wouldn't come, or the miles between us were too filled with interference to allow his message to ram home. I should not have made this journey. I knew it was fated to end in disappointment anyway. Me not finding Tamara. Me finding Tamara and being told gently, but firmly, to leave her alone. Things had changed, the world had turned, we were all new now.

I kept up with this as I climbed those stairs, convinced that my feet were pooling in cold fluid that was pouring up from the car park. Seawater. Blood. It didn't matter. It would consume me before I made it to my deck and then what was prowling around would be able to find me at its leisure.

The Craw, I thought. *You know it's the Craw.* Finding out about it in that fusty little museum antechamber meant it had somehow cleaved itself to me. I had unlocked it yet chained it to me, perhaps in the reading of those terrible letters in their painful childish handwriting. Misery likes its own company. We were bonded, bound.

My fingers shivered with the piece of card at the slot of the lock. Finally I slid it in and was released. I did not look back as I shut the door. I had a drink and got into bed fully clothed. I slept, miraculously, but my dreams were filled with labyrinths and walls and something just on the other side of wherever I was, steam rising from it over the edges, swirling and curling into shapes too hideous for me to contemplate. At various moments throughout the night I was wakened, by what I couldn't understand. Screams continuing to rattle around the corridors but driven not by drunken revellers this time. Shattering glass, but nothing that held beer or wine. It sounded dense, splintered. I imagined people scared solid, scared to glass, pitching over and fracturing against the bulk of the thing that had petrified them. A path of cold, red shards. Jagged moments of horror: shock-widened eyes and open mouths trapped in pieces of mirror. Glass globes of hearts impacted open into segments along fault lines, like blood oranges peeled apart for sharing.

My forehead was peppered with sweat all night, despite my swiping it away, despite the temperature hovering around a mark that turned my breath white. At times I was convinced something stood on the other side of that flimsy door and was leaning against it, testing its strength, measuring its resistance. I heard it creak and groan. I thought I could see it bulging, minutely, inward, the gaps between the hinges fattening.

And then a shrill *bing-bong* alarm and a tinny voice yanking me out of this unsleep, telling me we were approaching the Dutch coastline and would be docking in half an hour, time enough for us to enjoy breakfast in the ship's restaurant. More messages followed, about returning to cars, about the weather, about breakfast again, go on, have breakfast. There was no way to shut it off. I shed my clothes and stood under the shower head, face gritted against the rose. I took the water hotter than normal and imagined it flaying away my skin, layer by layer, until it could get at my brain and needle out all the bad.

ROTTERDAM WAS COLD, blunted by thick fog. I looked back once at the ship and it was something slowly being consumed by wet, white fire; the sodium lights clustered around and upon it shone with a corona so dense, you couldn't see the outline of the craft beneath it. I searched for the porthole to my room but could not work out where I had stayed. I turned away, deciding that I would only try to see some shape at it, staring out at me from the room where it had tried to take my life.

I took a road vaguely leading in the direction of the city, a path that meandered through a landscape devoted to the sea and the things that moved upon it. There were few shops, and those that were open were unwelcoming; little bars or cafés designed to hold as few people as possible, serving coffee and feeding weak light to transients, ghosts.

I kept walking, looking around for a cab that never materialised. I tried thumbing rides, but none of the cars would stop for this Frankenstein's monster. Eventually a lorry driver pulled over and the driver agreed to give me a lift as far as the Park and Ride car-park in Zeeburg. He didn't, or wouldn't, talk to me. Maybe it was the scars. Maybe he was just a taciturn Dutch guy.

I caught a tram to Amsterdam. At Central Station I bought a coffee and sipped it too quickly, burning my mouth. The waitress saw me and fetched a glass of tap water. She wore a tight white blouse and a black skirt. I got the impression she had grown since putting the clothes on that morning, that it would be too difficult to undress without tearing her garments and that she simply kept them on all the time now. Her face was grey with tiredness. I thanked her for the water and sloshed it around my mouth. With my tongue I could feel a blister on the inside of my lip. I took some more pills and read the leaflet in the box. *In addition, some other side effects have been reported but definite relationship with the medicine has not been established: confusion, suicidal tendency, violent behaviour, stroke...*

A guy flew past on a bicycle to which a massive wooden cart had been bolted. Three children and about a fortnight's shopping were piled up inside it. The poor, grey sky couldn't take any more and started weeping. I felt weird, being here. It wasn't just that I might be face to face with Tamara within the hour. It was being away from Southwick. I'd been slotted into that place like a piece from a jigsaw puzzle for such a long time. Not seeing the same buildings, people and coastline gave me a strange, vertiginous feeling, as if I'd just looked over a familiar fence only to find a thousand foot drop beyond it; the nerves behind my knee felt highly strung, painfully feeble. I guessed it must be some sort of agoraphobia. Bizarre that a dense, highly populated city should set it off, when home was all big skies and expansive beaches and the endless blue-grey span of the sea.

I didn't want my coffee now; even lukewarm it made my injured mouth sing. I left a couple of Euros and returned to the street, pausing by a bank of leaflets at the door, where I selected a streetmap heavily bordered by adverts for bars and restaurants in the city. I felt my heart lurch when I realised how close I was to Tamara's apartment. She was on Oudeschans, the other side of Neumarkt from the place I had booked on Oudezijds Voorburgwal. A twenty-minute walk... which meant more like forty for me. But still, touching distance.

I found myself unable to breathe. I leaned against the wall and waited for this dizzy spell to pass. What if she didn't recognise me? What if she refused to answer the door, or slammed it in my face? What if a man opened it?

I checked in at my hotel, which turned out to be three linked buildings incorporating a café and a nightclub. The hotel part of things seemed to be an afterthought and I was dreading the state of my room when I found the entrance was next to a seedy looking sex shop with multicoloured plastic streamers in the doorway barely concealing a row of glossy DVD covers depicting hairless, rubbery slits and a cornucopia of penis-shaped objects designed to fit them.

I had to climb a steep flight of stairs into a corridor that smelled sharply of old cigarettes and reefer coming up through the floor from the club below. There was a different kind of odour too, behind that, of something left to burn in a pan. I opened the door and found myself in a pleasant room with large windows looking out on to the canal. If anything, it was too big for me. I was used to close walls and the same view every day. I ignored the TV and went over to the window, watched the canal boats churning up the muddy water, and pretty girls in sensible clothes chatting earnestly as they headed into the Red Light District.

I went out and dawdled around the shops, staring in at piles of sepia-coloured junk and once-polished bronze and brass that now seemed to suck in the light rather than reflect it. The amount of traffic was staggering. I watched it play out behind me in the windows, the endless milling of people on foot or on bicycles or in cars or in trams. There seemed to be a hierarchy system going on. It appeared that cyclists had right of way over everyone. In reality it was one great mash-up waiting to happen.

I was stalling. My angle of attack was increasing beyond the point where lift began to decrease. I started laughing, then, and that helped. It didn't bother me that the act of laughing hurt my back and my head, or that people in the street gave me a wider berth. It was a positive reaction, no matter where it had come from. It was a surprise to be caught out by an old definition from the pilot's handbook. I still thought in terms of flight, it seemed.

Flight. There was an attractive prospect. I was distracting myself needlessly. Things were very, very simple. It all boiled down to her either taking me back into her life, or saying no. Everything else was just noise. I gathered myself and took a few deep breaths. Then I began my hobble over to Oudeschans.

I liked Tamara's apartment. She had intended to sell it when we sold the flat in Camden, but I insisted she keep it. We could come away for weekends, when we reached a point where we could employ a manager to look after the B&B and grew so sick of the hard summer work that we needed breathing space away. But we seldom managed to get over here. Either there was too much to be getting on with, or the logistics of such a trip were prohibitive.

'I'll keep it, for when you dump me,' she said once, treating me to one of her challenging, come-on looks. 'Then you'll have to come and get me, because I'll have stolen all your underpants and hidden them under my bed.'

I wanted children. The idea hit me from nowhere, although thinking of Tamara must have sown the seed. Seeing the child play so unselfconsciously in the ball pool on board the ferry had flicked a switch in me, I now realised. Tamara would understand.

My reticence had been well-founded, back when we had to think about budgets and five-year plans. I wasn't the right person to be a dad. There was no point in it. I didn't want to have a child only to farm it out to minders and nurseries at an age when they ought to be bonding with the people who created them.

My injuries had been extensive, but nobody had said the chances of me becoming a father had disappeared upon impact. I could have taken it as a sign, if I was a superstitious man.

I was so preoccupied with thoughts of boys and girls that I didn't realise where I was. Too soon, it seemed, I was on Tamara's street. I stood there, taking in the scene. I wanted it to remain with me, a stillpoint between my remarkable past life and the important, defining years to come. It all hinged upon this.

I closed my eyes. I heard cars and trams, I heard bicycle bells. Music from an open window. Jazz. I could smell the canal and the coffee shops. I could see Tamara answering the door in her long grey cardigan and skinny jeans. She'd be holding a large cup of steaming Earl Grey tea with lemon. Maybe her hair would be damp from the shower. She'd be listening to Radiohead or Roxy Music. She'd drop the cup. She'd run to me.

I made my way to the door and climbed the steps, shaky now, blood sugar low kind of shaky. I wished I'd eaten something. I couldn't remember the last meal I'd sat down to, or snack I'd bought. Thoughts of Tamara were sustaining me alone. I rang the bell and waited. No answer. She was out, buying lunch maybe. Going for a walk. Meeting a friend, or a lover.

I kicked the door, then punched the buzzer to the flat next door. A lazy voice answered. I knew it, but I couldn't remember his name.

'I know you,' I said, and regretted the words as soon as they were out. They sounded aggressive, illogical, the random snarl of a madman. Thankfully he didn't hang up on me.

It was a surprise when he said: 'I know you too, come on up.'

I struggled on the stairs. I'd been here on a number of occasions in the past, when I was wooing Tamara, when I had a spare weekend and I wasn't required at the airport. I would bound up here in seconds. Now it took me the best part of five minutes, with frequent stops. I thought about Schiphol airport as I did so, to try to sidetrack me from my pain. I thought of its six runways and tried to remember how long they all were. By the time I was standing in front of her door, my shirt was stuck to my back with what felt like an acre of sweat.

I tapped lightly on the door, just in case the buzzer was broken, but I was already coming to terms with doubt that I would see her today – a suspicion confirmed when I pushed open the letterbox and saw the small hill of mail, bills and advertising fliers reaching into the flat. Beyond that, familiarity snagged at me. I could see one of her jackets hanging on a coat hook. I could see the lower half of a framed photograph, a picture of the two of us standing at the rear exit of a Boeing 737: she was wearing my hat and saluting.

The door across from Tamara's flat shot open and I turned to see a familiar face. Jeroen? I thought. Is that his name?

I tried it and he nodded. He wore a cement-coloured shirt; one collar was flicked up. There were three pens in his top pocket. His hair was gelled back, a wet look, almost black: the skin of his scalp looked tender in contrast. His ears twinkled with diamond studs. He seemed athletic, comfortable in his skin. I noticed that about people these days. I envied him for it.

'Who are you?' he asked.

'I'm Paul Roan,' I said.

'I think – I thought – I recognised the voice, but you're not Paul Roan,' he said. 'I know Paul Roan. Not well. I've only met him a couple of times. But I know him. Who are you?"

I realised how different I must look. Everything about me, almost. Height, weight, clothing, not to mention the scar tissue: none of it was how I used to be. I pulled out my passport, almost laughing now at the complications that were arising. It was like being involved in a Hitchcockian movie about mistaken identity. At any moment James Mason and Martin Landau might materialise at my shoulder and ask me to step outside. I handed it over.

'I *am* Paul,' I said. 'We had you over once, for a drink. You had a Spanish beer. You forced a wedge of lime into the neck so hard that the neck broke and foam went everywhere.'

It was coming back to me now. This guy, this Jeroen, he worked at a recruitment agency in Leiden, as I remembered. I told him that too.

'Okay,' he said. 'So what happened to you?'

I ignored that. 'Tamara,' I said, nodding at her door. 'Do you know where she is?'

He frowned, shook his head. 'I've been away for a while. Holiday. Travelling to see relatives. Work. I've only been back for about a month. Why? What's up?'

He gestured for me to follow him inside. I gritted my teeth; I didn't want to move away from Tamara's door. It didn't seem right somehow. It was the closest I'd come to being near her since she left me. Turning my back was not what I wanted to do.

Reluctantly I went after him and pushed the door to, making sure I stopped it before the latch clicked shut. His flat was spartan almost to the point where it seemed he was either just moving in or ready to move out. But I remembered that he had no wife, no children. The more I remembered, the more came back: he read books but only on his Kindle. He couldn't abide dust – something to do with an allergy, I recalled – so surfaces were at a minimum. There was a sofa and a flat-screen TV in his living room. Precious little else.

'What's up?' he asked again.

I fixed my gaze on the canal and told him everything. I told him about skulls and the Craw and Amy and the lack of children in the village, and in such a mundane way, as if I was reeling off a shopping list, that he didn't say anything. But now I sensed he was frozen, and when I glanced at him he was looking at me with an expression that said: *I wish I hadn't asked.*

'Don't you have a key? A spare?'

'Sure,' he said, apparently grateful for something to do. 'But I'll have to find it first.'

I stood by the window while he checked through a series of coin envelopes neatly filed away in a recessed cabinet. He emerged with a keyring dangling from his fingers, wearing an expression of distaste, almost. 'Drop it back when you've finished, if you want,' he said.

'Thanks.'

'I hope you find Tamara,' he said. 'For my sake, as well as yours. She's a friend. She talked to me when I was lonely. She's a good woman, Tamara. It concerns me that you say she's missing.'

I gave him a telephone number, so he could contact me should Tamara return after I had gone, and left him in his living room. There was a sense of relief as I shut the door behind me. I slid the key into Tamara's lock. I felt a presence; Jeroen perhaps, on the other side of his door, listening to what I was doing. Or, too late, as I pushed open the door against the mass of mail at its foot, the presence was in *Tamara's* flat and I had made a fatal mistake in coming here. But no, the flat was empty.

I struggled to pick up all the mail – irked that Jeroen hadn't popped in to keep on top of it – and hefted it through to the living room. I suppose I wanted to see some evidence of recent activity, some clue that she would return soon, but the amount of unshifted mail seemed to have put paid to any hope of that.

Green sofas. White walls. The pendant lamp in the centre of the room that I always bashed my head against but she effortlessly swerved around as if she was in possession of radar. Thick rug with a simple petal print. White units. A TV and a mini stereo. The table by the window overlooking the canal where we breakfasted. I went over to it and drew up a chair. This was my chair. She sat opposite. On sunny days the light would catch in her hair and...

I sorted through the envelopes. Nothing of great interest. All of it formal, boring. I checked the drawers in the unit beneath the television: just video tapes, DVDs, a notebook of films she wanted to watch.

In her bedroom I checked the cupboards. Lots of clothes, neatly folded. A notebook by the bed. I found some documents of mine, with my signature on them. I pocketed them, hoping that any further passport hassle might melt away if I waved them around.

Tamara's smell was all over the place. Why had she not come here, if she was leaving me? Where else was there? I sat on the bed and clenched my jaw at the obvious answer to that. I wondered about her ex-lovers. She'd told me about them, talked to me about them. I'd seen photographs. None of them seemed to have captured a particularly special place in her heart. While we were together, she displayed no desire to drop in on any of them to say hi. No lunches. No phone calls. No birthday cards. Which counted for nothing, of course. Trust means never checking. She might have been having illicit meetings; she'd have had plenty of opportunity. I was often away.

But it wouldn't sit right with me.

It was March now. Eight months since my accident. Two months since I'd awoken from my coma. There was post on the table franked with dates from the previous summer. I couldn't accept that she had not been back to this flat in the meantime. She'd have needed clothes. Even if she had found a new man, she would have had to come home first. Set up a mail redirection service. Let the flat, maybe. You didn't just move from one man's bed to another. Not her.

Which meant what?

I couldn't stop thinking about what Ruth had said about the rapist. He'd taken off after he assaulted her, but she couldn't shake the fear that he was still around. I wondered if there was more to him that being a sex criminal. I wondered if the little boy, Kieran Love, had died at his hand. I wondered about me. The hit-and-run. How much damage could one man do? I thought too about DI Keble. There had been a massive police presence at the bed and breakfast, summoned swiftly. I knew nothing about police procedure, other than what I had gleaned from newspaper articles, and fictional takes, but it seemed a lot for such a small village, such a crime. This was no fresh corpse. This was a skeleton. This was old news, surely, like the skulls dredged from the Second World War hunting grounds of the North Sea.

I thought of Tamara in some shallow grave in the marshes outside the village, frozen solid beneath a thin blanket of soil. Bruises on the skin that would never fade.

I wrote her a note asking her to call me urgently. I left it propped up on the table and was going to the door when my bag snagged on one of the kitchen cupboard handles and pulled it open. I went to shut it and stopped. Inside the cupboard, next to the Weetabix and muesli, was a small box, the size of a toothpaste tube. The word Clearblue was written on the side. A pregnancy test. Its seal had been broken. I stared at it for a long time before hobbling down to the street. I hailed a cab.

'Waar?' the driver asked me.

'Schiphol.'

43

HER FINGERS WERE raw, but The Man had not noticed. Not yet. She didn't understand how he could have missed what she was doing. Perhaps he had seen it after all, and knew that it would come to nothing. She might very well detach herself from the wall, but the door was always locked. She would not get out. So why bother locking her up at all? She reasoned there were two possibilities. He didn't want her going near the door because the building was in a heavily populated area, which meant someone might hear if she screamed. She preferred this avenue of thought. It made sense. They played music to cover the noise, and the bare earth walls would absorb much of the sound she produced. But if she could get up close to that door, no doubt the acoustics beyond would help her voice to carry.

The alternative was that they had to keep her chained to the bed because they didn't want her to see what was behind the curtain.

It was chewing into her mind, that curtain, with its skirt of blue-black mold, like some offbeat grunge addition to bathroom chic, like a curtain she had once seen for sale in an ironic shop that was patterned with bloody red handprints and arterial sprays.

To take her mind off it, she returned to the eye bolt. It was thick, collared, impacted into the wall much farther than it had been intended, its head – the size of a doughnut – battered into the surface. Picking at it had cracked and splintered her nails. Her fingers were bloody and swollen, and returning to the task after a night's sleep was almost incapacitatingly painful, but after forcing herself, after getting back into the habit of picking and prising and teasing, the task grew easier. Not that the bolt was shifting at all. What she'd discovered was that the wall was less secure than the bolt. If she worked at the plaster, she could get to the brick behind it, which was old, crumbly, compromised by decades of dampness and, possibly, flood water.

It was painstakingly slow work, but she relished it. It honed the mind. It shrank everything down to one action, drew her attention away from too many things that could begin to undermine the bolt that kept her fastened to reality, to sanity. When a piece of music was played on the radio that she recognised – she knew Fauré's Pavane, and Lieutenant Kije, and Brahms' Violin Concerto – it helped to dull the pain and blur time; hours would go by and she'd have to suddenly stop working because she would hear the key in the lock, and the footfalls creaking on the wooden steps, pushing before it the smell of her dinner.

She'd shift the pillows so that her work was concealed, all the while aware of the brick dust and the blood on the cotton, certain that The Man was aware too, but he never said a thing, or made to repair the damage she had caused. He stood and watched through his ghastly orange mask, an ecstasy of bug-eyed pouting and ragged breathing, sweat turning the fabric of his coat patchy with dark. She would scoop up the soup or the stew or the risotto, and push away the plate with its blood-printed spoon, wishing she could conceal the cutlery from him and spare her poor hands. But, without fail, he watched her finish each day and he always took everything away that he brought to her.

It was on the morning of the 43rd day in captivity – she did not know what she would do if her watch alarm should stop working – that a third possibility reached out to her from her mind, with its filthy, thin claws. What if The Man was doing nothing to stop her because the time was fast coming when what he was planning would come to fruition? Maybe he knew she would be dead before she managed to work the bolt free.

She intensified her efforts. She dislocated her thumb, but she enjoyed a breakthrough. A chunk of brick the size of an apple fell clear of the bolt and she was able to drag it clear. For a dumb moment, while she stared at it – thick and rusty, its threads impacted with pulverised brick – she didn't know how to proceed: options spread out before her like too many choices on a menu. While she thought, her hands moved to put the bolt back in the wall. She had to throw it away to stop herself. She swung her legs off the bed and felt the ground beneath them for the first time in what felt like years. She was weak, and unsure. She stared at the curtain and moved towards it, but it was as if there were some kind of forcefield around it: two feet shy and she could go no further. Now she knew what she wanted. She wanted never to see what lay behind that thin, horrible barrier. She wanted more than anything to be through the door and out into the world again, where the air was not tinged with the smell of old dinners, or ancient, damp earth, or rat spoors. She wanted to find Paul and love him back to health, to tell him everything. To apologise. To at least give him a way out that was paved with the truth, rather than the sham she had lived in the weeks up to his accident.

She turned away from the curtain, the skin on her back drawing close as if in preparation for a blow, and rushed to the door. She was through it and up the wooden stairs to the door at the top – which was locked, as she had expected – in seconds, her confidence growing, in both her belief that she would be free and her own physicality.

She pressed her face to the jamb, felt the glorious gust of fresh air kiss against it, and screamed hard and long for minutes, until her throat felt stripped raw and the breath in her lungs had turned to dry, desert fumes. She listened above the roar in her chest but could not hear anything. No returning queries. No sounds of a door being broken down. She called out again, trying to remove the trapped animal from it. She asked for help. She asked if anybody could hear her. And then there was a sound. Of a door opening, snagging perhaps on grit, or its own age. And footsteps descending, which killed her, because that meant she was deeper underground than she'd initially thought. And she knew these feet. This was no rescue attempt.

She ran back downstairs. But there was nowhere to go. The room – her room – was a dead end. Then she must grab a weapon, anything to assist her, but the curtain tugged on her reins. There might have been a weapon behind it, but that would mean having to approach it, having to pull it back, and she was not up to that. The fight left her. She climbed back on to the bed and waited for The Man to catch up with her and reshackle her to the wall.

Chapter Thirteen

RISK OF COLLISION

MOVE. MOVE AS fast as you can. Into the terminal and across the polished floor. Up to the ticket desk and there's a flight to Heathrow in an hour-and-a-half. A Qantas connection. A 747-400, for fuck's sake. It's pretty full, but there are seats available. So, 500 passengers, or thereabouts. Nothing else. You have to take it. More trouble at passport control. An interview in a small room; a call to the British Embassy. A quick coffee and a volcanic melted cheese sandwich you take one bite from. You're too full of fear to eat. And as much as you try to read the newspaper, as much as you try to distract yourself in the cloying mists of the duty-free perfume displays, as much as you try to unburden yourself of nerves in a toilet cubicle, there's no getting away from the fact: there are monsters out there on the concrete apron.

The palms of my hands were sweating. This used to be me. This was my life. Airports and uniforms and pre-flight checks and thousands of hours' flying time. I knew my way around a cockpit display blindfolded. I had fighter-pilot reactions. And now I was ruined because of something that had never happened. The lure of the train and the ferry was great, but I had to be back home soon. If Tamara wasn't in Amsterdam, then she was in Southwick, or nearby. She had been by my side all that time in hospital, and then not. How did that happen? It sat uneasily with me, the thought that at the time of her disappearance, Ruth had been raped. DI Keble would want to talk to me. Hopefully he'd see I'd skipped town and have me arrested as soon as I set foot on Surt Road. And that was fine with me, because I wanted to ask him some questions too. Like, what was he doing to try to nail this fuckhead that was attacking women and, maybe, killing children?

I felt better after this. It was the distraction I needed. I splashed my face with cold water and passed through to the departure lounge. I bought a large gin and tonic at the bar and drank it down in three gulps. I made my way to the gate. Passengers were boarding, walking past the corridor I was taking, moving what seemed miles and miles further along the boarding bridge to the stern entrance. Big bird. You forget.

I did not look at it. I did not look at the plane.

I got into my seat and fastened the belt so tight I could hardly move against it. The Jumbo filled up. A woman with a small handbag and a large paperback sat next to me. She gave me a small smile, a kind of 'it'll be all right' smile. I realised how I must look. I felt as though I was sweating myself inside out. All the while, all over the planet, jets were taking off and landing, taking off and landing. No crashes. No collisions. No engine failures.

I suffered an engine failure taking off from Manchester airport once. The portside engine flared out once we'd gone beyond V2. No stopping then. We took off, established that a runway had been cleared for an emergency landing, circled and got down in one piece. We came in on the spicy side, but we managed it. The tyres caught fire. But everyone lived. There were a few injuries, but only as the passengers used the emergency chutes to leave the plane. My pulse hardly increased, I was so caught up in procedure. I'd been trained for it. It was second nature. Now I looked out at the engine nacelles as if they were alien objects.

'Ladies and gentlemen, this is your captain speaking...'

Push back. Taxiing. I imagined the captain and his first officer going over their routine checks. A forty-minute flight. My hands squirmed against each other in my lap. I responded to every sound change in the cabin. I found myself inspecting the wing for missing rivets, or cracks in the infrastructure. I checked the faces of the cabin crew for expressions of concern. The faint smell of exhaust became, to my mind, a raging fire in the belly of the fuselage. We were going to smother in here. The fuel tanks were going to catch and we would become molten, fused with the plastics and metals of all this unholy tonnage.

'I've got to get off,' I said, but I buckled myself in tighter and thought of Tamara. She might be suffering, and if she was, she was suffering a thousand million times more than me.

'Is this your first flight?' the woman next to me asked.

I let out a nervous little laugh, little more than a puff of air. 'You could say that, yes.'

We reached the runway and as we turned into it, I could see there was no queue. Even before the jet had straightened up, I heard the throttles open and I was pressed back into my seat by a giant, invisible hand. The engines roared. Along the road beyond the airport perimeter, cars were parked. Enthusiasts with cameras and binoculars here to enjoy the shuttling of various aircraft. We used to wave at them out of the cockpit window. It never once occurred to me that they might be rubberneckers hoping to see some moment of spectacular carnage.

I said to the woman: 'Do you know that the Wright brothers' flight, that *first* flight ever, the entire duration of it, could have taken place inside this economy section?'

She gave me a forced little smile and went back to her book. I stopped myself from gripping her elbow and screaming into her face.

There are six million parts on this fucker. This fucker has a hundred and seventy miles of wiring inside it. This fucker's tail is as high as a six-storey building. You could park around fifty cars on this fucker's wing. What could go wrong? WHY DOESN'T IT GO WRONG MORE OFTEN?

I reckoned the speed in my mind. Two hundred and fifteen miles per hour. Sixty seconds on a runway over a mile long… I whispered to myself – *rotate* – a moment before the nose lifted.

Nine hundred thousands pounds. Four hundred tons. This. Is. Not. Right.

I tensed for the explosion as the engine parts disintegrated and flashed back through the tail, slicing through the hydraulics, resulting in a catastrophic loss of control. *Brace, brace*. The screams and the piss and the vomit and the fiery end. Sudden hair ignition. Smoke inhalation. I envisaged being a black icon in an air accident report. All passengers and crew killed. Direct thermal assault. *Controlled flight into terrain*. Which meant: smithereens. Which meant: unidentifiable body parts. *Oh God, oh my Christ*.

A hand on my shoulder. The flight attendant. She was smiling. 'Are you all right? Can I get you a drink?' I wondered if all the cabin crew have those smiles impacted on to their faces, a part of the job requirement when they join the airline. Did the tinkickers pull their Joker faces from the disaster sites? Tamara didn't smile like this. She smiled when something pleased her. Her smile was natural; it touched the eyes. It touched everything.

I nodded. I asked for two G&Ts and a beer and washed it down with a dozen various painkillers. By the time we crossed into British airspace I was starting to nod off.

A loud bang jolted me out of it. The woman next to me had dropped her book. Her hand was a white claw on the headrest of the seatback in front of her. Her eyes were wide and restless, hunted, like a small animal's. Flames were tricking from the exhaust of engine number two on the port side, through what appeared to be a solid column of black smoke. There were noises of distress rising all over the cabin. No screams, yet. Whimpers, yelps, moans. The screams would come. People were glancing at each other as if searching for permission to do so.

The cabin crew were flitting around the aisles, trying to get people to calm down, saying that everything was in control and panicking would not help. I caught the wrist of the woman who had served me my drinks and told her I was a pilot and could I help? She squeezed my hand and held up a finger, then she hurried up to the cockpit.

I studied the engine. The condition had not worsened. Beyond the smoke I could see the north-easterly bulge of Norfolk. I imagined the plane turning into an unrecoverable bank and becoming a part of that countryside. Microscopic parts of me would embed themselves in the soil on those tilled fields. In time my molecules would fuse with the skin of potatoes or swedes, and they into me. In time I would become part of a roast dinner.

The flight attendant tapped me on the arm.

She whispered in my ear: 'Captain Purley would be grateful if you'd go up to the cockpit.'

As I was staggering up the aisle – not sweating now, no nerves, I was actually excited... I was psyched about getting back into a cockpit with fellow fliers – the captain made an announcement.

'Ladies and gentlemen, as I'm sure you're aware, we've encountered a slight problem with our flight this afternoon. May I reassure you that we are in control of the situation. However, we are diverting to Luton airport. Please ensure that you have your seatbelts fastened. It's likely that the landing will be on the rough side, but I'll remind you that we are trained for incidents like this and there's nothing to worry about. I'll talk to you again just before we make our final approach. Thank you.'

I knocked on the door and it opened inwardly. The cockpit was empty. I sat down in the left-hand seat and throttled up the port-side engine to full power. The plane yawed violently to the right. I took hold of the column and pulled as hard as I could, taking the plane into a sudden, twisting climb. The stall warning came on. I got out of the seat and staggered from the cockpit. People were screaming. People were vomiting. I saw a man trying to kill himself by stabbing himself in his own eye with a plastic knife. An insensate flight attendant with a bloodied face was flailing around the cabin ceiling like something without bones.

There was something in the cabin with us. It moved like ink in water, or fleet shadows on hot sand. You couldn't fasten it with your eye. It knew when someone was trying to look at it; it was as if its skin was reactive to light, or maybe it was fashioned in such a way as to disallow the angle of reflected light to meet the planes necessary to hit the retina. It was fascinating to watch, or to almost watch.

There were six children that I could see in this portion of economy. The shadow passed close by one of them and then there were five, without me being able to see exactly what had happened. The child was still there, kind of, but it was sagged into its seat as if it was apeing the bag of its clothes. I was reminded of something my mum used to say to me, if we were unlucky enough to get a tough bunch of chops from the butcher. 'Chew the goodness from the meat,' she'd say. 'Then spit out what's left.'

I thought I caught a fleeting understanding of what the Craw was, but it was chancy, dervish-like, dancing out of reach, much like its physicality.

And then there were four.

I stared down into the blank eye-holes of a child who could barely have been five years old. He was slouched in his seat like a pair of pyjamas that are in danger of losing themselves to the crack in a sofa. Boned. The jelly sucked clean of him.

Chew the goodness out of it.

I opened the passenger door and stared at the horizon as it became the verizon. And the light spilled and bent and warped into and around the fuselage as if it had become liquid. There was a loud crack and a grin appeared in the side of the cabin. A port-side engine sheared away from its cowling and thundered through the empennage, turning it to dust. The jet wailed as if in pain.

I could see the land as it swept south. If I concentrated I thought I could see the gleam of the lighthouse in Southwick, and the sweeping pattern of the pebbles as they were pushed on to the beach from the seichs that sloshed through the shallow pan of water in the North Sea.

Home at last, I thought. And stepped out of the plane.

'SIR? WAKE UP, sir. Or you'll have the cleaners hoovering under your feet.'

I snapped awake and, like a child plucked from a nightmare who is filled with fear and suspicion, waiting to see if the person who has rescued him will morph back into the monster, stared at the Australian flight attendant leaning over me. She was young and clear-skinned. Blue eyes and freckles. Short blonde hair. She didn't look right in that swirly silvery blue dress. She ought to be wearing denim short shorts and a halter top. Damp hair and tanning oil, fresh from the beach. I felt old and used and crumpled just looking at her.

The cabin was empty. There was no gaping crack in the fuselage. Through the window I could see Terminal 3 and the control tower. I apologised and stood up, feeling the muscles of my back leap and shiver away from the bonded column of bones, the stiff, unresponsive thing I had become. I politely waved away her offer of help and headed for the exit as the cleaning crew were coming in, encumbered by their equipment. Before I ducked between them, I cast a look back at the cabin, half-expecting to see something dark slide across the ceiling, or the carpet, and hunker in the shadows of the galley, waiting for the influx of new passengers. But I saw only the flight attendant checking the aisles.

I was ushered through passport control – no problems this time – enjoying the beautiful feel of firm ground beneath my feet, but trying to hurry, as if the sky-sized nightmare of what I'd just been through, what I'd just *achieved*, might prove too great for me and, the fear, like a planet, would trap me in its gravity for ever. Two, three, four hundred miles away from this airport could never be enough. Never again, I thought, wiping the sweat off my face. Never.

I caught the tube to Liverpool Street, barely conscious of how I had changed lines to reach it. I bought a ticket for the train heading to Lowestoft and waited on the platform and got on. I thought of Tamara all the way. There might have been other passengers on board. I didn't know. I didn't care.

I got off at Darsham and caught a cab. I fell asleep in the back and then the driver was prodding me and for an awful moment I thought I was back on the 747, being wakened by the flight attendant, and that this final leg of the journey was still ahead of me. But then I was standing on Surt Road and it was cold and the air was congealing around me and smelling of surf and hops and smoked fish and it was as if I had never been away.

And I didn't know what to do. Southwick was a small village, but now I was daunted by every place that Tamara might be. There were sheds and attics and garages and forgotten back rooms and plenty of duct tape.

Eventually I drummed up the courage to sneak along North Parade to see if there was any more activity at Tam's Place, but the mobile police unit was gone, as was the police tape. I might have gone to check on the building itself if it wasn't for the two men sitting in the black car outside. It might not have been plain clothes policemen waiting for my return, but I didn't want to chance it. Not yet. I went back to the bookshop and checked to see if Ruth had left a message for me. Nothing there.

I went to Amy's place and rang the bell for an age but the pale orb of her face did not materialise behind the warped, fractured glass in the front door. I went back to the beach and saw her immediately. She was staring out to sea again. I approached, trying to be quiet on the shingle, but it was impossible. I didn't want to startle her. I didn't want her to whirl around and fix me with those granite eyes of hers, shocked wide, too wide. She didn't turn around. She said something, maybe hello, but it was lost to the wind so I just saw her mouth move. Her hat was askew on her head; I could see the scar reaching down from under the edge like a fat, purple finger stroking the side of her face. She seemed thinner than I remembered, though I'd only seen her a few days previously.

'You all right?' I asked her.

'I'm okay,' she said. 'You?'

'Not so good. I can't find my girlfriend.'

'Where did you last see her?'

I laughed a little at that, despite the situation. She had a nice sense of humour, Amy, although she didn't seem to be aware of it.

'What's been happening?' I asked. I stared back towards the main road and the houses overlooking the beach. I could see the top window of Tam's Place. It was smeared with dirt and rain and the reflection of dark clouds, as if trying to gather as much obscuring material as possible to prevent what went on inside that room from being seen.

'You mean the body they found? In your bed and breakfast?'

'Have you heard anything?'

'They reckon he's been hiding out in there.'

'Who?'

Now she looked at me as if I was an alien. Or someone who had woken up from a long sleep. Maybe she realised that and softened somewhat. 'The killer,' she said.

'How do they know that?'

She shrugged and turned her attention back to the waves. The sea was the colour of steel. 'They found evidence of habitation. Plates with food on them. A kettle plugged into a wall. A box of tea.'

I bridled at the thought of a killer, a rapist, a kidnapper brewing tea in my building while Tamara cooled in a hole in the woods. Sipping Typhoo while he thought of which child to claim next. I thought of him putting his feet up and listening to the waves while Tamara struggled in a room, shackled and gagged, something for him to dip in and out of, like a book of short stories, like a hobby.

What if…

'Where are you going?'

I ignored her and marched towards Tam's Place. Maybe the police hadn't checked every room. Maybe Tamara was in there. I hadn't gone through all the rooms the other night. They might not have gone into the cellar. There was so much junk down there, why would you?

Just full of boxes, Sarge. I can hardly get my leg over.

Well don't tell your wife that, son. Get back up here, then. We'll tick it off the list.

How it might have gone. While he was sitting down there with a shotgun in one hand and Tamara's mouth under the other. *Shh. Quiet as a mouse.*

'Paul! Don't. Come with me. I want you to see something. I want you to come with me.'

I ignored her. I got as far as slipping the key into the lock before they came up behind me and told me to get into the car, there was someone who wanted a word. For a moment I considered resisting, but their hands on my arms were big and strong, and I was so weak. I was matchsticks.

Amy came too. We sat in the back of the unmarked squad car and ten minutes later we were sitting in an office in the police station. There was a photograph of a woman on the desk. Smiling. Happy. Miles from here.

DI Keble came in. He was humming a tune, something I recognised from my childhood but couldn't put my finger on. He unburdened his pockets of a wallet, a notebook, a tube of mints, a bunch of keys: put them all in his in-tray.

'I do that,' he said, as if anybody gave a shit, 'because the paper that gets put in there comes out so fast it almost shreds itself in mid-air. I don't like an untidy in-tray. I don't like...' he turned to face us. 'Pen-ding.'

He held up a file. 'This is pen-ding,' he said. 'This is waiting for action.'

'What is it?' I asked.

'This is child deaths. Kieran Love. And the thinnish boy we found in your chi-chi dirty weekender. Harry Parker. Six years old it turns out. He went missing a couple of years ago. I'd like to put this file in the out-tray. I'd like to stamp it with MISSION ACCOMPLISHED. I don't want to have to hand it over to the upper echelons while I stand there, picking trousers out of my arse and saying *I'm stuck sir, sorry sir.*'

'I want to report a missing person,' I said.

'Right,' he said, sitting down and putting the file, with a wince, back in his in-tray. 'Right you are, sir. I'll get my top men on it. They haven't got anything better to do. Just a couple of unsolved child murders but... fuck 'em, hey? It was probably their fault. Stupid little bastards getting separated from Mum. Not been taught the whole 'stranger danger' thing yet. Maybe a friendly old man with some ice creams in his hand. Want to see some puppies? Want to come and play with my toy trains? And in the car and off we go and hey, look at the bright side of it, you'll never have to worry about going to school and going to work and getting married to some bitch.'

'Her name is Tamara Dziuba,' I said, ignoring him. 'That's D-Z-I...'

He held up his hand and started writing on a notepad. He showed it to me. 'Like that?'

The note read: *FUCK YOU.*

'Professional,' Amy said.

'And who might you be?'

'I'm helping him.'

Keble stared at us both from under the brim of his hat, his heavy-lidded eyes penduluming between us as if he were watching a lazy tennis match. 'You look as though you both forgot to get out of the car before it fell into the crusher.'

'Are you going to arrest me for something?' I asked him. 'Because if not, I'm leaving. I'm going to talk to some real policemen who have got time for a missing person.'

'Oh, sit down Paul. We've all got time for a missing person. Plenty of time. We'll play anagrams with her name while we wait for her to turn up. I'm more interested in these dead kids. And why you fucked off out of town when I told you to stay put.'

'I was looking for Tamara. That takes precedence,

for me at least... Look, I'm as sick as anyone else about Kieran, and this other child – '

'Harry.'

'Harry. Yes, it's awful. But a, it was nothing to do with me – '

'It's what they all say.'

' – And b, there's nothing I can do about it.'

'You could confess.'

'You think I did it, you arrest me.'

We were both getting red in the face. His mask was slipping. I could see how torn up about all of this he was. He was probably coming under a lot of pressure from his bosses to feel a collar. I said: 'If we were at school, this would be called bullying. Just because you have no suspects...'

'Oh, I have at least one suspect.'

'You think I could kill a child? I can barely cut up a roast chicken, Keble. I'm a mess.'

'Yeah, and some quadriplegics play football in the park right after they've picked up their disability benefits.'

'So you can't help me with Tamara?'

He shrugged. 'You can do what everyone else who reports a misper does. Fill a form in. We'll take it from there.'

'And what about this killer. This rapist. Where are you on that?'

'Rapist?'

I found myself wishing I could disappear into the cracks in this cheap plastic seat. Amy was looking at me too. Ruth hadn't reported it. Shit.

'It sounds as if you know all kinds of surprising information, Paul,' he said.

'What else is a killer, if he isn't a rapist?' I said.

'Oh, you have a philosophical angle on all this too? I'm not *that* busy, I suppose. I *could* sit here and listen to you for hours.'

'How about my accident?' I asked him. He frowned.

'Your accident?'

I pointed at my face with both index fingers. 'You think I got this looking in the mirror?'

'Beg pardon,' he said, 'but this isn't information exchange day. I dragged you in here for questioning. *You* tell *me* what you know.'

I chewed my lip for a while. 'A friend of mine, Ruth Fincher – '

'I know Ruth.'

' – she was raped. She thinks the person who did it is still around. So do I. He could have been responsible for my accident. He could be responsible for Tamara's abduction.'

'Hold on, kidder,' Keble said. 'Rapists, kidnappers… it's a big leap from someone who was merely missing a minute ago.'

'Did you search the B&B?' I asked. 'I mean, really search it?'

'Top to bottom. Why, any nasty little secret passages you not telling us about?'

I sighed, shook my head. 'I just… I suppose it was wishful thinking. I thought he might be there. This rapist. This attacker. He might have kidnapped Tamara and was… I don't know… keeping her there. He might have planted that body to distract me, to keep me off the scent.'

'You're worse than a conspiracy theorist, you are,' he said.

'Maybe I'm just doing your job for you,' I said. 'Maybe I'm making connections that you'll make, eventually. You know, infinite chimps and typewriters, all that.'

He looked as though he might react badly and I thought I'd pushed my luck too far, but then he laughed; short, gruff, a tension releaser.

'I've been through the files,' he said, and he reached for his Pending tray again, pulled out a manila folder without looking at the label on the front. 'There's not much to pass on, I'm afraid. You were the victim of a hit-and-run, yes. All we had was a report of a black Land Rover Defender.' He fingered past a couple of pages. 'No registration number reported. No description that might help us locate it. It was going fast and it was heading south. That's all. And it probably didn't have bull bars. Or you'd be dead, most likely.'

He put the file away. It was very thin. He steepled his fingers. Looked at me from under the brim of his hat. 'Now tell me more about this rapist.'

'I don't know any more. Ruth told me he was passing through. A drifter maybe, looking for work.'

'A hitcher?'

'Maybe. But maybe he stole a car. This car.'

'We've had no reports of a stolen car that matches this description.'

'You might check.'

'It would be in your file,' he said. 'Something to check up on. We're like that, the police. We check up, follow leads.'

'So what are you saying? I'm lying? Ruth's lying? She's pregnant by this bastard.' I felt hemmed in, but it was not the usual imprisonment imposed by my too-tight skin, my realigned bones. I needed to be outside. Every second playing bullshit whiff-whaff with this clown was another second in which Tamara might be suffering.

'In my experience, murderers don't become rapists. And if they're rapists first, they're unlikely to move on to murder, but if they do, they're likely to rape first. And Kieran Love was not raped.'

'So you're saying we've got two violent criminals on the loose here?'

'I'd say one. I'd say that Ruth's rapist is long gone. And if she'd thought to report it, he might be behind bars by now.'

'So what now?'

'You go home. And concentrate on getting well.'

'I'm not a suspect?'

'No. You're a pest. But not a suspect. Which is not to say I won't be keeping an eye on you.'

'What about the children?' Amy asked. The question blurted out of her. It was like the stopper being removed from a bottle of shaken soda.

Keble sighed. It was the sound effect equivalent of *what now?*

'The bones, the skulls that were retrieved from the wrecks. What of them?'

'They're being carbon dated. They're not recent.'

'Doesn't mean there wasn't a crime committed.'

'Well our path man said they were pre-19th century. So whoever did it, well, I'm not going to dig him up and bring him in and ask him if he wants sugar with his tea. Sleeping dogs and all that.'

Amy stood up sharply, her calves barking against

the lip of her chair, forcing it back on the cheap lino floor. I wasn't sure if it was the chair leg, or Amy, or indeed Keble, that had squealed. 'Those children were murdered. Their parents did it. Something has to be done or –'

'What? Why?'

'I tell you something has to be done otherwise –'

'Sit down, Amy.'

'*Otherwise* –'

'Amy...'

'*It will happen again. It is happening again.*' She was screaming. I stood up and caught her arm. She was so tense I thought a piece of her might break off in my fist. I led her to the door and thankfully she didn't resist. I walked her through the reception and out on to the street. I flagged a taxi and we drove back to Southwick in silence.

Chapter Fourteen

BRYNING'S PIT

AMY PARKED HER Mini on the gravel in front
of a wooden café. Neither of us were hungry. A
determined couple in bright red fleeces were eating
chips from a polystyrene tray. The wind was such
that both of them were keeping the tray pinned
to the table with their hands. They ignored a dog
sitting on the floor beside them, staring forlornly
at their meal. I watched its tail wag. Every time the
man, or woman, lifted a chip from the tray, the tail
would freeze as if in anticipation of a treat.

'That's a form of cruelty,' I said.

'Maybe they fed it before they came out,' Amy
said. 'Maybe it's not even their dog.'

'Still…' I said. 'One chip.'

'How are you feeling?'

I looked at her. She was assessing me, like a doctor
searching for signs of disease. I guessed I appeared
as shaken by our episode at the police station as she
did. 'I'm all right,' I said. 'Keble's just a showman.
And a bully. I'm sorry you had to be a part of that.
You didn't have be, you know.'

'He needed to be told,' Amy said. Now she turned
her attention back to the café. To our left, the gravel
had been built up into a kind of wall; perhaps it had

been designed like that to protect this makeshift car park from stormy seas. Or maybe the wind had shaped it so. A tide clock indicated the times for high and low tide. There were no other cars here.

'Come on,' she said.

I struggled to get the door open. The wind kept trying to slam it shut again. Maybe it was trying to save me from what we were about to do. I followed her to the shingle and we hobbled over the rise to the spread of the beach. To our left, maybe two or three miles away, I could see the lighthouse in Southwick as it flashed its warnings out to sea. The tide seemed to be dragging the night sky into the village. Darkness was coming on quickly. Amy noticed it too.

'We don't have much time,' she said.

The dunes grew as we trudged south. Couch grass and marram bound them together to a point where the sand was disguised altogether. Rocks reared up ahead, pleated like a grey cloak.

'That where we're going?' I asked.

Amy nodded. Her breath was coming in stiff little stitches now. The terrain was affecting us both. The stones were loosely packed and kept falling away from each footstep. There was no feeling of firmness beneath, as if the shingle were suspended over an eternity of space; the camber of the beach was working against us. By the time we got to the rocks, the sky was a deep blue-green, as if it were trying to take on the colour of the sea. The cave resembled an open wound in this light. A large, dark stain on the sand in front of it could only have been sea water, but it resembled oil, or blood. The place was like an accident site. There ought to be ambulances. Police cordons. Helicopters. I didn't like it at all, and I said so.

'I have to show you,' she said. 'You have to see.'

She'd pulled a large Mag-Lite torch from her coat pocket. She switched it on and focused the beam, trained it on the mouth of the cave. Crabs skittered across the rocks. The gaping cave entrance was untouched by the light. It was absorbing it, sucking it out of existence, bending it like a black hole, unwilling to allow us to see what lay inside.

'They came here in 1772,' Amy said.

'Who did?'

'The parents. And again, a hundred years later. And they were meant to come here in 1972 as well. But something happened. There was no sacrifice that year.'

'Sacrifice?' It was difficult to pay attention to what she was saying and pick a route through the folds of rock at the same time. If I lost my footing here, it might set my recovery back months.

'There's strong death... I don't know what to call them... echoes? Stains? Something, anyway. There's something giving me the mother of all headaches whenever I go near this place. So the other day I went inside.'

The rocks increased in size. I was spending so much time navigating a route around them that I hardly looked up at the great, wet O of the cave entrance. The rock was like old flesh, damp and grey, hanging in wrinkles and creases as if it had melted and then hardened. I felt loath to touch it in case it had the same moist, springy feel of perspiring skin.

'Who was being sacrificed?' I asked, as much to distract myself from that horrible yawning entrance. 'Why?'

'Children, of course,' she said. 'Why do you think there are so few around here?'

'They're all being killed?' I stopped, shocked. I thought of Kieran Love and Harry Parker. How many more? I didn't want to go in there with her. I imagined the bodies of children – bulldozer loads – packed up against the walls, stalagmites rising from their cold, blue skin.

'No,' she said, and she stopped too, to catch her breath. I didn't know what was worse: keeping an eye on the cave myself, or seeing her standing before it, like some crumb that the mouth had temporarily missed. I saw the shadows of sharp rocks beyond the entrance, rows of them, like the inward curving teeth of a shark. 'But if they were here? Who knows? I think the families have left here, and stayed away. This is no place to bring up a child.'

We entered the cave. The temperature plummeted. Amy's torchlight, so bright when shone in the face, was incapable of picking out much detail in here.

'What's this place called?' I asked.

'Bryning's Pit,' she said.

'Sounds charming. There are better words, I'd have thought. Aperture. Opening. Cave, for God's sake. Why can't people just call things what they are?'

'There are worse words,' she said.

'Who's Bryning?'

'No idea,' she said. 'Person who found it? Dug it out? Died here? Some guy. Some girl.'

We concentrated on one foot in front of the other, until our eyes grew accustomed to the dark, and our feet felt a little more confident. 'How do you know about 1972?' I asked. 'You said they were *meant* to come here?'

She was staring at the rock, feeling it with her fingers, really digging into its crevices, as if she might find something tucked in there, like the prayers to God posted at the Wailing Wall. She seemed to suddenly remember my question. 'It's like those circles in a tree that's been chopped down. Age rings? I feel the same... space between events. Big shock in 1672. Another hit a hundred years later. Ditto 1872. And then... not a blip. Not here, anyway. Kieran Love? Harry Parker? Yes. Hard impacts to the gut. But... *different* here. There was desperation behind it. Not the same. There was a calmness too. It was as if...'

She tailed off, and I thought she might have closed down, like a robot whose power cell has drained, or whether her pain had come back, thick and hard, cutting off her train of thought. Her eyes streamed. Could be cold. Could be pain. Could be memories.

'Amy?'

'It was as if these deaths here in the cave...' She took a deep breath. 'It was as if the people – the children – who died... *wanted* to die.'

We moved deeper into the cave. Whenever I looked back towards the entrance – the exit – I felt a brief pang of panic; the sky seemed to be getting darker out there. I was worried that it might degrade to the point where cave mouth and sky were indistinguishable. If we got lost in here and the tide came crashing in, we were finished. I thought maybe it was some kind of optical illusion. Perhaps a consequence of the eye coming to terms with the gloom inside the cave was that the outside appeared darker than it actually was. I hoped so, anyway, as Amy drew us deeper beneath the Suffolk earth.

She actually said, at that moment, or rather, muttered: 'Suffolk earth. Suffolk hate.' The acoustics were so good that I could hear every scrape of her feet. I thought I could hear her breathing. I thought I could hear the triphammer of her heart. Or it might have been mine. The beam of light picked out insane shapes in the rock. Moments of shocking pareidol that the mind rejected almost as soon as it had assimilated them. Creations made of rock and shadow that ought to have remained in the dark. But it was just rock, after all. I had to keep telling myself that.

'Hang on a minute,' I said. I reached out a hand for the torch. 'What's that up there?'

I'd seen something gleam, a reflection from the torchlight as Amy ranged it around the jagged rock. My teeth were gritted together, hard. I hoped it wasn't eyeshine, light reflected from the retina of some near blind beast that, even now, was tasting us in the air with its salivary glands. Some kind of bat. Something worse. It was that kind of cave. It was a cave to rattle the child in you.

'It looks like some kind of bracket,' I said, once I'd played the beam on its length. It was a rod of some sort, bolted crudely into the rock. There was a cup at the top.

279 Conrad Williams 279

'Gaslight,' Amy said. 'Victorian. Don't worry, we're on the right path. I'd find this place in pitch dark.'

There were more brackets, some with, some without the rods that had held the gaslamps. Soot from long-extinguished flames speckled the rock above them. There were other shreds of evidence of human presence here, although not nearly so old. Takeaway coffee cartons, a page from an atlas, a single glove lying in the wet like something boneless and dead. I found a walking stick propped up at a fork in the cave. Perhaps it had been used as a marker. We used it too.

Now the acoustics were changing, or something was changing them: interference up ahead. It wasn't long before I had to raise my voice to be heard above it. It sounded like trapped thunder. We turned a corner and the beam from the torch disappeared.

'My God,' I heard myself say. It was like stepping out over a precipice. I felt suddenly sick with the impact of it, and could no longer trust the feeling of firm ground beneath my feet. I felt as if we were falling and had to reach out. I found Amy's hand and gripped it.

There was weak ambient light in this open space, this cathedral of stone. I couldn't work out where it was coming from. Perhaps it was being generated by the rock itself, or by the torrent of white water tipping from the ceiling, hundreds of feet above. It was enough, at least, to see that we had emerged into a huge chamber. There was a lake being fed by the waterfall. Off to our right there was either an echo of that storm of water, or there was a second fall, taking the lake's overflow even deeper into the ground.

'There,' Amy called out. She was pointing at a rock that stood by the edge of the lake. There was something odd about it, something different. Unlike the other formations, this one seemed smoother in places, and darker too.

'This is where it happened. Every century.'

'What?' I asked. But I didn't want to know. 'I think we should go. My feet... I'm sure it's wetter on the floor than it was. I'm worried about the tide.'

'Sacrifice,' Amy said. Her voice seemed awe-filled, as if she could grasp the logic of such an act. 'Look.' She trained the torchlight on the underside of the rock. Iron manacles had been driven into it. They had corroded badly, but not to the point where you couldn't tell what they were. Above the stump of rock, visible on the cave ceiling, was a broad, treacly patch.

'More soot,' Amy said. 'Lots of it. This is where they did it, Paul. This is where those children died, where they were burned.'

'To what end?'

A shape reared up to the left. I shouted and stepped back, felt the cave wall like fingers digging into me, testing me for tenderness. It was as if one of the faces I'd seen in these ancient crevices had come to life. I was getting ready to run, certain we were going to be attacked, when it breathed, it spoke, and I recognised him.

'To pacify. To appease. The Craw. It sleeps. But then. Every century. It wakes. It needs. We must. If not. The village. Will sink. Like Dunwich. Everyone drowns.'

Jake came closer.

I started speaking, as much to try to stop his approach. I didn't like his being here. I didn't really like him. 'What do you mean, everyone drowns?'

'The Craw. It takes. But also. It protects. Without it. We die.'

'But there was nobody sacrificed in 1972,' Amy said.

'You know?' Jake asked. Even in the dark I could tell he was taken aback by her statement. A change in his voice, a halting sound to his step.

'She knows,' I said. 'Trust me. So explain that. Explain why we aren't up to our throats in fish and seawater.'

'Interim measures,' he said. 'Trickledown oblation. Subtle rituals.'

'Do you speak a language other than cock?' Amy asked.

'Ask him,' Jake said. '*He* knows.'

And I did. Of course, I did. It was in the boxes I'd been burning. All those unidentifiable organic nuggets and spurs, the photographs and letters. Everything drenched in hope and belief and good old human DNA. I was the stop-gap, or rather, the agent delivering these piss-poor substitutes. The Craw was all things to all men. Yes, it was the grievous booty in the boxes left for me to destroy, and a psychological golem created from the fear-clay of all these villagers' phobias. But the Craw was as much mine as theirs. The Craw was the shattered bird and the claw marks on the beach. The Craw was the disease, or the lack in me, the thing that was missing, that allowed me to see the awful repercussions from the near miss had it been an actual collision. The Craw was Flight Z.

'Bad place,' I said.

Jake nodded. 'Bad place.'

'But it's not working,' I said.

'It doesn't. Seem so.'

'What about Kieran Love?' I asked. 'What about Harry Parker? Don't they count?'

'Desperate measures,' Jake said. 'Didn't work. Not native.'

'Then what?' Amy asked.

'You have to wait another hundred years,' I said, pleaded, even. 'Twenty-one twelve.'

Jake's head shook. 'Look around. The weather. The water. Storm coming. Bad things. Moves are. Afoot here.'

I had him in my fists before I realised what I was doing. Amy tried to pull me back but all that happened was that we lost our footing and went down against the jagged edges and the growing puddles of water.

'What do you know?' I hissed at him. This close, he smelled of dry paper and brass polish. Under it I detected notes from the endless drab lunches that he filched from his carrier bags. The sardine paste, the processed cheese squares, the pickle, the egg. I remembered what he'd said to me: *Helped us. Burned shit.* I wondered what it was I'd burned of his. Evidence, maybe. Something that would connect him to the deaths of Kieran and Harry. Something that could lead me to Tamara. 'You know Tamara? You know where she is? Because if you do and you're keeping it quiet… if you've got her… I'll… I'll fucking kill you.'

'The Craw. Needs offerings. Desires flesh.'

'Where is she?'

'I don't. Don't know.'

'Then what are you talking about?'

'The Craw. Demands flesh.'

'Then give him yours!' I pushed him away and hobbled back to the mouth of the cave, my fingers itching with the need to damage something. Amy caught up with me and we walked without talking, volleying terse, laboured breaths. I kept my eyes on the ground and my hands in my pockets. I didn't care if Jake was following us or stayed put in the cave. He could lose himself in there and die for all I cared.

Amy drove us back to her flat. Once we were inside, I made her a cup of tea and we sat down on the sofa.

'Something went on in this village,' she said. 'There've been deaths here. The police don't want to know because it's ancient history.'

'Keble's hands are tied. You heard him. What's he going to do? Arrest somebody's great grandchild?'

'Children were murdered by their own parents. Something to do with Winter Bay, with the battle there. I think the villagers saw the battle as the end of the world. They'd never seen anything like it before. Fire on the water. Bodies washed up on the beach. Their children stolen in the night by invaders. Maybe soldiers who wanted to rid the place of future generations of opposition. Neutralise the threat. The villagers equated, or confused, the terror of the battle with the loss of their families. A dragon, an erlking, a bogeyman came to steal their young. Who would want that to happen again? And so this myth was born. The Craw. Someone suggested an offering. It worked. No more children were taken in 1772. The village was not submerged. So it went on. And another sacrifice would have happened in 1972 – *should* have happened – but something went wrong.'

'Or went right.'

'How do you mean?'

I shrugged. 'Maybe the Craw had been satisfied a century earlier. Maybe the villagers didn't need to deliver any more children.'

She shook her head. 'I don't think so. It almost went ahead. There *was* a massing in that cave thirty years ago, a grand congregation. I felt it so strongly it was as if I was being jostled in a crowd. It was *meant* to happen. But there was a hitch.'

'The child didn't want to die? Or there was a parent who stepped in? Halted the whole thing from going ahead?'

'That's what I was thinking,' she said. 'That works for me.'

Her flat was a mess. Photocopied sheets of paper were scattered across the floor. All of her files had been stacked against the walls. There were books on Southwick's history, its people, its traditions and wars, and more general biographies of Suffolk piled up next to her favourite spot on the sofa. A notebook, half-filled with scribbles, loose leaves, references, Post-it notes. There was an Ordnance Survey map of the area pinned to the wall above her desk. Green pins scattered across the sea and the sand and the towns.

'I can't help you,' I said. 'It's important, I know. To you and the village. The truth is important. But I've got to straighten out a lot of things. I've got to find Tamara. And I've got to come to terms with who I am now. What I am. I've changed, I don't recognise myself any more, and I need to be able to deal with it. I need to find things out for myself.'

She nodded, finished her tea. 'Where will you start?'

'I don't know. Maybe I'll start with where it ended. The accident site. Maybe I'll find some clue that the police missed. I doubt they even did a thorough search. You think, a hit-and-run, someone makes a mistake and then gets scared, pisses off. You don't think hit-and-run because the guy wanted to actually *kill* you. I have to believe that now. I have to follow the hunch that he tried to kill me, and that he's got Tamara.'

'I dream of falling,' she said after a few moments of calm. 'More and more. I actually look forward to going to sleep. Falling asleep. When I fell, those few seconds… I felt more free, more alive than I've ever done before.'

She turned away from me and began leafing through one of her books. I left the room and went out into the street. It was cold, still, but there was something in the night, some granularity, some paleness. Something that took the edge off the rawness in the wind.

Spring was coming.

PART THREE

THE MONKEY'S FIST

Chapter Fifteen

THE NUCHIAL LOOP

I'M IN MY hospital bed. I'm still deep in my coma.
But I'm watching myself, as if I'm some disembodied
spirit escaped my corporeal self for a while. A bit of
a break from the breathing in and the breathing out.
The stutter of the heart. The spoiled limbs. Ghosts
don't limp. Ghosts don't have to worry about
myocardial infarctions any more. I could get used
to this.

I'm remembering something that happened, just
before the near-miss. A weekend away with Tamara
at an Isle of Skye hotel in the shadow of the Quiraing
Mountain. We were tired out from a long, long drive,
one shift from Camden – hitting the road at the
crack of dawn – to the hotel, and it was closing in
on midnight. The staff managed to find us some pea
and ham soup and a half bottle of wine. We bolted it
down and showered, then shared the wine wrapped
in bedclothes, looking out at the fantastic darkness
and all the stars and the kyloe in the fields, their long
horns gleaming in the moonlight. The shower and the
food had revived us. Tamara shrugged free from me
and, clad only in a pair of dazzling white knickers,
performed a *hopek* – a traditional Ukrainian dance –
on the grass in front of our hotel room. I was laughing

so hard I thought I might trip over the blankets and go crashing through the French windows. But I was also fired up with lust for her. She was so beautiful. Such a sexy, unselfconscious woman. We didn't even make it over the threshold back into our room. She smelled of ozone. She was so hot and clean I could have cried.

The door cracks open. Ruth stands in the gap staring down at my withered, pathetic body. She's wearing her crisp, freshly-ironed uniform. She hisses and rasps as she moves towards the bed. She puts a hand on my forehead, and up here, shivering against the ceiling, I feel it. Cool, dry, comforting. *Thanks*, I say, and she tilts her head slightly, as if she heard something. She checks the life support machine. She checks my notes. She turns and locks the door. She drops the blinds. She undresses me. She undresses herself. Her abdomen is tightening with the baby. Three months now. Maybe four. Her breasts are growing. Her nipples are a deep, chocolate brown. Her skin glows.

She wrenches my withdrawn limbs away from my centre. She straddles me, impales herself upon me. She rides me and I watch from the ceiling, feeling every stroke.

I fade. I'm going back to my body. But I can see now that there's no body to go back to. I see a tuft of hair, some pale fingers sucked into the Y at the top of her legs. She finishes and wipes herself clean and dismounts. She pats her distended belly and gets dressed. I stare down at the wet, empty bed and the scream stays inside me because there is no mouth to release it.

* * *

I WOKE UP convulsing, gasping for a breath that my lungs seemed incapable of drawing. My eyes were filling with black grains and it was only when I fell from the sofa on to the floor and the breath flew out of me that I realised I'd been doing nothing but inhaling and it was all trapped inside me. I sat there with my head in my hands, trying to calm down. I chased the feeling deep inside me, wondering if it might give me some clue as to why my dreams were so filled with death, with the utter destruction of the body, but I could only recognise hunger behind it. I laughed – a bitter little shock of air – and pulled on my coat, walked the fifty metres or so to the village fishmonger, suddenly, strangely ravenous for seafood.

It was a good shop, scrupulously clean, with attentive staff; I ate stuff from this place maybe three or four times a week. But something about the shop was off today. The fish smelled past its best. There were tiny holes in the swordfish steaks and I thought of worms burrowing into the flesh. The John Dory, like a grey dinner plate in the centre of the display, was drying out, its eyes shrunken and opaque. A fly danced across the carapace of a crab.

I was about to leave – forget dinner, I'd have a slice of toast and Marmite – when the fishmonger asked me what I wanted to get my hooks into.

'What's good?' I asked, feigning enthusiasm, and he gestured at a tray of squid. Unlike everything else, it looked fresh and bright, as if it would start swimming again if only it had some water to be dunked into. I selected one and asked if he could prepare it for me.

'I can't right now,' he said. 'I've cracked my wrist and my apprentice is late. He's on his way in if you want to wait.' He held up his hand to show me the cast that sheathed it.

I shook my head. 'How hard can it be?' I said.

He shook his head too. 'Not very. It's just a bit... strange.'

I took my white paper parcel back to Ruth's house and found a note from her in the kitchen: *Yoga! CU later. x*

Thunder coming. You can just hear it, miles away, trembling along the horizon.

I pulled back a corner of the wrapping. I hadn't eaten squid for years. It freaked me out. I suppose people living by the sea just think that everyone eats seafood, no matter what it is. There's no squeamishness here. But I was hungry and I didn't want to search on an empty stomach. I wanted to be blinkered. I didn't want to be distracted by the aroma of dinner being cooked in a thousand Southwick kitchens. Though I was put off by its alien looks, at least the squid smelled good: clean and fresh. Thrown in a blistering hot pan with some oil, lemon and chilli, it would do the trick with salad and what was left of a baguette in the breadbin.

I flicked through a couple of cookbooks until I found a recipe that included details of cleaning and preparing the old calamari. I was further put off by the reference to what was edible: tentacles, ink, body and *arms*. But I pressed on, gritting my teeth as I held the cold, moist body in my left hand while pulling out the translucent quill, like some piece of weird packaging plastic, from the sac.

No end to that thunder. It drones on and on as if the lightning that birthed it is endless, a static explosion that feeds itself, wrapping around the globe like a fishing net made of wet fire, snagging in the wrecks.

I thrust away thought of wrecks and concentrated on the squid. I peeled away the purplish membrane that clung tenaciously to the soft white flesh. I pulled away the hard 'ears' from either side of the body. The tentacles were curled inside the cavity, as if it were trying to withdraw into itself, or eat itself. I prised them clear with a knife, intending to cut them away, and core the beak from the very centre of the ugly thing, but saw that something was bound up in the knot of tentacles and slime and guts. I teased it clear with the knife, the dead tentacles reluctant to be parted with its booty: a partially digested fish slithered clear of the squid's clutches with a faintly audible suck. For a moment, before I turned away in disgust, I thought about cooking that too. But it was too pale, too unformed, like a hesitant child's drawing of what a fish resembled. I couldn't stop myself from imagining the knife slicing through its guts – too easily, no bones, no cartilage, like jelly – to find something else within. A finger or an eyeball or a pair of sea-shrivelled lips. Like some ghastly set of babushka dolls.

No longer hungry, I threw the whole lot into the bin and went to the bathroom, where I washed and rewashed my hands with soap and scalding water. It bothered me that I couldn't identify the fish. Its eyes had been almost the size of its head and black with mystery, probably reflecting the cold, benthic depths it had come from. I caught sight of myself in the mirror and my face was not contorted with the disgust of this aborted meal. There was something else there, hardening my features, something determined beneath the soft, broken shape, the jagged, brutal scars. I saw the hard metal of a black car dent my face; the glass of a windscreen crash open and peel back the skin of my arm like a sopping jumper sleeve. The figure behind all that shattered wet ruby and crystal, was he there, in my thoughts somewhere?

I shut the door and walked along Surt Road to the village centre. I turned west and kept walking, past the young couples with their buggies and the old couples with their walking sticks, past the water tower and the overpriced furniture shops, until the village was behind me and the fields muscled in. I walked while the thunder built up behind me in the monstrous shelves of cumulus being raised across the sea. I could feel the energy growing in all that condensing vapour; the hairs on the back of my neck were answering its call. I walked regardless of the fire spreading up my spine and along my ribs. I kept going until something in me felt a pang, a tiny echo of what it had run up against over three months previously. This corner. This hedge. This field. Bailey's Hollow. The car had been doing fifty, they reckoned. It was only because I'd half-turned, disturbed by the noise of an engine topping third gear, that I'd been spared a more serious injury, or death. The bumper connected with my shins and turned the fibia and tibia into a snowstorm of bone. I jackknifed against the bonnet and the section of skull cradling my eye was pulverised. At the same time, my arm disappeared like a magician's trick into the panel of glass. Like I was reaching in to shake hands with the driver.

I closed my eyes and imagined the illustrations in Gray's coming to life, wrapping themselves around me in a series of muscle maps and nerve highways. Him too. He was there, his face turned away almost coquettishly, like the picture of the flayed head revealing the route the arteries take through the neck. I envisaged the drawing as his face returned, allowing me a full-on view of his features. Eyes closed. I opened them. I applied colour. I felt the first fat spots of rain, warm, on my face and I was back on the ground, in a wash of my own blood. *Who are you?*

I felt a stab of panic, out there, standing impotently in the quickening rain, miles away from where I might be of use. I was more concerned than I probably ought to have been about the flood of colour on the flower heads of the weeds thriving in that cut where the accident took place. I wondered how much of my blood I had lost lying in the grass, how much had drained into the soil to feed the seeds and the weeds. It was small comfort to think that I'd provided nourishment for something while lying in my coma.

I set off across country. Staggering through fields helped mask my limp. For a while I felt almost normal. Once through a bank of silver birch, the edge of the village of Breydon made itself known to me, via a series of old metal fences failing to do what they had been intended for. I could edge myself through one of the gaps in the fences, the spars rusted back to the thickness of feathers; it flaked away in little brown avalanches whenever I knocked against them.

I emerged in a concretised parking space, forgotten by cars if not security guards; warning signs that patrols with dogs were frequently made were attached with nylon ties to rusting coils of poorly positioned razor wire. Weeds foamed from the cracks and buckles in the concrete and for a moment I had a sense of how the world would go, once we human beings were all ushered off it.

My panic over Tamara was now so persistent, so keen, that it was like tinnitus: I was aware of it all the time, but it had become a part of me. I was slowly coming to terms with it. Which didn't mean that I wasn't propelled by it, that it didn't fuel me any more, but I was learning to deal with such a heightened state; I doubted I would survive if I didn't. She certainly wouldn't. I felt that conviction deep inside me; it was the constant ache in my bones.

My breath was coming in a series of squeaks and grunts. The pain was so great it had no focus or location, and felt only as if my back meat had been parted to the chine by some diabolical butcher. I'd have no chance of getting away if I was accosted by the security patrols, but the place seemed deserted; worse, forsaken. There were a few sorry buildings that did not seem important enough to deserve the amount of parking space, never mind the protective fencing. All of the windows were boarded up, so I couldn't get any idea as to the purpose of the offices. Part of me stalled then, thinking that Tamara might be inside, but why here and why not any of these houses radiating out from a point fifty feet away from me? She was everywhere and nowhere, and if I searched this place and did not find her that was more time for her to fall into and become lost for ever. Still, it was gut-wrenching to leave the buildings behind me; to walk past a great articulated lorry with the cabin obscured by closed curtains; to avert my gaze from a man in a vest standing in his bedroom window, what looked like a rubber cosh dangling limply from his fist. She was somewhere, so why not? And why not? Why not?

Charlie lived in a house set back from the main road that ran through the village. It was a strange little house, almost something of an afterthought. Perhaps it had been a lodge, or gatehouse for some other, grander abode that had been removed from the landscape in the past. My boots crunched in the trail of sand and aggregate leading up the track to the door. A cement mixer with a crust of dried product ringing its mouth gaped at me as I rang the doorbell. Charlie's van was nowhere to be seen. Light glanced off the windows, making it difficult to look inside the house. I tried the doorbell again, waited, and went down the side of the house to the garage. I cupped my hands against the window and peered inside. There was a vehicle covered in tarpaulin; quite obviously, from the size and shape, different to Charlie's van. A few old tins of Duckhams motor oil and a rotten canvas bag revealing a broken sea fishing rod. Packets of seed mouldering on the windowsill.

I tried the door but it was locked. I stared at the tarpaulin. That shape. That size. I stared for so long that I began to imagine blood blooming through the material, on that blunt edge, for example, where the radiator grille must be. I raised my head and listened hard for a moment. Then I put my elbow through the garage window.

It put me in mind, instantly, of the hit-and-run, and I actually turned away, thinking I must be sick, but the sensation passed and I was able to deal with the edges of glass remaining in the frame without any further wobbles. I hauled myself through the gap, feeling every grind and squeal of my bones as they complained against each other, and stood gasping and sweating on dark, oil-stained cobbles. I fingered the knots keeping the tarpaulin in place. A Siberian hitch? A truckie's knot? It was easy to disentangle. I got my fingers under a corner of tarp and dragged it up. Deep red. Not blood. Paint. A vintage Wrangler Jeep. Charlie's little project. I checked the radiator grille. Old, but undamaged. No bits of me hanging off it. No impact scars. I struggled to reknot the ropes until I realised it didn't really matter; there was no point in trying to dust over my tracks when there was broken glass all over the place. Which meant that it made it easier for me to break his kitchen window too, although this time I did it with one of the rusting oil cans. Guilt was riding me hard by now. I'd expected to find a black 4x4 under that tarp. I'm not sure why. I was desperate. I was spinning out of control. I needed to pin something on somebody, and it was suiting me to do it to someone I knew.

I had never been to Charlie's house before. He had never invited me. But I'd sometimes see him pottering around his garden when I was being ferried around by Ruth, shortly after returning from hospital. He hardly spent any time here, though. Much of his waking life, from very early in the morning – before 5am, until midnight, maybe later – were spent either on the waves or in his fishing hut or at the markets. He used his house as a service station, little more. And that was reflected in the austere appearance. In the kitchen was a kettle; a pan and a plate and a fork were dried on a dish rack. The fridge had nothing in it. The freezer was full of fish bones, most probably intended for Ruth's stock pots. Cupboards broadly bare. One chair drawn up to a small table. A newspaper. A battery-operated radio. No pictures. There was a door that presumably led to a cellar, but it was sealed shut with old paint; I tried the handle but there was no give whatsoever. No keyhole, no cracks to peer through. Perhaps there had been a serious problem with damp – this region was prone to flooding – and the cellar had simply been filled in. But still, despite its plain accessibility, it was frustrating not to use the door for what it had been intended.

Every room was similar. It was like a house that had been gutted by people ready to move out. Only a few bits and pieces remained, as though awaiting the removal men. Upstairs there were two bedrooms, but only one contained a bed, which was more a thin mattress on a foldaway base. A cheap-looking plastic digital alarm clock stood on the floor next to the bed. I checked its settings: Charlie was wakened at 4am. I imagined him in the cold room, his breath solidifying around him, as he dressed in his thermals and his gansey and his blue overalls beneath the unshaded 60-watt bulb, the silence of the world piled against the house like an assault.

I didn't know what I was expecting to find. The bathroom contained a toothbrush, a razor, a bar of soap with a cloying aroma that seemed to seep through the house, a plastic cup with a faded design, a grey flannel hanging desultorily over a dripping tap. Anything that looked as if it might possess something to give me a direction – such as the chest of drawers or the wardrobe – proved to be so bare as to beg the question why bother owning it in the first place? In the four drawers I found only some woollen socks and a chart of seas I didn't know that contained alien sounding names: Charlie-Gibbs fracture zone, the Immarssuak seachannel, Great Meteor Tablemount. I felt the shock of the world I thought I knew going away from me. I had to clench my hands tight and, for a second, grope for my name. I'm Paul Roan. I am Paul Roan. No matter what. Despite and because. Et cetera and et al.

In the wardrobe there were a few dark, heavy coats, nothing in the pockets. An unopened bottle of whisky at the foot. But here was a box I almost missed because it was so dark, almost the same colour as the wardrobe wood. This was where Charlie kept his broken hearts and his forget-me-nots. Here, too, his many incarnations. Clipped photo-booth pictures of him going back in time. You could make a flicker book of him and see the colour of his hair undergo a rare alchemic change: silver to coal black. The shirt collars widened. The flesh on his face lost its sags and padding and became leaner, more elastic, wolfish. Handwritten letters from the 1950s, from him to his mother. From his mother to him, a pet name I didn't know about: *My Darling Fingal...* Later, letters to a woman called Sarah. I flashed through them, expecting a hand on my shoulder at any moment. Sweat from my forehead dripped on to a page, blurring ink that had been painstakingly shaped there half a lifetime ago. I blotted it dry with my sleeve and flicked deeper into the beautifully preserved deck: each envelope had been razored open; every page retained its original crispness.

The early letters were long and rambling; the later ones were shorter. All of them contained tender language, outpourings of love and devotion. After a date in the 1960s they dried up. Sarah became his wife, I guessed: you didn't need to write any more.

Other letters. In the 1970s he began to receive postcards from Gordon, written in ineligible handwriting. Reports home from the tent in the garden. Big expedition. Pleas for milk and jam sandwiches. That is, I thought they were from Gordon. But they were from Ruth. *Thanks, Dad. I love you, Dad. All my love, Ruthie. xxx*

So Ruth was Charlie's daughter. *Okay. Okay.*

I searched but could find no letters from Gordon. Surely his son would have written some too, especially if he was playing with his sister. And even if I'd got the dates wrong and Gordon had died before Ruth was on the scene, where were his pictures, his silly notes to Dad?

Here was a tin containing Charlie's birth certificate, and those of Sarah and Ruth (Sarah's death certificate was in here too, along with their marriage licence). There was nothing of Gordon's. I thought of how Charlie had related the story of Gordon's death, and of how there had been deep love in the telling. And I wondered whether that emotion might have been planted there. Gordon, I thought. I thought, Charlie.

Why would he lie about something like that?

The letters stopped after a while and I couldn't fathom why. Perhaps Charlie had started using email, but he didn't seem the type. And then I thought I might have been burning things for him. Or if he had been burning them himself. Stuff that was best not preserved. The people of this village seemed to be bent on doing things differently. I'd never really dwelled for too long on the reasons behind behaviour that had seemed quirky and detached, but now appeared more sinister the more I thought about it. I'd fallen in with the disposal idea readily, because – most of the time – it took my mind off the awful Technicolour frames of memory that showed me being sliced up by the car. I had a task that seemed to be important but, when you boiled it all down, it was just plain weird.

Downstairs was a living room that seemed an insult to the name. Precious little of anything went on in here, it seemed, let alone living. It was one of those rooms that feel colder than the rest of the house, possibly because they lack any human habitation. There was a bat-winged chair and a table. A fireplace filled with ash that might have been a thousand years old. No books. No television.

I decided to leave. I felt guilty about stoving in Charlie's window, and about harbouring bad feelings towards him. He was an easy target; my only target. I was desperate, lashing out, that was all.

I got back on the road and trudged towards Southwick. Almost immediately I saw Jake on his bicycle, powering his legs on the pedals against the wind. The remains of his lunch crackled and crunched in the plastic bag swinging from his wrist. I stepped back out of sight and watched him swing his bike into a driveway. He got off and unlocked the front door. He took his bike inside and closed the door. I waited and watched. An opaque window upstairs filled with orange light. I saw him move within it: dark hair, dark beard, dark jumper. Steam shifted against the glass. He was having a shower, or a bath.

I licked my lips and looked up and down the street. I hurried to his drive and slipped down the side of the house. No garage here. An untended garden with knee-high grass. A rusted lawnmower seized up and forgotten in the middle of its task, taken over by the lawn. There was a small shiplap toolshed painted black, with a sign on the padlocked door: *Gone Fishing*. Nets that needed mending, old lobster pots, a rusting grapple anchor and about twenty feet of corroded chain, a buckled water heater, orange Spongex floats, boss snaps and skiff releases. A plastic shovel and a scaling hammer. It really was a mess. I didn't know what to do. I couldn't break into Jake's house while he was in the bathroom. It was a dare too far. *Go home, you fool,* I thought. *Forget it.*

I was halfway down the drive when I thought

about that padlock. I went back and tested it. It was a fairly new padlock. There were no windows. I put my face to the thin crack between the door's edge and the frame. A smell of soil and engine oil and freshly sawn wood. The clean, cool metallic tang of well-kept stainless steel implements. I couldn't see anything in the darkness.

I whispered: 'Tamara?'

Thunder rackled across the sky. A sudden scattering of rain against glass, like stones thrown at the window of someone whose attention you are trying to grab.

Stop dallying. I snatched up the shovel and wedged it into the gap and tried to force it open. Nothing doing. My back was the more likely to cave in.

I had to get in there. I had to see.

I hunted around for a few minutes, the conviction that Jake would appear growing all the time, and clogging my chest like an obstruction. There were no more robust, tools however. What I needed to break open the lock was, presumably, inside the tool shed. In frustration I kicked out at a bucket of perished purse rings. My spine flared and I saw the familiar grey veil. But then, through that, there was the brilliant gleam of something flying thought the air with all those off-white Os, like so many pale mouths shocked by my find. It was a key – the key to the tool shed.

I got the padlock off the latch. I expected Tamara to tumble out into my arms and was braced for her delicious weight, her *thereness* against me. My disappointment when she didn't almost caused me to take another ill-advised kick at the bucket, but instead I breathed deeply and thought of pre-flight checks – routine as Dramamine – and it was then that I saw the wooden chest under a shelf of tools.

There were several packets of photographs in the chest but my fingers wouldn't settle for long enough to open one of them. I noticed my breath casting out and reeling back in, too fast to be of any use to my lungs. I was hyperventilating with fear. In for a penny, I thought, and pocketed as many of the packets as I could.

I retreated from the shed into hard rain and was wetted to the skin within moments. The garden seemed different now, somehow, but that could have been down to my new viewing angle, or the strange leaden sky. Or were these really recent boot prints in the mud fringing the lawn?

I hurried back along the side of the house, noticing an air duct in the base of the wall that appeared new. That gave me further pause. I wondered if he had Tamara locked up in there.

I CALLED LIAM Keble and told him what I'd seen, what I suspected, my thoughts filled with Fred West and Josef Fritzl. Within ten minutes there were three squad cars filing along the approach to the house, but although their lights were flashing, I didn't hear any sirens. For a moment I thought that was because the storm was stealing their sound away, but, loud though the thunder was, and the accompanying torrent, it couldn't mask the noise of car doors slamming, or boots scraping in grit. This isn't New York, I reminded myself, no matter how much Keble pretended it was.

It took seconds for the police to hurry over to the shelter of the front porch but they were all drenched by then. I was standing out of the way, out of sight but close enough to hear the swearing.

Keble was pulling up the collar of his raincoat. Water sluiced from the brim of his hat. I heard him say, 'This better be good,' before they went inside.

I couldn't risk being seen, but I needed to be there in case they found Tamara in the cellar. The only drawback was that if Tamara *wasn't* down there, the police would be on the look-out for me, which meant arrest for wasting police time and bureaucratic longueurs that I could ill afford.

The storm came on and on. I kept expecting to hear screams as the horrors were peeled back in that rotting onionskin house. I kept expecting the JCBs to turn up, and the white tents and the cordon. But it was just me and the forked lightning and the mushroom clouds obscuring the visible sky.

Eventually the police came out of the house. I heard Keble talking to Jake on the threshold and Jake's voice: 'No bother. I understand. Quite welcome.' He closed the door and the police got back into their cars. I heard laughter. I felt myself deflate. They couldn't possibly have searched the entire house, let alone investigated my suspicions regarding the cellar. I toyed with the idea of confronting Jake, trying to force my way into his house and searching it top to bottom, but I was not the man I used to be. What physical presence I once boasted had been battered out of me.

I headed back towards the village. The cold and the damp were in my bones now, it seemed; blue fire danced along my limbs. It felt as though a huge poker was being ground into the gaps beneath my shoulder blades, its tip sheathed in ice chips for millennia. I could feel myself seizing up. I'd had my hands balled in anger and helplessness for hours; now my fingers refused to straighten. I was like an acute case of rheumatoid arthritis. I was someone whose flesh was calcifying minute by minute.

An age later, as rain from the storm raced along the roads, I found myself traipsing into the centre of the village. The rain was so hard and thick here, it was almost impossible to see the edges of buildings. Rain hit the ground so forcefully that it produced spray coming in the opposite direction. There was a kind of fog out to sea. I could make out figures behind windows, warm and dry, perhaps gazing out at this shambling idiot coming up the road and wondering what form of madness – drink or pure insanity – was driving his heels. There were no buses to be seen.

I ended up flagging a cab and I was vexed to find it being driven by the same driver who had taken me to Ipswich hospital on my previous visit. He seemed too concerned by the weather to recognise me, thankfully. Nor my voice, as I asked him to repeat the same journey.

Chapter Sixteen

BRACE FOR IMPACT

IT TOOK LONGER than it ought, but maybe that was down to the foul weather, or to the anxiety chewing at my nerves. I had to keep checking the glowing green figures on the taxi's clock to remind myself it was still daytime. The sky had been shut down by the storm. The only suggestion that there was a sun shining beyond those clouds came at the horizon, where a thin line of light was scored. The taxi driver kept muttering about wanting to go off duty; he wasn't happy about driving in these conditions. The road was being erased. Driving had become an act of faith. Heavy goods vehicles on the near side were producing great plumes of spray despite the heavy aprons that skirted their wheels. The central reservation was the only indication we were on course, yet even that was warping and smearing in the runnels forming on the windows. There was no sense of individual spots of rain: it was bucketing.

Lightning forked across the black widescreen sky. Thunder fell from the gap it created, instantaneous, cataclysmic. The driver said: 'Jesus Christ.' It was like the end of the world. He could get no reception on his radio, only a tsunami of static that grew or faded depending on the strength of the monumental charge that was escalating above us. The buildings were dissolved. Nothing had any edge, apart from our voices as we attempted conversation. Though he was reluctant, the driver was making progress. I couldn't work out how he remembered the route. Maybe it was down to habit alone; his SatNav was dead, the screen full of question marks, unable to detect a signal. After what felt like hours, we pulled up in front of the hospital in Ipswich. I peeled myself from my seat, slick with a sweat of nerves and exhaustion. The driver didn't look much better.

'I'm going straight home,' he said. 'This is madness. There'll be deaths at the end of this day, you mind my words.'

I gave him a tip this time and waved him off. I was being slaughtered by the rain but I didn't want to get inside just yet. This was the calm before my own storm, I thought, no matter how messed up that sounded with the world apparently splitting apart around me. I imagined Tamara walking around in bad weather, a child growing inside her. I agonised over the reasons she couldn't tell me. I'd been such an idiot. Short of holding up my hand and telling her to shut it, I'd closed the door on even the most light-hearted debate on the pros and cons of starting a family by simply changing the subject at every opportunity. I whisked her past the displays of buggies in the department store. I ignored her as she turned her head to watch the children playing in the playground of our local school. I could always see that unspoken question on her lips, the ache to be able to give voice to it so obvious in her eyes.

But I was a driven man back then. I wanted to be

a success in my profession. I wanted to be a captain flying big jets into and out of the major cities of the world. I didn't want to be obstructed by nappies and sick and infantile chats about horsies and doggies and puss-cats. Perversely, I didn't want a child mainly because I wouldn't be around to watch it grow up. Which was kind of positive, but I knew Tamara wouldn't see it that way. She thought I was one of those people who just doesn't want to pass on his genes, whereas it was more a not yet than a not ever. But I couldn't tell her that. I didn't want to build up her hopes. I knew it was risky, that she was younger than me and might not want to run the risk of waiting until she was in her forties to conceive.

So many things get in the way. Time passes. Accidents happen. People go missing. Now, when it might be too late, my eyes had been opened and I could see what was important. It wasn't about pips on a uniform or flying hours or bringing the best part of a ton of aluminum, flesh and blood safely down on to a slick airstrip during a storm. I wished Tamara was here so I could tell her. I wished so hard, I believed I could pull a muscle.

Before I realised what I was doing, I was halfway to the maternity unit, my head down, not wanting to catch the eye of anybody who might have operated on me, or provided intensive care for me while I was here. The maternity unit was set apart from the main part of the hospital. It was accessed through a door near the café, but you had to walk a long corridor to reach it, to the northernmost point of the hospital, like some outpost discovered at the end of a spit of land. I wondered if it had been designed like that so that nobody would be able to hear the animalistic howls that came from it at all hours of the day and night. Maybe the hospital executives didn't want the people in the café, or the other patients, to be affected by those torture sounds.

I had to lean on a security buzzer for some time before a receptionist deigned to speak to me. I told them I needed to speak to someone, but they wouldn't let me in. Security, they explained. I could be anybody.

I told her it was my wife.

'Is she booked in?' she asked.

'No.' I closed my eyes, placed my fingers against the grille as if it could conceal this pathetic picture of me thinking, thinking hard.

'She… I think she's pregnant, but I'm not sure.' I shook my head. I started walking away. How crazy was I sounding these days? Then I saw a woman, heavily pregnant, waddling around in a gown, her face grey. She was speaking into a mobile phone. She was saying that she just wanted it out of her, it was taking the piss.

'It's not my fucking fault I can't produce progestin. They know that. So why don't they induce me? But no. Have a walk around, they said. Have a fucking walk. Fuck's sake…'

She keyed a code into the door and I slipped through after her. She didn't notice, but I was pretty sure the CCTV camera positioned in the wall would. I hoped nobody was keeping tabs on it at that moment. I followed the woman down the long corridor to the doors that led through to the maternity unit proper. She was tutting and swearing even more now, having lost her telephone signal. She rushed through into another corridor. I didn't know where to go, or what to do. I could hear babies crying. I could hear the lowing of gravid mothers-to-be. There was a woman behind a desk writing in a file. She might have been the voice that had forbidden entry, but I had to start somewhere. She smiled when I approached the booth.

In a sudden change of tack, I told her the truth. It blurted out of me. I told her about my accident and how Tamara had been by my side for much of it. I could feel the prickle of tears that would never come, by the time I'd relayed the details of the trip to Amsterdam. 'I don't even know if the pregnancy test was hers. But I need to know. I want to tell her it's all right, if she's going to have a baby. She thought I didn't want kids. But I do.'

My voice broke. The woman stood up and came around the side of the booth, opening the door and placing her hand gently on my arm.

'Come and sit down,' she said. 'I'll make you a cup of tea.'

I was shaking. I felt nervous about what I needed to do and frustrated that I couldn't find the woman I was desperate to be with. The idea of a blue flash on a small piece of cardboard was tricking around my head, as eye-catching as the feathers of a jay flitting through undergrowth. It could have been a pregnancy test belonging to a friend. They could have been sharing a bottle of wine waiting for the result, and then congratulations or commiserations. But if it *was* Tamara, and she was not safe…

Bright pain flashed through my palms and wrists and I looked down, appalled, as blood drizzled out from beneath the gouging white Us of my fingernails. I jammed my hands in my pockets and felt the thin cardboard lip of the photograph wallet I'd stolen from Jake's tin. I rescued it now and teased it open. Old photographs, some of them black and white. The usual stuff. Forced smiles and mugging for the camera. Lots of people I didn't recognise.

I paused over one of them. Charlie and Ruth leaning against the flank of an unidentified black car. It was a big one, boxy. Could easily have been a 4x4. Could easily have been a Defender. I wondered where that car was now. Sold on, quickly? Destroyed?

And here was a batch of photographs of children. Lots of them, candid snaps of them eating ice cream at a café bench, or playing on the beach. Was this Kieran, perhaps? Was this Harry?

I stuffed the photographs back in my pocket and spent the next minute or two wiping at my palms, cursing over and over. *What the fuck? What the fuck?*

I could see through the hatch that the nurse hadn't even made it to the staff room. She was talking to a colleague, someone with a clipboard containing a huge wedge of notes. She had it cradled in her arm like any one of the newborns being ejected into life in that suite of delivery rooms. Her computer was asleep. A screensaver had activated: streams of blue and pink text scrolling across an otherwise black monitor. *It's a boy! It's a girl!* I nudged the mouse, expecting a password prompt, but the screensaver blinked off to reveal a desktop littered with folders. One of them said ADMISSIONS. I opened it. My heart was on fire. A list of names, organised alphabetically. No Dziuba, T. I checked under ROAN: nothing. Thank God our names weren't Smith or Jones or Williams.

I closed the folder and frantically searched for anything else that might contain references to Tamara. My eyes were jagging all over the screen. Slow down. Relax. My host was still being grilled by the woman with the clipboard. Now she was peeling off sheets and handing them over. I saw the nurse glance my way, but she either couldn't see where I was positioned or hadn't really registered anything; she was looking for an escape route. I took a deep breath, squeezed my eyes shut for a moment, then reassessed the desktop and waited for her to come to me.

There. Another folder. APPOINTMENTS. It had been partially hidden under the ADMISSIONS folder. I dragged it clear then double-clicked on its icon. Another list of names. I stared at Tamara's for a long time, thinking, no, it must be somebody else, despite the chances of another Dziuba living within a thousand miles of this village being virtually nil.

I clicked on her name and a dialogue box opened. It showed me that Tamara had visited the hospital on half a dozen occasions before I had suffered my accident. One of the appointments had a little paper clip icon appended to it. I clicked on that. Another dialogue box. This one said: 12-week scan: 17/6/10. There was a host of jargon, stuff I couldn't for the life of me decipher, other than one word that I homed in on: *Healthy*.

Tamara Dziuba had been here for a scan on the seventeenth of May last year. The maternity unit. And someone – not just her – was found to be healthy.

It took a while to put the pieces together in my head. And then the nurse was back with my tea and she saw me staring at the screen and she swore and put the mug down and tea sloshed over the side on to my knee. I didn't even feel it.

'She's pregnant,' I said.

I didn't get to drink my tea. I was asked to leave. It didn't get any nastier than that, presumably because the nurse who had taken pity on me didn't want to lose her job.

I meandered through the corridors, not knowing where I was going, just content to keep moving. The chemical tang of the wards and the brisk shushing of starchy uniforms, the sunken bodies pushed around on trolleys, the sense of purpose everywhere, was reassuring.

But I couldn't stay for ever. I was no longer a patient here, and my purpose was beyond these walls. And I realised my progress through the hospital was anything but meandering when I found myself outside the tiny shared office that Ruth used. There was nobody inside. The door was unlocked.

All of the computers in this room were off, but a residual heat, and the smell of used toner from the printer, suggested that they'd been used recently. Three office chairs were in varying stages of decomposition, fabric worn or bare; stuffing poked through like frozen smoke. The tables were a mass of files and folders and cold, stained coffee cups. A shredder was packed to the lid with tapeworms of text.

I'd spent a couple of weeks in an office like this, during a summer job before going to university. A friend of the family who worked at University College London's haematology department. They were clearing out their archives, readying them for a digital makeover. They needed someone to go in and dig out years' worth of folders from dozens of filing cabinets and sort them into piles. I did all that and then watched a couple of doctors come in to trash about three-quarters of them, each folder flying towards an incineration pile along with a weary, barely varying phrase that seemed to go on for hours: 'He's dead, he's dying, she's dead, she's as good as dead...'

I'd left that office a couple of hundred pounds better off but appalled by the disaffected way of those people charged with saving life, and convinced that I was riddled with cancer. I felt for a long time less like a person with dreams and feelings and fears and more a sack of meat and offal that was staving off time somehow before it dirtied up a gurney for a few hours while someone sawed it open to see why it had stopped working. And then, of course, I started my pilot training and I was no more attached to the objects I forced through the air than the people who had worked for years studying blood and its deformities and diseases. The doctors and nurses couldn't afford to become attached; they'd never get through a single working day. They were untouched, but they were trying to save lives, and sometimes, in the face of seemingly insurmountable odds, they managed it.

Now time had slowed down for me, I could see all of this. Previously I hadn't noticed, or hadn't thought a great deal about it. I had an opinion, that was it, like a footprint trapped in cement. But I was prepared to be a bit more fluid about people these days. The only thing was, you saw every colour in the spectrum. Every portrait had its light tones but also its sombre shades, its cross-hatchings, its black.

Me, Amy, Charlie, Jake. DI Keble. There was darkness there, there was plenty of rust undermining the shiny, polished surfaces. I thought of Ruth straddling me in that dark room, the sweat wicking off her on to my torso, the tight swelling of her abdomen, like an angry, hot infection, drumming against my skin. She'd exorcised the violence of that rape by channelling it into me. I could still feel her in the tender ache at the tops of my thighs, and feel the ghost of those ropes at my wrist.

I thought of Tamara growing heavy with the baby and felt another stab of panic. Maybe she hadn't talked to me about it because it wasn't mine. Did you think about that, First Officer Roan? Did you consider the possibility? In her loneliness, she'd turned to someone else, or perhaps the rapist – that random Dad – had unwittingly forced another bastard upon the world.

The panic lessened as I began stroking the edges of paper folders, looking for ways in: names, references I might recognise, something to undo this tricky stopper knot: the monkey's fist that was tied tightly and prettily around the hard secret at its centre. It *must* be mine. She was devoted to me. We spent so much time together, especially after I walked away from flying, and there was no time to make new friendships, let alone intimate ones with other men. All of our thought had gone into the new venture. We'd spent hours, well into the night, talking and making notes and writing up a business plan, poring over maps of the British coastline, working out where would be the perfect spot to reinvent ourselves.

I felt a sting at not being with her to watch her change. It hit me how rare it was to see a woman come to terms, grow into, her pregnancy. There was Ruth, but I could think of nobody else. She was always moving, always sighing and wincing and shifting around, like a feverish cat trying to find a comfortable position. She didn't seem happy in this skin of hers. I got the impression she wanted the baby out as soon as possible. I imagined Tamara growing into the role, like an actor born to a particular part. I imagined her sexy with that bump, carrying it athletically, as if she were meant for nothing else. In the airline industry, the female flight attendants I saw on the jets either didn't get pregnant or, if they did, then that was it. You didn't come huffing into work with a burgeoning lump. You didn't fly if you were pregnant; the attendant health problems were unknown, but the kind of stresses the body felt in a pressurised cabin could not be good if experienced on a regular basis. And anyway, the aisles were too narrow.

Tamara's belly distending. My hand on the stretched, hot skin, feeling a hand or a foot press against mine through mere centimetres of flesh. Listening hard for a tiny, rapid heartbeat, hidden beneath its louder, stronger, slower counterpart;

(that shiver of something almost remembered again... that tip-of-the-tongue moment)

the tender jealousy that a baby would be a part of her and not a part of you.

The desk was locked. I jemmied it open with a paper knife and a screwdriver from a pen pot. I didn't care any more. Catch me, fine me, throw me in jail. I was making things happen, at least.

Ruth's work diary was in there, her name on a label stuck to the top right-hand corner. I went through it. Nothing beyond references to meetings, courses to attend, occasional after-work committee business. I didn't know if I should be concerned about that or relieved. I didn't know what I was expecting to find.

I checked the drawer beneath and found two more diaries, for the preceding years. I leafed through 2010, my fingers pausing on the page where my life had been suspended. There was an asterisk on the corresponding date. A telephone rang in the distance. I heard a voice call out for someone called Martin, telling him that he'd have to move his car or risk someone emptying the wet waste-bins all over it. Someone walked past the door, her perfume strong enough to make its way through the jamb and scour my nostrils.

Prior to the date of my accident, I spotted handwritten marks at weekly intervals. A single letter: 'T', and a time, and a place, away from here. The names of pubs. If that was Tamara, then she was talking to Ruth about the baby outside of her professional capacity. I thought: is that good? I thought: was she asking Ruth's advice on an abortion? Then why have a 12-week scan? I pictured her confused and frustrated, not knowing what to do. Is that why she went AWOL? I found myself grasping for that, because it would mean she wouldn't be raped and dead and cooling in some waterlogged marsh.

I closed the drawer and staggered out of the room. I wondered if Ruth was all right. I tried calling her from the hospital but nobody was answering. The world had disappeared when I reached the exit.

My back was grinding and flaring like something in a forge. Perhaps the weather had something to do with it. There was nothing but sky: the whole world was being smothered by a great dark grey blanket. Rain was its stitching, coming loose all over. Here and there were bodkins of lightning. The fabric tore in thunderous rents.

I got outside and the wind ripped at my clothes. The smell of the sea was thick around me. There were no taxis, no buses, no cars. I saw one other person bent against the storm, fighting his way into it. My foot charged against the kerb and I yelled out against the pain that tore through my spine, but I couldn't hear myself in the midst of all this howling. Slates fled a roof as easily as autumn leaves. The wind shaped the rain like ropes being weaved in a fishing yard. I was instantly drenched. I was close to screaming, feeling the untapped fury that had layered up inside me begin to crack and warp. There was plenty more beneath that. Rage and panic and fear and frustration.

And then I saw a flash of lightning and I was suddenly back at the harbour in Southwick, standing in the cold. Staring out to the mill with its denuded sails, its collapsed roof. The line of sheds along the harbour path, squalid and black. The tired decorations, the fishing nets and buoys, the oxidised anchors, the chalked signs. Colchester oysters. Brancaster mussels. Crab claws.

'You work here?' I asked.

He nodded. 'Work here. And harbour. Sell fish. Got hut.'

I knew where I would find her.

69

I HEARD SOMETHING break. I think it was this morning. Early. There was sound of glass breaking. And then someone walking around. Someone soft and going in circles at first, as if they were pottery (is that the right word?), as I used to in kitchens of people I meet for first time. I like to peek in the cupboards and check the spice racks while they are busy pouring drinks or putting on CD. The footsteps went away and I didn't hear them again for long time, but then they came back. These were different, though. They were footsteps with something on their mind. It was different person; it must have been. I thought maybe the first set of footsteps were Paul's. I was sure of it. He was like that, soft and pottery sometimes, especially in mornings at breakfast, and when he came back from long-haul. Like he was getting rid of locked energy from himself as he potter from bread bin to fridge to stove to table. But how would I know, now, for sure? He was so small and thin in his hospital bed, so weak and battered. How could his feet make any kind of weight or noise again? He must be in wheelchair. He might be dead. He might still be lying in bed, becoming like sculpture, like fossil, like foetus.

She's diminished, despite the good food and the regular supplies of drinking water, the portable heater and the Mozart. Gnawing dread will do that to a person, no matter how well cared for they are physically. The not knowing will cause the disintegration to begin, like an old rope with a poorly whipped end, unreaving, losing its shape, its purpose. Her earlier belief that The Man wore a mask because he wanted to protect his identity from her, thus negating the fear of murder, no longer rang true. She feared she might die here, whether purposefully, at his hand, or otherwise. She could begin to understand how people simply gave up. No matter how much the body clung on to life, the instinct that raged in us like fire, the intellect could overthrow it. If there were enough black marks in the AGAINST column, it was possible to find that internal switch and throw it. The lifelong sweethearts separated by death: how often did the partner follow soon after? Tamara had remembered reading about a serial rapist and murderer from her own country – the Wolf, did they call him? – a man who had terrorised Odessa during the 1980s and whose final victim, a seventeen-year-old student, was found a week after the killer was captured. She had been kept prisoner in a drain on the grounds of a disused factory by the railway in Malynivs'kyi. Her hands were tied behind her back. In this drain, which was filled with water almost to the grille, there was a ledge that she had been perched upon. If she remained on tiptoe, her face was just above the surface. If she lowered her heels, her nose and mouth were submerged. If she were to move forward she would drop off the ledge and sink. When she was found, dead, the Wolf finally deigning to give the police her whereabouts, it was broadly believed that drowning was the cause of death. But a post-mortem found no water in her lungs. There was no obvious answer to the question of what had killed her. It was thought that her body had simply given up; the severity of her depression had caused her to shut down. At the time Tamara had been shocked by the reports, had simply not believed them, thinking that youth was its own fuel, that its spirit was indomitable. The thought of death, to a teenager, was as far away as the faintest star in the night sky. It had been her first inkling of mortality. She never considered that her own body might come so close to following a similar path.

Those footsteps. Something is going on. I hope it's something to do with all water that's coming down steps. Even through walls I can hear thunder. It's been going on for days, it seems. Going away, coming back, like dogs in the street that can't leave their own mess alone. Maybe they're getting ready to move me somewhere else. The amount of walking around makes me think that they live in street where there are lots of houses. They are putting together plan, maybe. How to do it without someone seeing. How to make it look normal. What if they roll me up inside carpet? Or put me in suitcase? I don't think I would be able to cope with that. I'll fight. As soon as they remove handcuffs, I'll fight.

The footsteps finished their busy little circuits above then began, slowly, to descend. Little impact splashes, and the water coming a shade faster through the gap at the bottom of the door. What was chasing it pushed that barrier open and stood for a moment assessing Tamara in her bed. For a moment, she thought it was Paul, that the footsteps had been the choreography of violence, the skip and shuffle of cut and thrust and counter; that he had bested the evil that kept her here. But then the figure came out of the shadows, flicking on the light, and it was The Man in his orange fish mask, that snorkel hood with its matted lining of fur pulled over his head. Something was different. She could hear his breathing, fast and ragged, and this she had never heard before. And why that pause, where there had never been one before? As if he were gathering himself. She felt her heart jolt and a voice inside her tell her that this was it. There was to be no release from these cuffs, no moonlight flit between hideaways. She'd take the roll of carpet now. She'd gladly leap into the open mouth of a suitcase. She fought against the shackles, her voice in her chest shocked from her at each jerk of the chains. Whimpers and wails. She was able to snatch enough breath to try to scream but it wouldn't form in her throat and the pathetic sound fell dead in the room, unable to get beyond the metres of packed soil, and the churn of falling water. The Man came to her and reached behind her. An extendable lamp on a mobile base, like nothing she'd ever seen before, was raised over her head. It was alien-looking. Five dimpled glass circles were punched into a flattened plastic sphere. He flicked a switch and it was as if the sun had exploded into the room. She flinched from it. The light was almost physical. She could feel it scouring every wrinkle and crease of her skin. It opened up the squalid little room in which she had spent so much time and turned it into a different place. All shadow had been excoriated. The Man became something more than he had been. It was as if all that had gone before was mere figment; that her true nightmare was beginning just now. She noticed fresh detail. The unstitched thread in the seams of his coat. The spores of blue mould on the back of his gloves, like slow explosions of ink on blotting paper. The stain of something recently eaten, drying to an ochre smear on the sleeve of his arm.

'Bud'laska,' she said to The Man. 'Please. Ni... ni, bud'laska.'

The Man ignored her and moved to the curtain. The fight went out of her. She was frozen now, needing to see what was behind it in order to be able to go on, to decide how next to lose her mind. The Man struggled to draw it back; mould caused the plastic ties to hitch along the rail, but eventually he dragged it to one side and she could see a trolley beneath, covered with a dirty teacloth. The Man kicked off a brake on its castors and began to wheel it towards her. There were no smells of good food now. No warming cup of tea, or hot milk.

He set the trolley next to her and picked up the white board from the end of the bed. He scribbled on it for a moment, then held it up for her to see.
I'm sorry.

He peeled back the teacloth, and now she was able to scream after all. She screamed long and hard until the cold fire from the needle he'd jammed in her arm seized her brain and started switching it off. She was falling into oblivion trying to remember what she'd seen on the trolley, the most dismaying version of Kim's Game she had ever played.

scalpel
clamps
bone saw
pliers
cable cutter?!?

But it was what was missing that scared her most. She tried to ask, but it was beyond her. The question drifted in her mind while darkness closed around it.

No needles. No catgut. Nothing to sew me back together...

Chapter Seventeen

THE SURGE

I STOLE AN ambulance. I don't suppose it matters what kind I took, but in the end I plumped for one of the rapid response vehicles – a Zafira – the ones with yellow and green checks on their side. There were two of them parked askew in the parking zone reserved for emergencies. The keys had been left in one of them. I switched on the sirens and the lights and I sliced through the roads of Ipswich until I hit the A-road that would take me home. It felt less bad, somehow, stealing that car, rather than one of the proper ambulances, despite the mass of state-of-the-art kit, the life-saving gear in the back. What made me feel worse was the unopened sandwich on the passenger seat; something no doubt grabbed by the driver to tide him over until the end of his shift. I didn't improve my guilt by raking it open and wolfing it down. I didn't even like cheese and pickle, but I was hungry beyond tasting. I drove through what I thought was the Suffolk countryside, but it could have been a world of water. Rain beat against the roof and the windscreen, trying to get in. Across exposed bridges the wind felt as if it were lifting the car. I couldn't see well enough to dispel the fear that was exactly what was happening. Only the occasional sign, lit up through the slashing rain, and the cats' eyes in the road kept me from going off in the wrong direction, or leaving the road entirely. I missed the junction, shrouded by trees on the right, that would have taken me on to the B road to the village and had to do a blind U-turn in the carriageway. If anything was coming the other way I'd be dead meat. But there were few people out this evening. Only the idiots and the desperate.

I did take the car off the road down here. Right at the point where I had been maimed by the Defender. It was nothing serious. I was doing maybe 25 and misjudged the bend in the road. Both front tyres bounced into the kerb and I stalled it, mashing the bonnet into a hedge. I was able to reverse back on to the road without any problem, but it brought back memories of the hit-and-run and I was barely able to summon the strength to sink the accelerator once I'd got the engine going again. I concentrated hard – one of the headlights had been smashed in – and took the car steadily along the dipping, swerving road, past the school, past Breydon, and on to the mini-roundabout that marked the beginning of Southwick proper. Before reaching the main access route into the village, I turned right and drove past a pub and a junk shop, on to a more narrow road that led through the golf course. There was a sudden flurry of movement within the ribboning rain, avocets perhaps, and then it was just the rain again, and the futile sweep of the wipers trying to shift it from the glass.

You can't access the harbour by car at this point. There's a barrier blocking the way. Once I saw the gleam of the padlock I killed the lights and the engine and tried to fasten the shape of the old mill to the uneven black mattress of the marshes stretching out beyond the sunken lines of the river and the illuminated rise of the village. But there was no way through the white noise. I got out of the car and braced myself against the assault of the weather. The lighthouse was sending a pathetic beam out to sea. Lightning arced across the clenched fists of cloud, as if some diabolical being were throwing up a great enclosure of barbed wire to hem in the village. I spotted the mill within that flash, like a twisted, rusting bolt jammed into a rotten plank of wood. I'd begun to suspect it existed only in my mind. I opened the boot and sifted through the cases of medical supplies. I pocketed syringes, needles and two phials of morphine. I took some scalpels too, although they felt grossly unwieldy in the meaty traps of my hands. I took a waterproof LED torch from the glove box. There seemed to be nothing else that might help me, either to save life or to snuff it out. Stretchers, bandages, splints. A defibrillator. Fastened down with straps was a white tank of oxygen and, but for its green diamond warning sticker, it looked like my leg after I'd woken up from coma: pale, inflexible and swollen.

I ducked carefully under the barrier and struck out along a cindered path. The river had silted up over time, choking the waterway and limiting the traffic that could use it, but the high tides had swollen it to the point where it was close to breaking the banks. It trembled, right on the brink. I could hear the crash of the surf as it tore up and down the beach.

This place was like a strange, landlocked island. I felt both exposed and isolated; the creeks, marshes and reed beds stretched out around me for miles, but there was nowhere to go if it flooded. You'd have to rush to get in a boat or face a drowning out in the wilderness.

From a distance, the fish huts were invisible against the night. The only clue to something standing there was the slight dip in the strength of the wind as the conglomeration of old wooden walls and roofs acted as a break against the weather. I squinted into the night, training the torch on the path, and tried to remember where Charlie's fish hut was. If I found that, there might be a clue as to where Jake's hut was positioned. Intermittent pulses of lightning helped. Here was a stack of yellow trays bearing Charlie's initials, punched into the plastic with a bradawl. A rusted horse shoe nailed side on to make a C above the door. His boat flashed at me alongside a wooden landing stage. *There's Gratitude for you.* His stamp everywhere.

I knocked on the door. It was locked from the outside, a padlock hanging from a bolt. Music was playing inside, but the sound was all wrong. With my ear pressed up against the wood, the melody sounded far off, though indisputably from somewhere within. Muffled by a blanket, perhaps? He must have forgotten to turn off his radio before leaving.

I was about to move further along in what would no doubt prove to be a protracted bid to identify Jake's hut when the lightning came again and I saw my shadow cast against the wall. But my shadow was carrying a torch, not something long and thin, like a spear. I switched off the torch. Back in darkness, I could feel my ears tingle as I strained for something beneath the rage of wind and rain. I pressed myself against the wall of the hut and gripped the torch. I shifted to my left and heard a strange sound, something I'd never heard before. There was a kind of pneumatic *socking* noise, and a shrill, high-impact concussion of metal against stone, maybe centimetres away, where I had been standing not seconds before. Had I been shot at? I felt my bladder give way at the thought, and I staggered further to my left. The sound of something being forced against resistance, something catching. Loaded. I kept moving. At one point the wind fell away for a moment, perhaps because I was shielded in this position from the worst of it. I heard footsteps, slow and deliberate, and I watched the gleam of a harpoon dart slide out from the edge of the wall, followed by its long, silver shaft. I waited until I saw the gloved hand gripping the stock and, ducking underneath the point, switched on the torch and shone it into the face of my pursuer.

I swore when I saw it, giving away my position to him. He swung the harpoon down towards me; I was almost on my knees. I lashed out with the torch and caught him across the top of the shin. Something give there, like the shell of an egg under a spoon. I heard the harpoon as it was triggered again and felt heat explode through the right side of my body. I was on the floor, up to my elbows in water, mud and grass in my mouth but I managed to drag myself towards the fence and got through, losing my jacket in the process. He was splashing after me but there were no more shots; maybe he'd run out of harpoons. I could hear his breath ragged behind that staring mask. The eyes of it stuck in me like a hook; I couldn't shake away the shock of it, despite seeing it for less than a split-second. Bulbous and glassy, sunk into what looked like a swollen pile of orange grease, a black mouth agape, nonplussed, blank, emerging from a matted fur hood. I kept that nailed in my mind, that and the pain, which was good and fresh, distracting me from the old, insipid pain that had been slowly dragging me down. I knew about pain. We were old friends now. So tight you forgot how to say goodbye. I wondered how much of it I needed to experience before it finished me. How broad my threshold now.

Water was pouring over the sides of the river bank. The tide could clearly be seen now in a body that had rarely ever felt it before. I almost drowned on that incline: water kept crashing into my face and down my throat. I wasn't strong enough to lift my body above it. I kept having to arch my neck back to get some air. Whenever I did that, I felt a coming apart in my gut and wondered if, where I'd been shot, parts of me were escaping. It threatened a grey out; I could feel it shrouding me. I felt weak and queasy.

Lightning again. His shadow again.

He was closer that I'd given him credit for. He was standing over me, one hand on his knee, trying to keep what was left of it together. The point of a harpoon was grazing the back of my neck. Through the storm and the crash of my own breathing, I could hear his, stifled and harsh behind the plastic.

'Tamara,' I was trying to say. An appeal. I was coughing up seawater – what I hoped was seawater – and trying to hold up my hand against the harpoon, but my back was in spasm. 'Jake, please, I'm begging you.'

We moved back to the harbour barrier in this way, me crawling like a penitent dog, him keeping pace behind me, both of us growling with pain. The car was up ahead. I'd left the keys in the ignition. I was wondering how much of a chance I'd have to get in and drive off before he shot me in the back of the head. He stopped walking. I twisted around, carefully, looking for a rock or a stick, anything I could use as a weapon, but there was nothing and it was too dark to see. He threw the harpoon down. He sat down opposite me and reached up a hand to grab hold of the mask. I almost cried out for him to stop. His doing that marked a beginning to an end I wasn't sure I'd be able to cope with.

The thunder was fattening, out to sea. It seemed impossibly loud now, metronomic. The sky enjoyed no respite from it. Lightning sizzled around the clouds and occasionally escaped them. The man pulled off the mask and Charlie was standing there, suddenly diminished, as if my recognising him shed him of all his threat. He was just Charlie, in a big coat. And I could see that the fight had gone from him. It was as if taking that mask off had stripped him of his desperation. There were tears there, I could tell, even through the rain. His eyes were liquid with them, as if they'd turned to this shimmering blue wetness and if only he tipped his head forward it would all come drizzling out.

Through the tears and the snot he mewled: 'I can't do this. I can't do this. I won't do this.'

I sat back in the mud, staring at him. I thought I'd heard him say this before. A long time ago. But it might well have been déjà vu. 'Jesus,' I said. 'Charlie… it's you. It's… Tamara, she's in your hut isn't she?'

'Forget it, Paul. Y'should get out. Leave Southwick. Now.'

'Did you take her? Let me see her, now.'

I'd got hold of the tail of his coat and was dragging myself upright. I was going to get hold of his throat and I meant to squeeze until he did as I asked, or he died, whatever happened first.

'I never wanted… but there was no way out of it, y'see? It's all my fault.'

He seemed far away, tied up in his own thoughts and emotions. The tears were coming freely now, despite his efforts to conceal them. Exhaustion and shock had us both. We were slapping each other's hands away, trying to find new purchase, grappling in the mud like children.

'What happened?' I asked him. 'While I was out of it. While I was in hospital. What happened to her? What did you do?'

I felt I could have barked questions at him for an eternity, but I bit my lip and gave him space to answer. I had to know. It was hard to hear anything beneath that racketing sky. Our faces were centimetres apart. I could see the pain and the time etched into his; he could see mine too. I could see mine, in the mirrors of his eyes. He smelled of smoked fish and sugary mints and hot wax.

His mouth was moving as if trying on the fit of the words before speaking them. But nothing came out. His eyes took on a wounded, pleading look, like a dog caught stealing from the dinner table.

'I always wanted to be a dad,' Charlie said at last, and it was as if they were the hardest words he had ever uttered in his life. They came out strangled, on tortured puffs of air. I could only sit there in the freezing mud and water, listening to him. I got the feeling he'd have been saying this even if he had no audience.

'And then, at the moment I was going to become one, things happened. My wife died. She haemorrhaged right there, on the table, while my daughter was inching out. I held her hand and there was nothing I could do. She was gripping my hand so tightly, right at the end. She was full of strength. And then the baby was born. I held Ruth in my arms while the nurses and doctors were running around trying to save my wife. And Ruth was so quiet. No crying. Until I saw my wife go slack. I saw the life go out of her. And then Ruthie screamed so hard I thought she was going to break.'

His eye caught mine and he stumbled a little, as if embarrassed at the extent of his revelation. 'I couldn't go through with it,' he said. 'She wanted to die, Ruthie, that day in Byrning's Pit. *It's all right, Da. I'm going to see Mum.* She wanted to go. But how can a father allow that? I've never been able to finish anything. That day out on the sea, fishing, I was supposed to... y'weren't to come back with me. There was meant to be an accident.'

'You were *supposed* to? What, you were under *orders*?'

'We're trying our best,' he said. 'We're trying our utmost to cleanse the soul by eating its filth. Like you, son, on that beach, with y'little burning piles of hurt and regret. What a role model y'proved to be.'

'Cleanse the soul? By kidnapping my girlfriend? Tell me where she is, Charlie. Or this time there *will* be a fucking accident.'

His face changed. It became sneering and furious, but there was a tremble beneath it all, as if it was underpinned with sorrow and doubt. It was not a face designed for violence.

He said: 'You would never understand. The one hope you had was that Ruth loved you. That saved you. And it would save... it might save...'

He punched me and I went sprawling. My nose became a hot, melting centre to my head. The pain was astonishing; I almost laughed out loud, I was so surprised by it. Shreds of Charlie's coat were trapped beneath my nails where I'd torn it as I'd been launched backwards. He stood there in the wind in his raggedy coat like a scarecrow blasted into life by the storm. He seemed incapable of making a decision and rocked there on his thick limbs as if torn between one direction and the other. Then he stumped towards the car I'd stolen.

'Stop!' I called out, but blood was pouring down the back of my throat and the plea turned into a choking fit. 'What about Ruth? You have to go to the police, Charlie. You have to do what's right.

There's a child in the middle of all this. You… Ruth is having a baby. You can't just walk away!'

I started retching and sneezing. I thought I would drown out here on the floodwater and the stormwater and my own fleeing juices. I had to stop him. Something awful had happened to Tamara. I was sure of it. 'Give me the key, Charlie. To your hut. Do the right thing.'

He was looking at me, shaking his head, his teeth a clenched white rectangle. Eyes creased into confusion and pain and fear. His hand reached for the car door. I dragged myself upright, but my foot slipped in the mud and I went down again. I opened my eyes, blinking away mud and grit, and the gleam of the harpoon was there, directly in front of me, the very tip of its point fizzing with its own lightplay. Panic leapt in me like something alive in my stomach. I picked up the harpoon, disconcerted by how light it was, and screamed at Charlie to stop. And he did, for a moment, although that could have had as much to do with the violence in the sky as the warning in my voice. I saw him turn his head to the right, to the east, to the mass of folding, imploding cloud piling against the headland. It seemed impossible that the atmosphere could contain all of that, that the weather had somehow transgressed nature's boundaries, and that the storm was now trespassing in space. But I glanced at it too, and there was something else in that cloud, adding to its noise, providing a weird, black countermeasure to the cacophony. I thought it must be my heart arresting. I thought the injuries I had sustained might be life-threatening, that the harpoon that had sliced through me had taken some vital organ with it, or nicked an artery and I was now bleeding internally, had lost so many pints that there was nothing left for the heart to pump around and it was sucking in and chucking out little more than a red mist.

I didn't mean to fire the harpoon right at him. I meant for it to be a shot across the bows. Something to halt him, give him pause, make him come back so I could reason with him about Tamara. I needed him alive.

But he had slid in behind the wheel and the red lights of the car came on and my finger tightened on a trigger that needed many less pounds per square inch in order for it to execute its job.

At first I thought the car had been hit by lightning. There was a shower of sparks and a great belch of black smoke that leapt from the opened tailgate. I could hear the ricochet of hot metal fizzing against metal. There was fire now, so bright, so hot in such a short time that I was pressed back, despite standing over ten metres away. The tank of compressed gas. I must have ruptured it with the harpoon. I saw a shape jerking within that fierce orange glow. The driver's side door opened and Charlie collapsed on to the floor; the water put him out instantly. His clothes were smoking and his hair had been scorched down to stubble. He was writhing like a cut worm, trying to get away from the car, or out of his steaming skin.

I ran to him and dragged him clear of the wreckage, mindful of the petrol tank, but he was dead. What was left of his mind just hadn't caught on to the idea yet. There was a ragged fist-sized hole in the side of his neck; it looked like some animal had taken a great bite out of him. The heat from the explosion had cauterized it immediately. He kept shrugging, as if it were no more irritating than the remains of a haircut that had fallen down the back of his shirt.

He was flopping there like any one of the fish released on to the deck of the *Gratitude*. He was opening and closing his mouth. It was as if the mask was still on him. He had become what he was using to hide himself from the world.

'The Craw,' he managed. 'The Craw. It's coming.'

He died then, and I held it together long enough to frisk him for the keys to his shed. I slithered away from him through the mire, mouth rigid with shock. I was completely black with mud and blood. I eventually threw away the harpoon, which I was clenching so hard my fist had seized shut and I had to bite at the muscles in order to relax their grip. I was exhausted. I couldn't tell if the clouds were real or merely the cross-hatchings of my brain trying to shut me down for a while and feed me some desperately needed rest. Lightning might only be so much brain activity sparking around my lobes. Bad weather was in me. Here was a low.

I blinked. The cloud was changing. Something monstrous was pushing the ghost of its own shape before it. This thunder was man-made, mad-made. Thrust and lift. Approach speed. ETA.

Charlie was wrong. The Craw was not coming. Whatever held sway over this village, it had nothing to do with some childhood shade, a bad bedtime story, a hex. I closed my eyes. I said:

Flight Z
ARRIVAL

LADIES AND GENTLEMEN, *this is First Officer Roan here.*
Good evening. We have commenced our descent.
The weather is dead wet, dead windy. The present
temperature is dead cold. Death is all around. We'll
be landing shortly. Please take off your seatbelts
and observe the no smoking signs. This does not
extend to the aircraft, which is already on fire. We
apologise for the turbulence you're experiencing at
the moment. It won't get any better. In fact, there
are fatigue cracks the size of a tree trunk already in
the fuselage. If you look out of your windows on
the left hand side of the plane, you'll see your life
flashing by.

I CAME OUT of a dizzy, grey spell and was sick
again, although it was little more than a thick cord
of spit that hung from the back of my throat like a
squeeze of glue. I was losing blood. I was dying. I felt
something hard and hot against my thigh. I thought
maybe it was the harpoon, that it was still embedded
in me, and that would be good – I remembered from
my first aid training – that would be much better
than it having gone straight through me. But no, it
was just the knot. Charlie's old piece of string that
he'd given me to practise my sailor's bindings. I

pulled it out now; its shape was comforting to me, coming as it did from a time when things were much simpler. I slept, I burned, I walked, I tied knots.

I kept that weird little indented pile of string in my fingers and it helped keep my mind on staying conscious. That and the slap of the freezing wind was distracting me from the heat spreading through the right side of my body. My hand came away black when I felt there. I was numb. No pain. I guessed that was a bad thing. I stared up at the sky and saw the bulge of clouds, like something alchemic being fomented in a maniac's laboratory flask.

Flight Z tore through that weather like something being birthed out of nightmare, something emerging from a membrane. I saw pieces of it raining down into the sea and only realised they were bodies when I saw the pinwheeling of arms and legs, hideously illumined by the daggers of lightning. The engines were on fire, and screaming as if they possessed voices to give shape to the agony of their disintegration. I saw the two fuselages disengage with a soft, popping sound. One wing was sheared off and flipped lazily towards the sea. A great deck of seating fell out of the fissure in the belly of the aircraft. I could see the hair on the belted passengers snaking above them as if they were thrill-seekers on a fairground ride.

The wind dropped and the rain lessened, as if paying respect. I whispered something... it might have been *Advance the throttles*. But I was losing my grip on things. The jet hit the water. The noise and the fire might have become the thunder and the lightning. It might all have been the jags of pain shooting through my head.

Burning aviation fuel marked out the crude trajectory of the jet's final approach. Already I could smell it, charging inland, pressed on by the winds. I thought I saw a seal's head bobbing some distance away, perhaps curious about the commotion. But then there were more, and they weren't seals' heads. They were human. Some of them were still attached to bodies that ponderously trudged out of the sea, weighed down by waterlogged clothes and carry-on luggage. They came silently up the beach and crowded into the harbour, ovine, as if searching for the queue for passport control. A child carried in one hand a teddy bear that was singed and saturated, and in the other, the naked leg of a woman that she used as a walking stick to help her move the molten clubs of her own feet. A man whose face had been sealed shut with heat puzzled over a flight itinerary. Oxygen masks were fused into faces. Lifejackets and flesh were seamlessly joined. An elderly woman dragged herself and the metal skeleton of the seat she had burned into up the cindered path like a charity marathon runner whose choice of costume has backfired.

One of these victims came up to me and opened his mouth. A tide of blood and sand gushed from it. In the end he was able to get out what was on his mind. He said: *This accident was not survivable because impact forces exceeded human tolerances.*

The passengers reeked of aviation fuel. Now the fire that had fled across the bay came hunting for what it had missed. I watched the flames catch up with them outside the first rank of fishing huts. *Please burn this for me, please,* the man said, and pulled back

346 Loss of Separation

the lacerated shreds of his torso to show me what remained of his heart. The aorta had become detached from the internal wall and it hung out of him like a cat's plaything. The fire raced up him. I watched them all go up as if they had been born to this moment, that it was what they had been intended for.

The knot, somehow, had come undone under the blunt nubs of my fingertips. There was a jellied plug of blood at its centre. I threw away the cord in disgust and wiped my hands against the sodden, mud-streaked flanks of my coat. I watched the passengers burn until there was nothing but ash on the floor, then I waited to see if I would come out of this, wake up in some warm bed with crisp sheets to find Ruth leaning over me with a cool drink and a handful of pain relief.

It wasn't going to happen. Which meant I had to do this. I had to stare at the door of Charlie's fishing hut. I had to stare at the handle on the door, the fingerprints picked out by the smouldering coals on the harbour path.

I stared until my hands tingled, and then I realised they were tingling because the metal had sucked in the heat from the fire and I was burning too. I sucked at the swift blisters that had risen on my palm, relishing the pain, glad that my nerve endings weren't part of just so much fossilised tissue. I was still breathing. I was still alive in this blackened, death-filled crucible.

On behalf of the crew I'd like to thank you for dying with us this evening. We hope to see you again soon.

Chapter Eighteen

DESCENT

THE RAIN HAD stopped. The wind was still gusting in. Halyards spanked against black masts. A real din. I opened that shack door. I stepped inside. One bare 100-watt bulb. Shelves of hooks, ledgers, lead shot. Buckets of fish-heads. Buckets of guts. A dried-up lemon air freshener. Calendar on the wall. Ornamental anchor. Off-cuts of carpets. A table. A large coffee tin. Tightly rolled scrolls. Knives for scaling. Filleting. Gutting. Waxy paper. A huge bobbin of string. Tailor's scissors. A chalkboard of prices. I stood there. I sucked it in. Blood poured from my abdomen. Pooled on the floor. I stared at it. That was me. I felt like scooping it up. Packing it back in. I was light-headed. Not long now. How many pints before black-out? How many pints before arrest? Every breath was an effort. Every exhalation threatened to spill me. I walked forward. I don't know why. My foot caught in the carpet. I went down. I hit my head. I thought about the sound. Not a flat knock. Echo in this. Empty head? I ransacked my coat for pills. Nothing. I needed a drink. I needed to sleep. I sat up. Rapped knuckles against the floor. This bit solid. This bit not. I pulled back the carpet. A hinged hatch. Water drained

through the cracks. I fumbled it open. Stairs fell
away. Black as the hobs of hell. Water chuckled
down there. Hello? I sank. Splashing through mud.
Close down here. The walls pressing in on me.
Another door. Soft music playing. Hello? I felt for
a lightswitch. Rivers of water. I flicked it on. Tensed
against electrocution. Shadows scattered. Signs of
life. A bed. Manacles on the bed. Chains bolted
to the wall. A table and dishes. Congealed food.
Medical items. A first aid kit. Bandages. Steel knives
on a steel tray. Shower curtain. A moan. I turned
around. In the shadowed corner. Ruth in and out
of blankets. Blood-stained and mewling. Cradling
something red. Cradling someone red. I went to
her. Ruth, what are you doing here? I held out my
hand. Shush. It's okay. Everything's fine. Her eyes
on me. Lightshine. Animal in her. Gripping the baby
like a weapon. Blood on her cheeks. Blood on her
forehead. Like tribal warpaint. Her eyes on me. Her
eyes flashing around the room. Ruth?

She draws her lips back. We have to go. Charlie...

Charlie... Charlie's dead, Ruth.

Charlie? Dead? Charlie?

He tried to kill me.

Her eyes. Red and wet. Unfocused. Another wild
scan of the room. We have to go. Now.

How's the baby? How are you?

She ignores me. Heads for the door. The water's ankle-deep. I switch out the light. Switch it on again.

Paul?

Now I ignore her. She had to go to hospital. Charlie's body. Keble would have to be informed. But. Something else.

Paul? We have to go. We have to go *now*, Paul.

Why?

Because. The baby. Charlie. Isn't it obvious?

What happened down here, Ruth?

It's over. I've just given birth. Can't you see? I delivered early. Come on. We need to get to hospital.

Blood moving through the water. Red ribbons in a current. The shower curtain darkening.

I wade towards it. What's behind here?

Leave it, Paul. We're going to drown down here. Think about the future.

Frozen in time. The moment before everything changes. In that moment there is potential. I could recover. Tamara is a splinter. I could tease her out. In time. I could fall in love again. Ruth would take care of me. I would take care of her. And the baby. We'd move away. Charlie would be forgotten. In time. I don't want the slow heal. The easy path. I can't not look. I'm a rubbernecker on the motorway. I disable the safe search. The not knowing is impossible. I'm there. I'm right there. In the horror film. With the guy in the bathroom. Who pulls back the shower curtain. Every time. Every time. What black, blasted secrets lie behind?

The truth. What's the truth? Don't believe the truth. *Don't believe that Ruth*.

Paul!

I got my hand around it. Tight fist. White knuckles. Pulled that fucker off the rails. And Tamara was there. And I screamed at her. How stupid she was. How fucking stupid I was. I'd been here before. Baiting Charlie's hooks. I could have saved her. I COULD HAVE FUCKING SAVED YOU. Where had she been? And all the while I was looking for something that wasn't soaking wet with filthy seawater, something I could tuck inside the gaping hole in her, something to staunch the blood and pack her up with hope, with a chance. And I heard Ruth splashing through the water as she came to drag me away and she had the baby by the hand and she was jerking it around like some sock puppet, but at least it was screeching, at least it was alive. Unlike Tamara. Unlike me. But she didn't want to drag me away, she wanted to put me under, and I felt the burn in my abdomen matched with another in the back of my head and I keeled over, trying to turn to see what it was she'd hit me with, to see if it was survivable. Can't not look. See how much of my brains were dangling off whatever she'd clouted me with. But it wasn't a gaffe or a meathook. It was only an aluminium table leg. The screw-in end of it was black with blood and hair. But that was kids' stuff. I'd come back from a ton and a half of four-wheel drive collapsing around my puny bones. I was more than this.

Her hands had been soft on me, pressing cool dressings into the freshly knitted creases of my injuries. Shushing. Soothing. A brand new mother.

She came for me again, and for a moment I thought she was going to try to hit me with the baby. She had it tight in her fist around the ankles and her balance suggested that was what she was going to do, but she seemed to think better of it and, instead, backhanded me across the temple with the table leg. It wasn't so hard this time, but she cut me and blood fell into my eyes, blinding me. I couldn't lash out because of the baby, so I held my arm across my chest as a barrier and kept myself between Ruth and Tamara. When she came again, I heard rather than saw her and was able to block the blow. I grabbed for the leg and got hold of it. We pushed and pulled each other across the room. I got my hand around the blanket on the bed and pulled it clear, sending boxes and trays clattering across the floor. I checked I hadn't hit Tamara with anything, and I was horrified and exhilarated to see her groping around in the water, her face millimetres away from it. She was alive. She was scooped clean like a child's ice cream bowl. She was going to drown.

Ruth caught me again in the chest, and I felt, I *heard*, the flesh tear like tissue paper. She drove under my arms, punching me in the stomach with the grisly end of the table leg. I felt something give in my back, felt the woeful separation of metal and bone and thought, *this is it, this is me gone*. And I must have fainted, but only for a second or two. The cold water revived me as I hit it. She was standing in front of me, blocking my view of my Tamara, her eyes blazing, her clothing hanging open on her flat, flat stomach, the baby jouncing in her bloody fist.

There was no rapist, I said. And now what? Bryning's Pit? The next level? Newborns, Ruth? Is that it?

Ruth said: You had to keep at it, you stupid bastard. You couldn't let things go. You're a wreck. And wrecks don't get fixed, Paul. Wrecks know their place. You stay quiet, you stay deep. You're a wreck. The pair of you.

I heard Tamara. I heard her, and Ruth did not. That voice was mine, and mine alone. I'd heard it whisper in sleep. I'd heard it sing for me, and call out as it was lifted and changed during her climax. I'd heard it through laughter and tears. Weak as it was, now, and as long as it had been since I heard her speak, I *did* hear her, through all the stormwater and the ragged breathing. And it was a beautiful voice. And she said: *I am not fucking wreck.*

I saw the victory go out of Ruth's eyes in a shot. Shock dragged her features south. I saw her try to step forward, but she began to topple and she was unable to do anything about it. Tamara was revealed as Ruth fell. She was holding up a scalpel. I scrabbled over to the baby and plucked it free of Ruth's hand as she struggled in the water beneath my boot. Her heels were grinning red where Tamara had slashed through the Achilles tendons. I clutched the child – a boy, *my* boy! – to my chest. The poor thing was freezing. I shushed him and kept him warm inside my coat, talked to him over the awful sound of choking and gurgling. I kept my boot down hard and long against the screaming of my muscles and the long, lazy spasms that rolled through Ruth. I talked to him for as long as it took for her to stop moving. Then I took the baby to his mother and held them both and, straight away, I felt the horses' hooves again – one strong and steady, the other fast and distant, catching up – and I understood and I loved them both beyond words, and I knew… I hoped, but no, I *knew* everything was going to be all right.

Chapter Nineteen

WAKE TURBULENCE

I USED TO soar.

Much of my life was about charts and checks and mathematics and budgets. Fuel estimates. Weight distribution. Pre-calculated decision speeds. Sign this, sign that, duplicate, triplicate.

But nobody becomes a pilot for the paperwork.

Above it all was this gleeful, childish impulse. The playground game of spreading your arms and running so fast you could believe, almost, that the wind charging into you was going to lift you into the sky. Being a pilot was all I wanted. And then it was all I knew. And all I ever wanted to know. The thrill of the engines powering up as you squint down that runway. One hundred thousand thrust horsepower paid out beneath the fingertips.

All these cars and houses and factories, the so-called skyscrapers. The billions of people shuffling and scuffling around in the dirt and smoke and chemicals. Goodbye to that. I'd power up that bird, so ungainly and helpless on the tarmac, and drag it out of the arguments and ill will and those dangerous, blood-spattered roads, through acres of dark cloud, into a blue so fresh and free and clear you might reach out and snap some off, suck it like a mint.

Up here it is safe and bright and you can see for miles. You can see the softly rounded horizon of the Earth, and the darkening blue above, and you know that there exists no living being between you and the curve at the end of the universe.

I miss all that. I miss that everyday miracle of flight. But there are others...

I don't know how I did it, but somehow I got Tamara and the baby (we'll call him Andriy, after your father... our little man, our little warrior) out on to the cindered path. I covered them with my coat and hobbled down to the pub and battered the door until the landlord came to see what was wrong. I managed to tell him what and where and then I promptly fell unconscious.

I underwent an operation that night, as did my wife. She nearly didn't make it, they told me, but I shook my head at them. Nearly doesn't count. After what she had been through, an operation was but a minor obstacle for her to bat aside. Physically she is a good healer, Tamara. Good and fast. But I could tell that there was a place now, inside her mind, where I would never be allowed to go. I hope she stays away too.

I was told I was lucky I could still walk. The brace had split clear of my spine and a jagged edge was one centimetre from cutting my spinal cord. The harpoon wound was clean, but I'd lost a lot of blood.

I wasn't bothered. Physical pain was something I could cope with now. What mattered was lying in a ward nearby. The baby had suffered mild hypothermia but was making good progress despite being born... despite being *taken* a month earlier than planned. My life had been kickstarted again. I couldn't have been happier.

Keble came to visit me. He said he was spending more time with me than he was with his wife.

'I hope she's prettier than me,' I said.

'Oh yes,' he said, peering up at me from beneath the brim of his hat. 'But she doesn't stare at me with quite the same degree of naked sexual longing.'

He asked me how he was, but I could tell he was itching to be away. 'I just came to tell you...' he said, and then he faltered. Now he didn't meet my gaze. All of his little gimmicks and affectations had vanished. 'Amy killed herself yesterday.'

'She jumped?'

He nodded. 'The water tower.' Now he stood up. I saw him to the door. He apologised. 'I think I might leave this place,' he said. 'And policing. I've had a bellyfull. Things are getting... nastier. I don't know if I can hack it any more.' Then he said goodbye.

I saw him pause as he stepped away, peering along the street in both directions to see if he could spot who had left the letter outside the door. My name was not on the envelope. *burn this, if you want* was all it said on the outside. All lower case letters, unjoined, slanting left. You didn't need a graphologist to see the depression in those words. Keble gave me a look, as if he wanted to share with me what was on that paper, but then he left.

Amy had been in a rush. I imagined the page making a fluttering noise as she spread her arms and pushed off into the blue. For a brief second, she would have been flying. I knew that when they found her she would have been wearing a smile.

*   *   *

dear paul i cant do this i'm not going there with
you if you want to go and check then thats your
lookout honest i think youd have been better off just
burning this note rather than opening it god knows
why i wrote it in the fucking first place. so its up to
you and if you think this is just me sending you on
a wild chicken hunt then fair dos and i'm so sorry if
thats how you feel. but anyway theres dead people
on cold acre marsh. the sacrificial lambs. the poor
babes. shallow graves most probably if you want
to go prodding around. i've been distracted by the
old bodies that fell at the battle of winter bay. i've
been stupid. slow. i reckon these poor loves were
buried under its disguise, to keep people like me off
the scent maybe. i don't know. i might be wrong.
i'm probably wrong about all of this and it doesnt
matter any more. the bodies are there, or they are
not there. whatever – i hope i've been of some help
to you. i know you were to me. dont feel bad. dont
feel as though you are to blame. i hope you find
your woman. i hope you are happy. i hope you can
live with your scars. i cant live with mine. i've tried.
last night i had a wonderful dream paul. i dreamed
i was made of light and i had no scars, no metal
pins or braces. no clumsy limbs. no heartbeat to fret
over in the middle of these insomnia nights. i was
pure and weightless and innocent and fast. i could
move, i mean really move. i was everywhere. i was
brilliant. and it is in us all, paul, i think. don't you?
we're all of us got this ancient carbon in us. old and
unknowable and magic. billions of years old. we're

all born of light. whos to say that when we die we
dont become it again? be well. love, amy

WE LIVE IN Scotland now. Oban. Land of my
grandfather, on my mother's side. It's quiet. The air
is clean. The people are good; friendly and open,
without wanting to stick their noses in your business
all the time. And it's miles and miles away from
everything.

I help Tamara; she helps me. The fact that I can see
her again, every day, is more of a salve to me than
all the pills and creams and physiotherapy. Andriy is
strong, and getting stronger by the day. We pay for
some help, because neither of us can properly pick
him up, even though we're both improving. I stare
at Andriy for many, many hours at a time, when he
is asleep, and I think about how I almost missed
him, lost him – through one set of circumstances or
another – and how I will never allow anything to
come between us again. I love him. And I think of
my childless self for the past forty years and I think,
what a waste. This is what it's about. Children are
what it is all about.

I've had children on my mind a lot since Southwick.

I read the newspapers in the little one-storey stone
library in Albany Street. Tamara won't have them
in the house. Sometimes I'll switch on News 24
when she's out in the garden with Andriy. *Breaking
news. We'll keep you up to date with events as they
unfold.* I began to hoard pages and pasted them into
a scrapbook. Amy was right. The corpses are being
dug up on a daily basis from Cold Acre Marsh, not

three hundred metres from Bryning's Pit, like treats snatched from a bran tub. They all bear the same injuries. Forensic evidence suggests that their hearts had been removed before they were burned. Many children gone over many years. Files on missing children were re-opened. Residents are being questioned. People are moving away from the area. Older graveyards are being dug up for clues. In one newspaper photograph I saw Jake being led away by police officers to a waiting car. He was wearing handcuffs. Police had seized many documents from the museum, and a harddrive belonging to his computer. There was talk of ancient curses. Of burned offerings. Of Jake's photograph collection.

I followed the story for weeks. I washed my hands often. Whenever I smelled burning I felt as if I might vomit. I thought of Ruth, despite what she had done. Ruth had always meant to be one of the 'lambs', but Charlie had smuggled her to safety. He believed her inability to carry a child to term was punishment for his actions. Ruth resented him for that. When Tamara confided to Ruth, it was a temptation too great to ignore. None of this would have happened if I had been approachable, if Tamara hadn't feared my reaction at being told I was to be a dad. Had Andriy been meant for Bryning's Pit? Or did Ruth want to keep him, raise him with me? Did he see my survival as some kind of sign? She probably thought it was poetry. Destiny. It was almost sad.

I woke up one day and the sun was crashing into the bedroom. No sounds of breakfast, of Andriy crying or lalling. No sounds of the television and Andriy giggling happily over his obsession for *Show*

Me, Show Me or old episodes of *Morph*. Needled, I got out of bed and shuffled along the corridor to the living room. Nobody there. Nobody in the garden.

The doorbell rang. I felt a swelling of grief in my gut, something I had not felt for months, since Southwick. The shadow at the door. The policeman with his hat in his hand. The downturned eyes.

But it was Tamara. Andriy was in his buggy and he smiled when he saw me. Tamara was smiling too, but it was a sad smile. She looked as though she had not slept well. In her hands was a box. She held it out to me. 'Please,' she said. 'Burn this for me, please.'

I didn't know what to say. She kissed my cheek. And she said something in Ukrainian: 'Zabuty.'

Forget.

I opened the box. My scrapbook lay inside. We went through to the garden and I placed the scrapbook in the centre of the lawn. The first match ignited. I touched it to the edges of the pages. The flame tucked in. I watched Andriy's face as he became rapt by the fire. I saw the glimmer in his eyes and I went to him and held his tiny hand and it was warm and soft and good.

THE END

A Thaddeus Blaklok Novel

KULTUS

RICHARD FORD

UK ISBN: 978 1 907992 27 8 • US ISBN: 978 1 907992 28 5 • £7.99/$7.99

Demonist Thaddeus Blaklok is pressed into retrieving a mysterious key for his clandes-tine benefactors. Little does he know that other parties seek to secure this artefact for their own nefarious ends. In a lightning paced quest that takes him across the length and breadth of the Manufactory, Blaklok must use his wits and demonic powers to keep the key from those who would use it for ill..

 WWW.SOLARISBOOKS.COM

Follow us on Twitter! www.twitter.com/solarisbooks

UK ISBN: 978 1 907519 95 6 • US ISBN: 978 1 907519 94 9 • £7.99/$7.99

Imagine a place where all your nightmares become real. Think of dark urban streets where crime, debt and violence are not the only things you fear. Picture a housing project that is a gateway to somewhere else, a realm where ghosts and monsters stir hungrily in the shadows. Welcome to the Concrete Grove. It knows where you live...

 WWW.SOLARISBOOKS.COM

Follow us on Twitter! www.twitter.com/solarisbooks

AN ANTHOLOGY OF HAUNTED HOUSE STORIES

HOUSE OF FEAR

EDITED BY JONATHAN OLIVER

UK ISBN: 978 1 907992 06 3 • US ISBN: 978 1 907992 07 0 • £7.99/$7.99

The tread on the landing outside your door, when you know you are the only one in the house. The wind whistling through the eves, carrying the voices of the dead. The figure briefly glimpsed through the cracked window of a derelict house. Editor Jonathan Oliver brings horror home with a collection of haunted house stories featuring Joe R Lansdale, Tim Lebbon, Christopher Priest, Rober Shearman, Sarah Pinborough and others.

 WWW.SOLARISBOOKS.COM

Follow us on Twitter! www.twitter.com/solarisbooks

UK ISBN: 978 1 907519 62 8 • US ISBN: 978 1 907519 63 5 • £7.99/$7.99

Jordan helps kids on the run find their way back home. He's good at that. He should
be - he's a runaway himself. Sometimes he helps the kids in other, stranger, ways. He
looks like a regular teenager, but he's not. He acts like he's not exactly human, but he
is. He treads the line between mundane reality and the world of the supernatural. Ben
McCallan's urban fantasy debut takes you on a teffifying journey.

 WWW.SOLARISBOOKS.COM

Follow us on Twitter! www.twitter.com/solarisbooks